GHOSTS OF YOU AND ME

MIRANDA VALENTINE

AUTHOR'S NOTE & CONTENT WARNINGS

Dear Reader,

Ghosts of You and Me has been a whole new adventure for me! Not only did I get to tackle a fun, emotional second chance romance, but I also really enjoyed creating Larkspur Island, Sunny Spirits Ghost Tours, the ghosts themselves, and all of the other elements that come with this fictional, haunted island setting.

Sage and Dawson go through quite the journey in this book, both individually and together. When I'm creating characters, giving them real, relatable conflicts and characteristics is something I aim for. Throughout the story, both are struggling with accepting themselves and feeling worthy in different ways. As humans, we all go through this at some point. It can be hard, and I wanted to use this opportunity to remind anyone reading that you are amazing and deserving of everything you have the courage to go after.

There are content warnings for the following: adult language, a few steamy scenes, strained family relationships, and discussions/portrayals of anxiety, depression, and panic attacks. Take care of yourselves!

I can't thank you enough for reading, and I hope you enjoy *Ghosts of You and Me*.

Love, Miranda

To the perfectionists and non-perfectionists alike.
Your best is always enough. And even on the days you can't be at
your best, you're still enough.

PROLOGUE

Like every other day this school year, I know he's coming before I see him.

The sun is high in the sky as Caroline and I traipse across the bustling (well, as bustling as a campus with 367 total students can be) courtyard to our final class of the week—our final class of high school. Maybe my final class ever, since college is a permanent floating question mark above my head these days. I squint into the bright afternoon light, locking my gaze on the bumbling group of classmates coming in my direction.

That's where he is. Right in the middle of them. Always surrounded by a minimum of six admirers. The sun hits his dark brown hair just right, creating a golden orb around his head.

Appropriate, I think, then scoff to myself.

"Oh my god," Caroline gasps and reaches for my arm. "I just realized this is the last time you two will get to have this little flirt session."

"Ew." I shake her off and glare at her out of the corner of

1

my eye. "That's *not* what this is. More like an *I can't freaking stand you and I want you to know it* session."

"Whatever you say." Caroline sniffs. "All *I'm* saying is, you and Dawson Aiken are a missed opportunity."

Ignoring her, I force my leer away from the approaching posse and pretend to admire the blooming crape myrtles that line the courtyard. I always refuse to make eye contact with him until the last possible second. The point of this daily interaction is that he's supposed to

feel like it's a burden for me. If he knew I expected it (and somewhat looked forward to it), I would simply die.

"Heyyyyy, Caroline." One of the posse—Dawson's best friend, Cole—blows a kiss at *my* best friend as our paths finally cross. I wrinkle my nose at him, not even trying to hide my distaste. He unattractively mimics my expression, earning a laugh from the remaining bunch of bozos. All of them except Dawson, anyway.

Caroline waggles her fingers at Cole. A mysterious yet familiar force pulls my eyes straight to Dawson. The yellow aura still dances around his dark hair. His hazel eyes are crinkled in the afternoon brightness, and his expression is the same as always—relaxed with the tiniest hint of a smirk.

I hate it.

Slowing to a stop, we continue our stare-down, remaining silent while Caroline and the goon squad fall into animated conversation around us.

"I can't believe high school is over!"

"We'll keep in touch, right?"

"I'm going to miss you guys!"

Blah. Blah. Blah.

"Ghost Girl." Dawson bobs his head in acknowledgment, like he's only just noticed me standing in front of him.

"Golden Boy." The greeting rolls off my tongue with a little less malice than usual. I cross my arms over my chest.

"Any plans for the summer?" he asks. "Buying more black eyeliner? Perhaps finally starting your own coven? Or adding to your ouija board collection?"

"How'd you know?" I feign surprise. "I would give you tips on the coven thing, but you already have...whatever this is." I sweep my hand in the direction of his friends, who are trying to impress pretty, strawberry-blonde Caroline by having a painfully cringey shoving match.

A salt-filled breeze blows through the courtyard, casting my bangs into my eyes and ruffling Dawson's Larkspur Island High School athletics T-shirt. The football-wielding otter is front and center, waving one of its little paws at me. I almost smile. Our mascot has always been far too cute to be intimidating.

Focus, Sage.

The two-minute warning bell trills throughout our tiny campus. I stare down at my checkered Vans and scrounge around in my brain for a final Dawson dig. A *truly* final Dawson dig. After today, these courtyard duels will cease to exist.

"You'd better get going," I say, backing away from him. "Golden Boy can't be late for class. Would be a shame to ruin that perfect attendance record now."

It's far from my best work, but it will have to do.

He hoists his backpack further up onto his shoulder. "A pleasure as always, Ghost Girl. Enjoy your last English hour. Don't put any hexes on Ms. O'Neal. She might not let you graduate."

"If I curse anyone, it will be the valedictorian. AKA: you." I pretend to flick an imaginary wand in his direction. "I sure hope you don't forget your big speech."

Dawson's infuriating smile doesn't falter one bit, but all of his friends begin to look slightly nervous. I grin at them mischievously. There are pros to being the daughter of the local ghost tour operator. It doesn't even matter that other than a love for black band T-shirts and temporary hair dye, I look just like almost every other teenage girl living on Larkspur. Most kids (and even some paranoid Larkspur adults who believe in the island's haunted history) are still kind of scared of me. I've learned to use it to my advantage over the years.

And it's worked on everyone except *him*.

Dawson Aiken, who so kindly "blessed" me with the nickname Ghost Girl when we were lab partners in sixth-grade science, and who has worked incredibly hard over the years to make sure the nickname remains relevant. Dawson Aiken: straight-A student, kicker of the football team, son of the local millionaire who owns most of the island, and of course, the Golden Boy of every teacher, peer, and Larkspur resident.

The courtyard around us turns to chaos as students begin shooting off in different directions to beat the tardy bell. For some reason, Dawson and I remain rooted in our spots, stares locked, just a couple of feet apart. Which of us will be the first to back down for the last time?

Caroline grabs my elbow, breaking my focus and knocking me off balance. "See you at graduation, Daws!" she says brightly.

"Bye, Caroline." Dawson flicks his attention to her for a brief second before returning to me.

All at once his expression changes. His brown-green eyes soften. His smirk loses its slyness. He releases his backpack strap with his right hand and reaches across the distance between us. I scrutinize it briefly before placing my own hand into his. It's the first time we've ever touched each other in any capacity, and I can feel the calluses on his palms, weathered from many summers of working his family's fishing charter. He shakes my hand, pumping it once, twice, three times.

"See ya later, Sage."

Before I can realize what's happening, I smile at him. And

it's not one of my *I hope you trip and fall before the day is over* smiles. It's a real one. A rare, genuine one.

He lets go of my hand and walks away before I can think about getting another word in. My palm hangs suspended in the air, tingling in the wake of the handshake. More salty air gusts through the courtyard, and I shiver despite the midday heat.

He called me by my name.

"Sage, come *on*." Caroline tugs me harder, and I shuffle behind her, bumping into her shoulder as I quickly speed up to match her pace. I look down at my hand one more time, feeling my usual grimace slide into place to mask the weird sincerity of the moment with Dawson.

"He's the worst," I grumble, partially to Caroline, but mostly to myself.

"Whatever you say, *Ghost Girl*." The gleam of a giggle is in Caroline's voice.

CHAPTER 1

PRESENT DAY, SEPTEMBER 2022

S omething, somewhere falls and thuds loudly atop the bookstore's worn wooden floor, and a scream fills the air.

I breathe evenly through my nose, fighting the urge to roll my eyes deep into the back of my head. So close, I think. We were so close to wrapping up quickly and peacefully. I was so close to getting out of here and having my dinner before midnight, for once.

Kicked into gear by the unidentified noise and the scream, the group around me begins twittering nervously, grasping on to each other in the semi-darkened shop and looking to me for guidance. Tonight's screamer is packaged in the body of a middle-aged blonde woman. Her eyes are the size of saucers and her mouth still hangs agape in a perfect little O. She clings to her teenage daughter, who glares at me like it's my fault her mother is causing a scene.

My impulse is to glare back. But, I'm unfortunately an adult. Also, that wouldn't be very professional. Though, one could argue, how professional does a ghost tour guide really need to be?

Professional enough to keep this business afloat, is the answer I give myself almost too rapidly.

"What was that?" a bespectacled gentleman at the back of the small crowd asks. "Do you think Madam Roberta is attempting to make her presence known?" His eyes dart around, searching every nook and cranny of Ghost to Coast Bookshop for signs of a ghostly woman he won't see tonight. A ghostly woman he, nor anyone else, will never see. Because she doesn't exist.

Well, Madam Roberta did exist. She owned and lived in this building from 1850 to 1879. History is real. Ghosts are not. Growing up with a paranormal-obsessed father has made me more and more certain of my own views on the subject the older I get.

I guess the joke's really on me for being the manager and head guide of my family's ghost tour business. People always say life is funny. That might be true, but sometimes its sense of humor is cruel.

"Oh, Madam Roberta doesn't usually like to draw attention to herself." I clear my throat, giving myself a few seconds to figure out how to address the situation in a way that will get these people out of here, but also be on brand for Sunny Spirits Ghost Tours. "Maybe we should investigate the source of the noise?" Clicking my flashlight on, I hold it beneath my chin and raise a single shadowy eyebrow.

"Absolutely not!" Screaming Lady says shrilly.

"It sounded like it came from that direction." Defying her mother, the daughter points to the back of the shop with a bright pink fingernail, where heaps and heaps of used, dusty books live haphazardly stacked in a never-ending abyss of mismatched shelves. The bit of street light filtering through the store windows barely illuminates the first row of shelves before disappearing into the gloom that surrounds them.

Everyone nearly breaks their necks looking in the direction

Grumpy Teenager #1 is pointing. I could technically remove the #1 since she's the only "grumpy" teenager in tonight's tour group (there are also Know-It-All Teenagers #1 and #2), but my brain has been committed to the #1 for the entire tour.

"A draft probably just knocked a stupid book off a shelf," Know-It-All Teenager #2 says, right on cue.

"Let's go look then!" I say a little too brightly, pointing my flashlight at the used book section. I begin to walk and look over my shoulder to make sure the group is following me. Everyone is trailing behind except for Screaming Lady.

"I'm not going back there," she refuses.

"No problem, you can wait for us here," I offer.

"Leah, stay with me!" She reaches for her daughter's hand again.

"No way!" Leah (still Grumpy Teenager #1 in my heart) snatches her arm away. "I want to go."

"I'm not staying here by myself!"

The two continue to squabble and it takes everything in me not to blatantly check my watch. I once again envision the leftover pepperoni pizza waiting for me at home, and my stomach makes a noise so loud I'm surprised no one screams again. I continue walking and don't stop until I've reached the first row of used books. Everyone, including the mother-daughter duo, stumbles into place around me. It's quieter closer to the back of the shop, away from the late-night Main Street hubbub that flows through the frame of the front door. Heavy, nervous breathing fills the stale air.

I point my flashlight down the first aisle, illuminating floating dust particles and hundreds of ripped covers, cracked spines, and yellowed pages. Ms. Knox, the shop's owner, stopped trying to keep up with the used section decades ago, other than making sure the books are picked up off the floor. She focuses all of her attention on the front of the shop, where the new releases, bookish merch, and art created by Larkspur Island locals are merchandised to perfection.

When islanders clean out their personal libraries, they bring the books that didn't make the cut straight to Ghost to Coast for donation. From there Ms. Knox or one of the other shop employees price them, then quite literally toss them into the pit that has become the used section. True readers don't seem to mind. They love the thrill of the hunt—the opportunity to seek out and find a hidden gem that may be buried on the lowest shelf in the furthest corner.

Sunny Spirits Ghost Tours also doesn't mind, because it's the perfect creepy location to end a tour. Know-It-All Teenager #2 wasn't wrong when he said it was probably a book falling. In a building this old, it happens all the time. A customer most likely left some 1000-page tome perched precariously on the edge of a shelf, and one wrong footstep reverberated through the shop's floor and sent it falling to its death.

"Nothing here," I say, sweeping my flashlight across the empty floor and moving to the next row of shelves. "When Madam Roberta lived here, this room was split by a wall, with her formal dining room on one side, and sitting room on the other. She was well known for hosting tea parties for all of the Larkspur women."

"Did anything bad happen here?" Bespectacled Man asks, peering around the corner of the second aisle. "I feel...energy. Negative energy."

Dad would love this man.

"Actually, yes." I pause at the end of the third row. "In 1875, there was a fatal accident at one of Madam Roberta's famous tea parties, involving two women—Clara Atwood and Alice Bartholomew. Rumor has it, both women were in the running to enter a courtship with Edward Aiken I, the island's most eligible bachelor. Edward chose Alice, and they were engaged the day before Madam Roberta's fall women's party. Clara didn't handle it so well."

The flashlight beam lights up another empty expanse of floor and I continue moving, feeling my heartbeat quicken as we get closer and closer to the sixth aisle.

I always avoid the sixth aisle. Visiting only occasionally on tours when I have no other choice. And it's not because of a paranormal experience. Although, what happened there does seem like a transcendental occurrence over a decade later.

If this book fell in aisle six, so help me, I think, shivering as I'm flooded with memories that I'm somehow still fighting off well into my thirties.

Pizza, my stomach yells at the same time.

"What did Clara do?" Grumpy Teenager #1 asks.

"Well, no one could prove that it was Clara," I begin to explain. "But about halfway through the party, Alice suddenly fell out of her chair. The other guests tried to revive her, but she was gone before she even hit the floor. According to the local newspapers from that time period, she had been poisoned. No one at the party saw it happen, but gossip eventually pointed back to Clara and her strange demeanor at tea that day."

"Was she arrested?" Screaming Lady clasps her hands against her chest.

"Nope," I say, shining the light down aisle five. Empty. "She passed away here on Larkspur. Never married. No children. She kept to herself after that day, only coming out into public for necessities."

I run my free hand down the length of my ponytail and force my feet forward. Halting at the end of aisle six, I close my eyes and attempt to gather my wits.

It's just a row of books, Sage. It looks no different than the eight other aisles in this section. You have to let go of this at some point.

Before I can spiral any further, I turn the beam of the flashlight down the aisle. As I already suspected, there are not one, but two ancient, massive dictionaries on the floor. Their red covers shine like puddles of blood against the dark wood grain.

"HA! I told you!" Know-It-All Teenager #2 crosses his arms smugly over his chest.

"Those could have already been there though!" Bespectacled Man argues. "I don't believe that's what made the noise. It was too loud."

Screaming Lady pushes her way through the crowd to get a closer look. "What if *something* threw them to the floor?" she asks, moving a hand to her neck to clutch an invisible strand of pearls. "Maybe it was Clara!"

Leah rolls her eyes and sighs audibly.

Chuckling, I take a couple of wobbly steps toward the dictionaries. "As much as I'd like to give you a more exciting answer, it probably was a draft. In a building this old, anything can sound like an explosion."

I bend to collect one of the books, trying to ignore the frisson that seems to be building in the air around me. The hair on my arms stands at attention. My hands start to shake and the flashlight clatters to the floor and rolls to a stop at the base of one of the shelves. To the exact spot I can still pick out of this used book maze years later. To the exact spot it happened.

My fingers brush the rough wood of the shelf as I collect the flashlight. A shiver shoots through me at the contact, conquering my refusal to reminisce and taking me back to that night so long ago.

My back is pressed against the shelves. The splintery wood scrapes the sensitive skin of my shoulders and neck. Heated breath comes in bursts against my lips. Considerate yet curious hands roam over my body. There's an outline of a face in the dark. *His* face.

For a second, it feels like I'm actually there. Back in the body of 20-year-old Sage.

Then the sadness comes to sit on my shoulders, pinning me in my crouched position on the floor, reminding me of my current reality. The memory is too much. I've already said I don't believe in ghosts, but that's somewhat of a lie.

There is one ghost I believe in. It's the ghost of him, and he's not even dead.

While my back is turned, I take a moment to collect myself, then stand and slide the dictionaries into place on one of the shelves. I feel heavy, drained. Like I've just been possessed.

This is why I avoid aisle six.

"Well, that was an adventure!" My voice comes out so high-pitched it should bring all of Larkspur's dogs running. "Looks like we've gone over our time a bit. Any questions before we depart?"

I lead the group back to the front of the shop, where Sunny Spirits headquarters resides off to the left of the bestseller table. It's nothing more than a corner with some tour T-shirts for sale and a desk where we sign guests up and check them in before showing them around the most "haunted" spots in downtown Larkspur. That's why we always end back here in Ghost to Coast, with the grand finale of Madam Roberta and her deathly tea parties.

Ms. Knox has been renting the space out to us since Dad started the business nearly twenty-five years ago. It was supposed to be a temporary setup, but demand for Larkspur real estate doubles every year, and with the high rental and purchase costs, finding our own building has been a fiasco. Although, that could finally be changing soon.

"Thanks for an informative tour!" Bespectacled Man tells

me as I finish ringing him up for a Sunny Spirits keychain. "I learned a lot. Larkspur Island is officially my second favorite haunted place in Florida."

"What's your first?" I ask, humoring him.

"St. Augustine, of course."

Of course.

"If you're ever back in the area, you should set up a VIP tour with my dad," I tell him. "He's a major nerd for all things haunted Florida, too. No offense!" I add quickly at the end, biting my tongue over the nerd comment.

"I'll do that." He tips an imaginary hat at me. "And none taken."

He saunters out of the shop, just ahead of Screaming Lady and her daughter. The know-it-all teenagers linger to snap some photos in the used section, then eventually take their leave too, waving awkwardly over their shoulders. The bell on the door tinkles when they close it behind them, and then I'm cocooned in the most beautiful sound on the planet.

Silence. Nothing but the creaks and moans of Ghost to Coast Bookshop, which I'm so used to that they really may as well be nothing.

I lock up and walk behind the desk, bending at the waist to rest my forehead against the cool surface for a moment. It wouldn't be too difficult to fall asleep standing right here. I was tired and hungry *before* the incident in aisle six. Now I feel absolutely drained.

Straightening back up, I return my attention to the computer to finalize my closing reports and check our numbers for the day. The results are bleak—another day of earning less than half of what we would during the summer. All Larkspur businesses tend to experience a lull in September. Summer vacations end, kids go back to school, and less tourists visit.

But October is right around the corner, and it will be

enough to sustain us through the winter months until the saving grace of spring break comes around. During the spooky season, everyone wants to do spooky things. Maybe I'm biased because I've lived here my entire life, but there's no better spooky place to visit than Larkspur, with its eerie past, friendly locals, and the cheesy yet endearing ghost-themed shops and restaurants that many of the downtown business owners have created and embraced. Like Sunny Spirits and Ghost to Coast.

Of course there's the beach, too.

My eyes unwillingly flit to the used section a few times while I'm wrapping up. Each time I repeat the same mantra—one so familiar it's practically tattooed on the surface of my brain.

Don't think of him. He's in the past.

I guess I should feel somewhat lucky that my issues with being here late at night by myself have nothing to do with the supposed creepy things hiding in the dark. However, what people don't tell you is there are much scarier things in the real world than whatever lies "beyond." Things that never quite leave the corners of your mind, and leave you wondering "what if" and "maybe things would be different if I was different."

The computer shuts down, taking the glowing light of the screen with it. The shadows around me multiply, and I fumble beneath the desk to pull my phone and bag from the lock box. The bell on the door sounds muffled as I step out onto the sidewalk and lock up behind me.

Just when I think I've escaped, the shop's window display brings me to a pause. Suspended above tables of carefully arranged featured books are at least two dozen stained glass suncatchers, each one portraying a different tiny scene. Book-shelves, stacks of colorful books, sunsets, rainbows...They're meticulously crafted, and though they hang in shades of gray as we move closer to the early morning hours, I know they are all far from lackluster.

They're beautiful, but they're also just another painful reminder.

Don't think of him. He's in the past.

CHAPTER 2

PRESENT DAY, SEPTEMBER 2022

"Dad?" I whisper-yell as I let myself into his apartment above Beans N' Boos Coffee House with my key. "It's me! You still up?"

The front door clicks gently shut behind me and I slip off my Vans to creep down the hallway to Dad's study. Like usual, he's at his desk, hunched over his old laptop. Its fan is running so hard it could potentially blow up any second. Stacks of papers of varying heights and shades of white and yellow cover every surface of the study, immediately lulling me into the comfortable feeling of familiarity.

What I don't expect to see is Whitley sitting cross-legged on the threadbare couch in the corner, still awake at 12:45 A.M. with her own stack of papers in her lap.

"Mama!" she exclaims when she sees me in the doorway. "You're back!" She sets the pile aside and comes to hug me around the waist.

"And you're still up too, huh?" I hold her tightly and raise an eyebrow at Dad over her auburn head, which seems to grow closer and closer to my line of vision every day. I'm learning to cherish these hugs a little more lately.

"I'm proofreading for Grampa." She looks at me like I should have already known that and runs to flop back onto the couch, pulling the papers into her lap again. "You would've had to wake me up to take me back home anyway."

She's not wrong. Dad watches her on the evenings I work the late tours. Waking her halfway through the night to transport her back to our house across the island isn't ideal, but it is what it is for now.

"Oh, of course." I take a seat beside her and stare at Dad. "I didn't realize proofreaders were starting so young these days."

"She couldn't sleep." Dad removes his gold-framed glasses and props them on top of his graying head, which has a yellow cast in the study's dim lighting. "She wanted to help. Who was I to say no?"

"He's almost finished. Look!" Whitley shoves one of the papers in front of my face and taps the number at the top. "Page five hundred and forty-three. Of course, I've only read a couple of them..."

Dad has been writing a work of nonfiction on Larkspur Island and its history for as long as I can remember. Definitely since I was Whitley's age—around eleven. Maybe younger.

Twenty-plus years later he insists he's still "perfecting" it. Even after a couple of complete rewrites, rounds and rounds of edits, and a brief period of time where he attempted to turn it into a piece of paranormal historical fiction, it hasn't seen the light of day. There have been no query letters, no attempts to find an agent or self-publish, and no public declarations of "It's finally finished!"

When I think about Dad, he and Larkspur go hand in hand. He was born and raised here, but didn't really begin to delve into the island's background and supposed supernatural atmosphere until he was in his early 20s, around the time he met Mom. His growing obsession eventually led to the founding of Sunny Spirits Ghost Tours, then when that was no longer enough, he started his book and everything (and everyone) else took a back seat.

Me. My brother Sawyer. Mom.

I know he loves us all. But I've accepted that he might not love us as much as this island. That's why Mom left. That's why I'm stuck here keeping Sunny Spirits alive so we can all pay our bills. That's why Sawyer constantly begs me to toughen up and ask Dad to help me more than he does.

"One more draft. Then I'll be ready to query." Dad flips his glasses back down and hits the backspace button on his keyboard a few times.

Sure you will, I think, stewing in my eternal pessimism.

Then I look over at my daughter, who is so diligently pretending to be interested in the Larkspur humdrum in front of her face to make her grandfather happy, and I feel the familiar fifty-pound weight of guilt add itself to my body mass.

For a long time, I was the same way...always wanting to make Dad proud, feigning enjoyment of this island's past even when I couldn't care less. Now I barely even pretend to be interested.

I love Larkspur because it's my home. But I hate it for the same reason.

"How did the tour go tonight, Sage?" Dad asks without breaking the rhythm of his keystrokes.

"It was fine." I collapse against the back of the couch and lean to rest my head on Whitley's shoulder. She reaches to absentmindedly pet my ponytail. "A couple of books fell in the used section."

"Madam Roberta was up to her antics then." He scoots his chair back to peer at me around the corner of his screen. "She hasn't been very active lately."

"It was probably a draft," Whitley and I respond in

unison. She looks at me and winks. She wants to make her Grampa proud, but she's also her mother's daughter.

Dad harrumphs and returns to the three-thousandth draft of his manuscript. "Have you eaten?" he asks. "I have stuff for sandwiches."

"There's leftover pizza at home, but thanks." I sit up, taking the papers from Whitley's hands and reaching to plop them into the only empty space on Dad's desk. "Let's get moving, my future book editor."

"Pizza at midnight? Let's go!" She shoots off the couch and runs down the hallway to find her things.

"One piece, and then it's off to bed for you!" I yell after her.

"But it's the weekend!" I can hear the defiance in her voice from somewhere on the other side of the small apartment. I sigh.

"I know I say it all the time, but she's just like you." Dad pushes up from his chair to walk me to the front door. "Maybe a little less ornery, though," he jokes.

I side-eye him before bending to put my shoes back on. When I stand, exhaustion floods my veins, like the wall holding it all back was ruptured by me sitting down for a couple of minutes. My limbs feel heavy and when the first yawn comes, I don't attempt to hide it.

"Mama, you look awful. You need to sleep more than I do," Whitley says bluntly, stopping in front of me with her backpack clutched to her chest. It's unzipped and various folders, clothes, and other random things eleven-year-olds keep in their bags spill out the sides. I shove it all in and zip the backpack up, then take it and slip it over her shoulders. Dad snorts.

"You always know how to make a lady feel good about herself, Whit." Rolling my eyes at Dad, I open the door with one hand and place the other on top of my daughter's head to steer her into the hallway.

"I'm sorry you're stuck with so many late tours these days." Dad leans against the doorframe. "Leo only has a couple more weeks of paternity leave and he'll be back. The book is taking too much of my attention, but I'll be able to help more again soon."

It's an excuse as old as time, but I'm too stubborn to call him out on it. And I love him too much.

"I know, Dad. I'm fine. Everything is under control."

Whitley shoves herself between us, wanting to be a part of the grownup conversation. "Yeah, she's fine, Grampa! She's tough."

"She certainly is." Dad taps her gently on the tip of her freckled nose. "I just hope she knows how much I appreciate it. Without your mom I wouldn't be able to focus on my dream. When this book sells, all of our lives will change." He looks from her to me, his face full of so much hope I wish I could believe what he says.

Instead, my first instinct is to ask, *What about my dreams?* Then I remember that I don't have any. Haven't for a depressingly long time. Which is fine. I have Whitley. I have Dad and Sawyer. I have Mom, though we only see her once a month or so now.

Dreams aren't meant for everyone.

The corners of my mouth turn up as I study Dad's face. The lines around his eyes seem to multiply every day. His tan skin is rough and weathered from a life lived in the island sun, but he still has a boyish quality to him. His eyes are the same shade of green as mine and Whitley's—sage, if you will. Though they seem to grow paler as he ages. I lay a hand gently against his rough cheek.

"I know you appreciate it, Dad. Whit, tell Grampa thanks for watching you."

"Thanks, Grampa! See you tomorrow night!" She skips off toward the door to the stairs and I follow behind. The lights in the historic building flicker, casting us in darkness for a brief second. We don't startle because we're used to it.

"Oh, Sage!" Dad calls after me. "Any word from Caroline on the old ice cream parlor?"

"I'm meeting her at nine to tour it and talk numbers. Keep your fingers crossed."

He holds a pair of intertwined fingers in the air and grins at me. "It could be perfect. Just think...a real home for Sunny Spirits."

Despite everything—my exhaustion and hunger and hot-cold feelings toward the ghost tours—a thrill shoots through me at the idea. I can already imagine it all. An on-brand sign to complement the classic charm of the building. Room for a desk, an expanded line of Sunny Spirits merch, a waiting area, and maybe even a tiny museum for guests to peruse. A true brick and mortar for our family business.

Maybe some people don't get to choose their own dreams. Maybe Sunny Spirits is the dream that the universe chose *for* me.

Feeling hopeful is nice. I should let myself try it more often.

Dad and I exchange a final wave before I herd Whitley down the rickety stairs. Back on Main Street, the salty humidity keeps us company on the two-block walk to my car. The Friday nightlife is quickly dying down; a welcome ocean breeze blows a few stray plastic cups along the sidewalks and cobblestone road. Whitley lets go of my hand to collect them and toss them in the nearby trash can.

"Throw your shit away, people!" she says, annoyed.

"Excuse me?" I reprimand, mainly because I know it's the responsible thing to do as a parent. Sometimes it's difficult to remember she's not just my little best friend—she's my daughter, too.

"Sorry..." she grumbles. "It's just, you adults can be very irresponsible."

My delirious screech of laughter ricochets off of the old buildings around us, and by the time we reach the car I'm still giggling so hard I drop the keys twice before successfully unlocking the doors. "Sorry," I apologize to no one in particular as we finally collapse into our seats.

"What's so funny?" Whitley asks while buckling herself into the back.

"You are." I steer us past Beans N' Boos and Ghost to Coast, then away from downtown. The last couple of streetlights disappear in the rearview mirror, and within seconds we're enclosed in the depth of the night. The moon is full and bright, and its illumination grows brighter and brighter against the surface of the Atlantic as we near the coast.

This is always one of my favorite parts of the day, no matter how tired or hungry I am. Most of Larkspur is sound asleep in their beds. It's just me, and the person I love most in the seat behind me. With the windows rolled down, we can hear the soft sound of waves crashing in the near distance. Every now and then the headlights catch a sand dune just right and reveal a spray of the red Spanish Larkspur flowers the island is named for.

On our right, a sprawling beachside mansion crawls out of the darkness and into the lights of our approaching car. Once upon a time, I would let this house ruin my peaceful drive home. Then one day I realized, he no longer lives there. What I once knew as his truck hasn't been parked in the driveway for many, many years. He no longer calls the showy house his home. He hasn't for a long time.

It was one of the easier memory triggers to push out of my head. I wish the rest of them were as simple to eradicate.

By the time I pull into the driveway of our own humble

cottage, Whitley is sound asleep. I throw my bag over one shoulder, and her backpack over the other. Then I half carry, half assist her up the front steps, through the front door, and into her bedroom.

CHAPTER 3

PRESENT DAY, SEPTEMBER 2022

"Did you pack sunscreen?" I poke my head into Whitley's bedroom, already knowing the answer from the way she avoids eye contact with me.

"I don't need it..." she says simply.

Scoffing, I walk into her room and begin rummaging through the drawer that holds her swimsuits. I locate the sunscreen and toss it to her. She catches it with narrowed eyes.

"Yeah, you very much *do* need it," I tell her, watching to make sure she puts it in her beach bag.

"Uncle Sawyer won't make me wear it."

She's in a mood today, but what she doesn't know is that I'm in more of a mood. After I got her to bed and had my dinner last night, I couldn't sleep. I ended up on the couch in the sunroom, my favorite room, where I fell into a fitful sleep thinking about the unwanted experience in aisle six. A short three hours later, I'm up for another full day, with the end of it nowhere in sight.

"He will if I threaten him within an inch of his life." I slash a finger across my throat in a cutting motion and Whitley widens her eyes. "Now hurry, he'll be here to get you soon and I also have to go."

My brother Sawyer works on an offshore oil rig, usually two weeks on, then two weeks off. Whitley loves Sawyer, and he thinks she can do no wrong, so he spends a lot of time with her when he's home. Today, he's taking her to the beach, then for lunch at The Phantom Eatery. Whitley has been looking forward to it for days.

I rush to the bathroom and begin spraying dry shampoo all over my head. Wash day should have been two days ago, so the white cast seems to float above my light brown hair until I ferociously rub it in. The plan was to wash and style it for today's tour of the old ice cream parlor—for a little extra luck and confidence—but oversleeping has ruined that plan, so up into a ponytail it goes. Hopefully the orange sundress I've chosen over my usual uniform of cutoff shorts and a Sunny Spirits T-shirt will make up for it.

"Mama, you look amazing!" Whitley appears at my elbow, startling me. A streak of mascara now runs halfway up my forehead. "Can you move though? I need to brush my teeth."

"Of course, your highness." I move to the side and she takes my place in front of the tiny pedestal sink. Leaning over her shoulder, I use the mirror and a Q-tip to clean off the erratic makeup. There's a knock at the door as I finish and toss the Q-tip in the trash.

"I'll get it!" Whitley somehow says while spitting a mouthful of toothpaste into the sink. She rinses it away but tosses her toothbrush into its holder unwashed. Before I can say a word, her footsteps are pounding down the hall, our little cottage shaking with each one. I purse my lips and pick the toothbrush up with two fingers to run it beneath the water she's also forgotten to shut off.

This girl, I swear.

"Heyoooo!" My baby brother's voice booms through the house. "Your favorite uncle is here!"

I walk into the sunroom to find Whitley suspended in the air, her head mere inches from the ceiling fan as Sawyer spins her in circles. They both laugh maniacally, and I find myself grinning while I watch, momentarily enjoying the feeling of having zero cares or worries. The feeling of just existing with and appreciating two people I love.

Sawyer sets her down on the floor and she continues to spin in a show of over-dramatized dizziness before falling face-first onto the couch. "I'm dead." Whitley giggles into a throw pillow. "I'm going to haunt the cottage with Buster."

"I think you're *almost* too big for Uncle Sawyer to do that," I say, moving to give my brother a quick hug. His light brown hair is long and shaggy, curling up around the edges of his ball cap. His face is sunburnt but freshly shaved, making his signature golden retriever–grin stand out even more than usual.

"Never too big!" He grabs one of the other throw pillows and softly tosses it on top of her. She continues to pretend to be lifeless.

"Thanks for hanging out with her today," I tell him, searching the floor of the sunroom for my Vans. "You're always saving my butt."

"How many times do I have to tell you that I *enjoy* spending time with you two, Wedgie?" He plops onto the couch at Whitley's feet and tickles them, forcing her to sit up.

The use of his childhood nickname for me makes me smirk, which is always funny considering it used to make me want to murder him. It started as "Sagey Wagey," then over time, in that way that only kids have, he turned it into something more offensive. I was eighteen before I stopped trying to fight him on it.

"You say that," I reply, finally locating my shoes beneath

the coffee table, "but I was twenty-five once too, which means I know that most twenty-five-year-old guys would much rather be out with their friends, meeting girls on a Saturday."

"Meh, overrated." He leans into the couch and pulls his cap over his eyes. I slip my shoes on and turn my attention to finding my keys.

"Uncle Sawyer, Mama said she was going to threaten you within an inch of your life to make me wear sunscreen," Whitley says in a voice of mock innocence. "But I told her you won't."

"Oh, did she now?" One of the pillows hits me in the back of my calf and I turn to find Sawyer innocently staring up at the ceiling while Whitley convulses in another fit of giggles.

"Yes, *she* did." I pick the pillow up and throw it back in his direction.

Where the hell are my keys?

I dash into the kitchen to search the counters. The clock on the stove shows 8:51, which means I need to be at Beans N' Boos to meet Caroline in less than ten minutes. But my keys are still nowhere to be found.

"That Buster, he's always hiding our stuff!" my dad used to say when we all lived here as a family, back before things fell apart.

Like most other places on Larkspur, Dad believes the cottage is haunted, but not by a human spirit.

By a dog.

Whitley's and my stuff *does* get misplaced just as much as my family's did when I was growing up, but that's because all of us, except for Mom, are terribly disorganized people.

Though, if ghosts were real and we were going to have one, a canine version wouldn't be so bad, right?

"Looking for these?" I bump into Sawyer's chest as I turn to exit the kitchen. He holds my keys out to me and I snatch them from his hand in relief.

"THANK YOU." I grab his shoulders and shake him. "I'm sorry to rush off, but I have to go."

"Dad should be doing this with you, ya know." Sawyer follows me to the door. "Every time I see you, you're more and more stressed."

"I don't have time for this right now, Saw." I bump the screen door open with my hip. "I've got it all under control."

"You're his daughter, not his personal assistant," he keeps pressing.

I brush his comments away. "Whit, I love you. Uncle Sawyer will drop you off at Grampa's later, and I will—"

"You'll get me after the tours tonight. I know, I know." She waves her hand at me then blows me a kiss.

"Please lock up!" I yell over my shoulder as I trot down the stairs. I stare at the cottage as I back out of the driveway, making my daily mental note that the fading seafoam green exterior desperately needs a fresh coat of paint.

One day, maybe I'll have the time to look into it. Along with the crack in the sunroom window.

It's 9:04 when I drop into the seat across from Caroline at Beans. "I know, I know, I'm sorry I'm late!" I say.

"Sage, chill the fuck out." She slides a frozen coffee—my absolute favorite—across the table to me. "I know this is technically a business meeting, but don't forget I'm your best friend and I know how you operate."

I take a slurp of the coffee, which is already starting to melt in the end-of-summer heat.

"I overslept, then I had to get Whit ready for a day out with Sawyer, then I couldn't find my keys." A brain freeze begins to develop between my eyebrows, and for what feels like the first time this morning, I take a deep breath.

"Buster up to his shenanigans again?" Caroline asks, grinning around her sip of iced coffee. Her strawberry blonde hair is pulled back into a chic french twist and all of her clothes are free of wrinkles. I look down at my orange linen dress, which is more wrinkled than not, and try not to think too hard about the flyaways I know are escaping my ponytail.

"More like I was so freaking exhausted last night that I couldn't remember where I tossed them."

"You're doing too much right now, lady." Caroline reaches across the table to squeeze my forearm. "I know the possibility of getting this building is huge for Sunny Spirits. For your family. But you need to find some time for yourself amongst all of this."

"Leo will be back from his paternity leave in a couple of weeks," I tell her. "Then things will be better."

She raises an eyebrow at me, and the action is all I need to know exactly what she's thinking. Even when Leo returns and I cut back on the late tours, there are still the day tours. There are still the numbers and the marketing and now, a potential move into our own building which will bring a completely new set of things to figure out.

Leo is our one full-time employee. Our other three tour guides work part-time or seasonal hours, depending on the time of year. Dad is supposed to be my boss, *my* guide, but I still feel like I'm in this completely alone. He wants Sunny Spirits to grow and thrive just as much as I do, but he's not willing to put in the same effort. He only has his book and the VIP tours (which are rarely a point of interest) to worry about.

I have everything else. Lately, I'm pretty sure I know how Mom felt just before she left.

Caroline continues to study my face as she leans back into her chair and crosses her arms. I know I'm hiding absolutely nothing from her at the moment, but it doesn't hurt to pretend that she's buying it. We're not here to talk about my problems today. We're here to talk about the old ice cream parlor, which might become a problem at first, but will hopefully, eventually, be a solution for some of the pressure I'm feeling.

"I'm planning us a night out." She grabs the straw from her empty cup and chews on it, a bad habit she's had since I've known her. "Just me and you. No kids."

"No husband either?" I ask, pointing at her.

"Yes, definitely no Cole either."

"Fine. But make it"—I pretend to flip through an imaginary agenda—"three years from now."

She snorts. "Okay, let's start this meeting over. Hi, I'm Caroline Rogers, your realtor," she starts, exaggerating a British accent. "I understand you're interested in potentially buying the old Larkspur ice cream parlor and making it home to your family's ghost tour business?"

"Why yes, Mrs. Rogers. It's a pleasure to meet you. I would love to buy this place as long as it doesn't quite take *every single penny* I have." I mimic her accent times ten.

"We have some wiggle room then!" She claps her hands together.

"Can I just start with a very, very blunt question that could possibly save us both some time?" I ask, quickly becoming serious.

"I'm scared now, but yes." Caroline bites her lower lip.

"Knowing me and my finances on the deeply personal level that you do, is there a chance in hell of Dad and I getting this space?"

"Yes," she says matter-of-factly.

"Okay." I stand, grabbing my bag and coffee and trying to suppress my excitement. "Let's go see it."

"Sage, wait, there's one—" Caroline reaches for my wrist but I shake her off.

"I know, there will be a lot more to talk about, but right now I'm running on caffeine and adrenaline," I say, heading for the door.

We leave the coffee house and cross the street toward Ghost to Coast, then walk all the way down to the last building on the right—the only business on Main Street that didn't have a business name. And not just a ghost-themed business name, but a name period. Everyone just always called it what it was: the old ice cream parlor.

In my opinion, they really missed out on the opportunity to capitalize and name it *The Olde I-Scream Parlor*. Instead, the owner decided to purchase an ice cream *truck* and take his business mobile. As a result, the parlor is the first space in our price range to open up in years.

The parlor is a tiny space, but as Caroline opens the front door and guides me inside, it seems much larger with the lack of freezers and high-top tables. A bar with squishy red stools lines the length of the back wall. There are cobwebs in the corners and the large front window is covered in a thick layer of grimy dust, which seems excessive after being vacant for only a few weeks.

"Spooky," I say, turning to look at Caroline. The sun shines in rays through the dirty window, creating flickering patterns on the walls and floor.

"This building is almost a century newer than the others on Main." Caroline walks to the bar and runs a finger through the dust. "It was built in the 1930s, and was kind of just tacked onto the end of this strip. Since it's only one story, it was a sore thumb for a long time, but eventually became a Larkspur landmark when the ice cream parlor moved in during the '50s."

"Wow, that was a really well-delivered timeline," I say. "You sure you don't need a side gig as a tour operator?"

"You're hilarious." She sticks her tongue out at me. "My job revolves around the island's history too. Just in a different way than yours."

"Good point." I stick my hands in my pockets and walk over to the door of the kitchen.

"I know you don't necessarily need a space with a kitchen, but don't let that discourage you." Caroline steps up beside me and flips the kitchen light on. "It's really small, so it could be perfect for an employee break room. You would only need to make a few changes."

I raise my eyebrows, considering the idea, then continue to walk the remaining perimeter of the building. "It's actually a really decent size," I say. "Plenty of space for what we would need."

"Is there anything you don't like about it?"

"It lacks a little of the character the other Main buildings have," I say, doing another scope of the minimal, square interior.

"That's one of the reasons it's a fraction of the price," Caroline points out. "And who knows, it could be haunted, too." She scrunches her nose at me.

I intentionally ignore her second statement. "The lack of charm isn't a deal breaker—that can be fixed. I actually feel like this could be perfect for us."

"So do I." She steps toward me and grabs one of my hands. "But there's something else we need to talk about first, Sage."

"Okay?"

She leads me over to the red stools and wipes one off. "Maybe you should sit down."

"Why...?" I ask skeptically, even as I smooth my dress and lower myself onto the stool.

"You oughta know, there is...someone else coming to look at the building this weekend."

"I would assume so. You just started showing it."

"Someone who, without a doubt, will be willing and able to offer more than the asking price if they like what they see."

"Is it someone local?" I ask.

"No." Caroline shakes her head then scrunches her brow. "Well...yes? They used to be."

"Do I know them?"

She shuts down, staring at me with wide eyes. Her red lips twitch every couple of seconds, like she's at war with herself over whether or not to give me the information. She plops onto the stool across from me and takes a massive breath.

"Before I say it, please know that I'm on your side here, and if you want to put an offer on this place, I'll make sure you have a fair shot."

"Well, thank you," I say, feeling my heart soften briefly before it hardens again. "Now tell me who my new nemesis is!"

She swallows, then speaks so softly I can just hear her above a passing motorcycle.

"It's Dawson."

CHAPTER 4

SUMMER 2009

The sound of waves collapsing against the shore infiltrates my headphones despite the music being turned up to the highest possible volume, but that's exactly how I like it.

AFI's "Silver and Cold" starts playing as I press up to all fours and flip over onto my back. The towel is comfortably itchy against my freshly tanned shoulders and sand spatters across my torso when I fling my arm over my eyes to shield them from the relentless sun. My toes tap along to the music on their own accord. The waves eventually line up with the beat, rounding out my perfect, summer moment.

Then an alarm goes off, piercing through both my music and the sounds of the beach, and I want to sink into the sand and disappear. How is it already that time?

Sitting up, I pause my music and yank the headphones off. I dig through my backpack and find my phone at the very bottom. 30 MINUTES TO TOUR CHECK-IN, the reminder on my screen yells. I slide the screen up to cancel the alarm, then forcefully snap it shut again.

"Time for work, huh?" Caroline mumbles into her towel beside me.

"Yeah..." I sigh, throwing my phone, iPod, and head-phones into my bag. "I'm leading all of the evening tours for the next two weeks."

"Yuck. Have y'all hired anyone else for the summer yet?" She rests her cheek on the towel to peer up at me.

"Mom is interviewing someone as we speak." I slip my Sunny Spirits guide tee over my bathing suit and stand to brush the sand off my legs before I pull my shorts on. "Hopefully it works out. We're spread thin while Dad focuses on his book."

"Hopefully! If I wasn't knee-deep in working on my real estate license, I would help out."

"You worry about you." I grin down at her, swiping my backpack and towel off the ground. "Mom and I are good. Plus, there are worse jobs out there."

"Text me later?" Caroline asks.

"Will do!" I slide my sunglasses into place and head through the dunes for the parking lot. When I reach the edge of the pavement, I bend to brush the sand from my feet and slide into my trusty Vans.

My cherry red moped—my new pride and joy—waits exactly where I left it. Ms. Knox sold it to me a few weeks ago for half of what she bought it for. *"I just don't use it like I thought I would,"* she'd said. I promised her it would be in good hands, and used well.

So far, it certainly beats the rickety bicycle I've been pedaling around the island for as long as I can remember.

The leather seat burns my exposed thighs when I sit to roll it off its kickstand. I start it up and the engine purrs quietly to life, activating the serotonin in my brain. After waiting for a couple of cars to pass, I pull onto the bumpy road and gun it toward downtown, reaching a whopping 28 miles per hour.

With five minutes to spare, I pop into Beans for a frozen coffee before walking across the street to Ghost to Coast. Ms.

Knox is perched on her stool behind the cash register when I walk in and she grins at me. "Lookin' good on that hog," she jokes, motioning to my parking spot across the street.

"I'm not trying to brag or anything, but we almost hit thirty on the drive from Primera Beach." I fold my arms and lean against the counter, wiggling my eyebrows.

"Danger becomes you, Sage." Ms. Knox laughs and tucks her gray-streaked black hair behind her ears. "But let me pretend to be a grandmother for a second. Where is your helmet?"

"I ordered one, I promise." I use my finger to make an X across my chest. "It'll be here in the next couple of days."

"Smart girl."

"Busy day?" I ask.

"Yes!" Ms. Knox fans her face with a spare sheet of paper, turning the many bracelets on her wrist into a wind chime. "Summer is definitely in full swing."

"No joke." I finish my coffee and walk behind her desk to toss it in the trash can. "The tours are fully booked for the next month."

"Even more reason for this interview to work out for y'all." She nods in the direction of her closed office door, which cracks open the second I look at it.

Excellent. I was hoping to catch a glimpse of the interviewee.

Mom never did tell me who it was.

"Thanks so much for your time, Mrs. Murray." A male voice floats through the parted door. "I'm looking forward to this!"

At the sound of the voice, I freeze. It's familiar. Too familiar.

"Welcome aboard," Mom's voice replies. "We're excited to have you for the summer."

I shake my head and try to relax my shoulders. *There's no possible way it's...*

The door opens wider and Mom walks out, followed by none other than Dawson Aiken.

My knees buckle and I follow my first instinct and dive beneath Ms. Knox's desk.

No. Please no. This isn't happening.

"Sage, what in the world?" Ms. Knox gently kicks at me with a bare foot. She hates wearing shoes, even inside her place of business.

"Shhhhh!" I hiss.

"Oh, is Sage here?" Mom's voice is closer now. Through the crack between the desk and floor, I can see Dawson's Sperry-clad feet walk up to stand next to her. "Perfect timing to meet Sunny Spirits's newest guide. She'll be happy to see a familiar face."

No, Mom, I WON'T, I yell internally, shoving a fist into my mouth to keep it from actually coming out.

"She's down here." Ms. Knox rats me out and I consider pinching her calf.

I stand quickly, flipping my ponytail out of my face. "Sorry, I, uh...dropped something!"

Mom furrows her brow at me and I force myself out from behind the desk and closer to her. Closer to him.

Over a year later, he still has the same expression on his face. Over a year later, I still want to punch him. The corners of his mouth turn up even more as we stare at each other. Why is he here?

"You know Dawson." Mom looks back and forth between us. "He'll be working with us this summer."

"No, he won't." I clap my hand over my mouth but it's too late. I've already said it out loud.

Mom widens her eyes at me. "Sorry?"

"I just mean, uh, nothing...never mind." My brain spins in circles, exactly like it used to every time Dawson and I crossed paths. "Welcome...*Gold*—I mean, *Dawson*."

"Nice to see you, *Gho*—I mean, *Sage*. It's been a while."

He sticks his hands in his pockets and rocks back and forth on his heels. He looks pretty much the same...preppy clothes, tan biceps, neatly styled chestnut hair. There's a slight five o'clock shadow covering the bottom half of his face, which is... nice. I mean, new.

His eyes flick discretely from my head to my feet, but he isn't fooling me. I know he's sizing me up too—trying to figure out if he still despises me. I wish I looked different somehow—hotter maybe, or more interesting. But I'm still the same tall, thick-thighed girl covered in beach sand who he went to high school with, the one exception being that the tips of my hair are currently blue, and I'm pretty sure they were purple at graduation.

"Aren't you supposed to be off at college? In Georgia, or wherever you were going..."

"Virginia," he corrects. "I'm home for the summer."

Is his voice deeper?

"Doesn't your dad own a fishing charter or twelve you could work at instead?" I ask.

"*Sage*," Mom hisses under her breath.

A few people enter the shop and Ms. Knox directs them to the Sunny Spirits desk in the opposite corner. How am I supposed to guide a tour after this? How am I supposed to work with *Golden Boy* all summer?

Am I being pranked?

"I wanted something new." Dawson reels me back into the conversation. "Thought I'd trade catching fish for catching ghosts."

Mom giggles and I widen my eyes at her. *Traitor.*

"That's not what we do here. Maybe this isn't the job for you." I shrug.

"Dawson is going to shadow you starting tomorrow." Mom changes the subject, giving me a look that lets me know it isn't up for debate. It's her *You're embarrassing me and we will talk about this later* look.

"Awesome," I say through gritted teeth. "Now if you'll excuse me, I have guests to greet."

I practically sprint away from them. When my back is fully turned, I screw my face into a silent scream, which I expertly transfigure into a polite smile as I awkwardly make eye contact with one of the tour guests. "Here for the 5:00 ghost tour?" I ask in a screechy voice.

"Sorry about her, I think she got too much sun today," Mom tells Dawson when she thinks I can no longer hear. But *oh*, I do hear.

Mom is already under *his* spell. Another one bites the dust.

By the time I've checked everyone in, Dawson is gone. Mom joins me behind the desk as I'm making sure my backpack is stocked with all of the tour essentials—water, a few printed photos of supposed ghostly encounters from past tours to show at each stop, a giant umbrella, and a small digital camera. (For more supposed ghost photos, of course.) Her arms are crossed and one white-sneakered foot taps impatiently on the floor. I pretend not to notice her, which only works until she clears her throat.

"Oh, hi," I say with mock brightness. "Didn't see you there."

"Are you ill?" she word-vomits.

"What? No. Why?"

"You were kind of rude to Dawson." She bumps me out of the way with her hip and opens our booking system. "Is there a reason?"

I reach over her and pluck my cell phone from its spot by the keyboard. "You just unknowingly hired my enemy, but whatever. It's no big deal."

Except it's a huge deal.

"Your enemy?" she asks. "What exactly makes him your enemy? You haven't seen him in a year."

"He used to call me names." I poke my bottom lip out, immediately feeling the effects of age regression. "Well...a name," I correct.

"*What* name?" she presses, looking me in the face. Her expression is slightly worried.

"Ghost Girl," I mumble.

"Ghost Girl?" she clarifies. I nod.

Her shoulders visibly relax. "Is that all?"

I nod again, realizing that none of this sounds bad enough to make her want to take my side. At this point she's staring through me, my older mirror image with the exception of our eye colors and my blue hair. She reaches out to smooth a flyaway behind my ear.

"Did he do anything else? Bully you? Hurt you in any way? I need to know if I should retract his job offer."

Something that feels strangely like panic shoots through me. Bully? Hurt? I can't stand Dawson Aiken, but he never did anything like that. For the first time, I feel a little silly.

"No! He was just...annoying."

"I see." Mom tries to hide a smirk but doesn't do a very good job.

It reminds me of Dawson's stupid smirk and my blood starts to boil again.

"Last question. Will you be able to look past that 'annoyance' long enough to train him?"

Staying silent, I wrinkle my nose.

"I've gotta get this tour started," I say, trying to slip around her.

"Sage, please answer the question. We need the help. He seems nice, and genuinely interested in guiding. Plus, he's Ed Aiken's *son*. We don't want to piss off Ed Aiken by firing his son the day after we hired him."

She's not wrong. Though something tells me Ed doesn't know about Dawson interviewing for this job in the first place.

"Yes," I hiss. "I'll train him. It will be fine. Great. Wonderful. Fun!"

I push past her and walk around the desk to stand in front of the group waiting for me by Ms. Knox's favorite display of classics. "Hi, everyone! Thanks for choosing Sunny Spirits Ghost Tours! My name is Sage and I'll be your guide this evening. We have a big group, so I just ask that you all keep up and try to stick together as we go. Let's get this show on the road!"

The group files out of Ghost to Coast and onto the sidewalk. I wave at Mom and step out to join them, our conversation and my interaction with Dawson still playing on repeat in my brain. Getting through this tour is going to be a challenge.

As of thirty minutes ago, getting through this *summer* is going to be a challenge.

Clearing my throat, I force myself into my tour persona. "We start all of our tours in Larkspur Square, home to the well-known statue of the island's first mayor, Henry Howell. Let's just say, more than Henry's statue is rumored to hang out in the square these days..."

CHAPTER 5

SUMMER 2009

The first thing I do upon arriving home from work is disappear into my room with my cell phone in tow.

Flopping on top of my twin bed that seems to shrink every second, I push the screen up to expose the phone's tiny keyboard, and my thumbs take on a mind of their own.

> MEET ME AT BEANS TMRW, 10 A.M.
> SHARP. THIS IS AN EMERGENCY, NOT A
> DRILL!!!

I let the phone fall to the mattress and bury my face in my pillow. My feet dangle off the end of the bed and I kick them ferociously, unable to contain my frustration any longer. The exertion produces a sheen of sweat over my entire body, and I roll dramatically to the floor to crawl over and turn the window unit on. I sit there on my knees for a few minutes, letting the cold air blast directly into my face. Every summer seems to get hotter and hotter, and every summer our three measly window units seem to cool our little cottage less and less.

"What are you *doing*?" A weasel-like voice makes me jump,

and I look over my shoulder. Sawyer stands just outside my room, holding the sheet that serves as my door open with one hand, and a melting orange popsicle in the other. He slurps his tongue around the popsicle and a chunk of it falls to the floor with a *plop*.

"Contemplating my existence." I scramble to my feet and use an old paper towel from my dresser to clean up the popsicle before it becomes an even bigger mess.

"I don't know what that means," Sawyer says through an orange-rimmed mouth.

"You'll understand one day." I pinch his chubby cheek. "What happened to knocking, by the way?"

"You don't have a door." He shrugs.

"So knock on the side or something." I bang the wall for effect. "I'm an adult and I need my privacy."

"Nineteen is an adult?" He swallows the last bite of popsicle and shoves the stick into the pocket of his pajamas. "If you're an adult, why do you still live at home?"

Because it's impossible to find an affordable rental on this island that isn't reserved for tourists. Because we're too poor for me to go to college. Because Dad isn't even close to selling his book yet. Because I have to be here to help Mom with Sunny Spirits so we don't starve to death and lose this cottage that is so small it can barely house all of us! My brain produces an angsty list of answers, but none of them need to fall upon Sawyer's ears.

"Because I would miss you all too much if I left," I say instead. To be fair, that's also true.

"Oh," he says simply, then walks away. The sheet swings back into place.

"It's past your bedtime, by the way," I yell after him.

"You're not my boss!"

Sighing, I look around the tiny den that became my bedroom when Sawyer and I got too old to share. It used to be Dad's office, but he moved all of his stuff to the sunroom so I could have my own space. It's never had a real door, and it barely fits a twin bed and a dresser, but it's mine.

My phone chirps, and I make a dive for it to read Caroline's reply.

CAROLINE
I'll be there. U ok?

It's 2 much 2 type

CAROLINE
Give me a hint???

I stare up at the ceiling and slide my phone open and closed while I think of a response.

Dawson. F-ing. Aiken.

Ten minutes later, Caroline still hasn't responded. Dawson is no stranger when it comes to being the subject of conversation between Caroline and me. By the end of high school, she was practically begging me to stop complaining about him. Now, I'm bringing his name up for the first time in over a year and she's probably wondering, *What now?*

That's what I wanted to ask Dawson when I saw him in Ghost to Coast today. What now, Golden Boy? Are you here to bestow upon me another nickname that will now follow me throughout my post–high school life? Maybe you'd like to remind me how smart and perfect you are? Would you like to tell me about everything grand you've accomplished in your first year of college?

After putting my phone on the charger, I find a pair of pajamas on the floor and head to the bathroom for a much-needed shower. Sawyer is in front of the TV in the living room and I haven't seen Mom since I got home, which means she's probably asleep. I can see the lamp in the sunroom glowing at the end of the hall, but I don't need the sign to know that Dad's still up writing.

I don't really feel like chatting right now, though.

"Sage?" Dad's voice stops me just before I turn into the bathroom. Apparently, *he* feels like chatting.

"Yes?"

"Come here for a sec. I haven't seen you all day."

The sunroom is undoubtedly the best room in the cottage, even covered in Dad's cluttered mess of used coffee cups, rejected manuscripts, old Larkspur newspapers, and books with too many dog-eared pages to count. Three of the four walls consist of bay windows that, during the day, provide a picture-perfect view of the ocean that begins a few thousand feet away. At night, like right now, they reflect everything from the inside, making you a little leery of who (or what, we do live in "haunted" Larkspur after all) could be creeping around in the dark, watching from afar.

Our cottage might be old and small, but it's worth it for the location. It was a lucky find for Mom and Dad. It's the fish out of water amongst the newer oceanfront homes that have been built on this part of the island in the past decade, but we don't care. It's our home.

Even on my worst days—days where I'm angry at the world because I feel stuck, days where all I can think about is what it would be like to leave Larkspur and go to college or chase some other dream I'm not aware of yet—the cottage grounds me. Maybe it's because I know nothing else. Regardless, I don't know what I would do without the consistency... even if I am too tall for my bed and the humidity makes everything inside feel sticky for much of the year.

"What's up, Dad?" I perch on the corner of his desk and shoot a couple of finger guns at him.

He clasps his hands behind his head and leans back in his chair, then nods to his laptop screen which is packed full of so many words my eyes go crossed trying to focus on them. "You're looking at it."

"Getting there?"

"Slowly but surely!"

There's a beat of silence.

"Did Mom tell you she hired someone?" I ask, figuring it'll be better to go ahead and get the inevitable topic out of the way.

"She did?" He looks genuinely surprised. "She must have forgotten to mention it."

My eyes wander to the pillows and blankets that cover the loveseat on the other side of the room. When Dad first started sleeping out here, I assumed it was because of his messed-up sleep schedule, due to the writing. It only took a couple of weeks to start noticing other strange things between him and Mom, though.

Like the way she seems to glare at him when she knows he isn't looking. Like the way they only seem to talk about work anymore. Like the way they stopped kissing, or touching each other in any way.

They used to be like magnets. Dad's hands would find Mom's hips or the small of her back during something as simple as squeezing past each other in the hallway. Neither of them would leave a room, let alone the cottage, without a goodbye kiss. Now, Mom yells goodbye to him from the front door whenever she leaves, usually not even bothering to tell him where she's going.

That's probably because it isn't necessary though. If Mom isn't home, she's out giving tours or borrowing Ms. Knox's office at Ghost to Coast to work on bookkeeping for Sunny Spirits. It used to be Dad who ate, drank, and breathed the business. Somewhere along the way Mom took his place, and the older I get, the more I feel myself following in her footsteps.

"Who did she hire?" Dad asks, pulling me back to the conversation. "Anyone I know?"

"Don't we technically know everyone on Larkspur?" I joke.

"Not *everyone*, smarty pants."

"Trust me, you know this person."

"Just tell me, Wedgie." He thumps me on the forearm.

"Fine." I cross my arms. "Mom hired Dawson Aiken."

Dad's mouth falls open. "Really? Ed's son?"

"The one and only." I pick at a sticky spot of coffee on the desk. "He starts shadowing me tomorrow."

"Wow…" He stands and stretches. "An Aiken, working for Sunny Spirits. Maybe we've finally made it."

He grabs the empty glass next to his keyboard and heads to the kitchen. I follow behind, feeling my cheeks heat. "What do you mean? Why does everyone in this town act like the Aikens are celebrities or something?"

"Around here, they are. You know that."

"But *why*? Because they have money? Because they have a big, fancy house?"

"Well, yes." Dad turns the faucet on and sticks his glass underneath it. "They have influence, Sage. Something we could use. Most of the locals are still skeptical about Sunny Spirits. Dawson working for us could change their minds— make them see that what we do isn't about gimmicks, but about Larkspur history. About *their* history."

I stay silent, considering everything he said. My entire school career was spent as one of the students floating along in Dawson's wake. For years, I watched my peers and teachers fawn over him, just like the people of Larkspur fawn over his parents. I watched him grow into the Golden Boy he is today.

Am I going to have to spend my summer doing the same thing? Watching him become better than me in every way, and driving me crazy along the way?

"Why is he doing this?" I whisper to myself.

"What?" Dad asks between gulps of water.

"Nothing, nothing. I guess I'm just wondering why he chose Sunny Spirits over helping with the Aikens' fishing charter like he usually does."

"Let's just be thankful that he did!"

I scoff and start to walk away. "I'm taking a shower and going to bed."

"Sage." Dad stops me in my tracks.

"Yes?" I say over my shoulder.

"Be nice to him."

"What, like I wouldn't?"

"Don't mess this up. One wrong move and we could be ruined."

The comment stings. *Make sure you kiss the rich boy's ass, Sage*, is what he might as well have said. Luckily my back is turned so he can't see the hurt in my eyes. Never mind that I've given Sunny Spirits my all and picked up Dad's slack since I've been old enough to work. Apparently he still doesn't trust me.

"Mom and I have already talked about it. Don't worry. I'll roll out the red carpet for Dawson and if it isn't available, he can walk on me instead."

He sighs heavily behind me. "Good night, Wedgie. I love you."

His footsteps disappear from the kitchen, heading back to his lair. I run to the bathroom and shower with water so hot, it burns even my thoughts away.

～

"I don't understand why you hate him so much." Cole pierces me with his gaze, making me squirm.

"He's your best friend, so you would say that," I point out. "Besides, you're not supposed to be here, remember?"

"Fine." Cole makes a show of standing and turning his chair around so his back is to me. His curls bounce when he flops down. "Pretend I'm not here."

Caroline puts a hand to her mouth to hide her growing smile. I wasn't exactly pleased to see Cole sitting next to her when I arrived at Beans N' Boos this morning. Their relationship is new and they can't seem to get enough of each other, so I should have expected it. The fact that Cole is Dawson's best friend is a mere coincidence, but somehow it seems intentional. It's like being in high school all over again.

"I swear, I didn't invite him!" she'd said, holding her hands up in surrender. "He was here already."

Larkspur really needs a second coffee shop.

"I actually think you and Dawson will get along great if you can stop picking on each other long enough," Caroline says. "I've always said that you two would work well together."

"What do you mean you've *always* said that?" Cole asks, glancing at me over his shoulder. "This is the first time they've ever had to work together."

"'Work' can mean different things..." she says, looking at me with wide eyes to gauge my reaction.

I hold my hands up in a time-out signal, hoping to steer the conversation away from Caroline's theory that Dawson Aiken has been harboring a secret crush on me for the better part of our lives, but it's too late.

"Oooh, you mean like a relationship?" Cole swivels in his seat, face eager.

"I thought you weren't here?" I glare at him over the top of my frozen coffee.

"Get over it. I want in on this." He flips his chair back to face our little table in the corner of the cozy coffee house and places an arm around Caroline's shoulders. It's deeply tanned against her fair skin. Physically they're almost opposites, which means they look striking together.

"In on what?' I ask.

"This conversation. I have my own theories."

"Theories?" Caroline turns to look into his face and he gives her a quick peck on the lips.

Gag me.

"Daws-slash-Sage theories."

"This isn't happening." I slide down in my chair until my head is barely visible above the table.

Somewhere behind Cole and Caroline, the front door opens. Everyone in Beans does that small town thing where they turn to see who's coming in. Unable to help myself, I sit up in my chair and do the same.

I should have stayed under the table.

"Those *theories* are going to have to wait," I tell the lovebirds opposite me through gritted teeth, nodding toward the door.

"Why?" Cole asks, just as Caroline says, "Ohhhh."

Ed Aiken stands just inside the doorway, seemingly taking up the entire coffee house with his large frame and even bigger social presence. He smiles, waving and bobbing his head at various patrons around the room. Dawson stands at his elbow, a polite smile plastered to his face too. The smile turns to a full-fledged grin when he spots us in the corner.

Please don't come over here, I think, already knowing there's no way he won't.

He whispers something to his dad, then weaves between the mismatched tables toward us, murmuring apologies to anyone he bumps into along the way. Eyes follow him as he walks. He's a prince amongst the masses, showing chivalry to his people. He may as well be tossing gold coins to them in his wake.

"Hey!" He stops at the end of our table, bending to give

Caroline a hug before fist bumping Cole. "Sup, man? Long time no see, Caroline."

His attention turns to me and I find myself back in the courtyard of Larkspur High, staring at him, just waiting to see which of us will speak first.

"Hey...Dawson." Thinking of my conversations with my parents, I forgo using his nickname. I've spent a lot of time cursing his real name in my head, but it always feels strange in my mouth.

"Sage, my new boss!"

Then he does the worst thing he could possibly do. He leans across the table and hugs me like he hugged Caroline. His hair brushes my cheek, and my nose ends up so close to his neck that I catch a whiff of his cologne. It smells, well...great. My body goes rigid beneath him, and I force a hand up to pat him on the shoulder before he pulls away.

"Have a seat, dude." Cole motions to the empty chair next to me.

Without a second thought, Dawson pulls the chair out and sits beside me. His knee settles against my bare thigh and his cologne settles into the air around me. I've never been this close to him for this long, and I halfway anticipate that I may somehow burst into flames. Like when a vampire goes outside during the day.

"Sorry," he says, moving his leg away from mine.

"It's okay," I mutter, feeling my cheeks heat.

Caroline and Cole stare at us like a couple of zoo animals, fingers clasped beneath their chins. If I could do it without confusing Dawson, I would kick both of them in the shins.

Dawson-slash-Sage theories. God.

This is far from the helpful vent session I was hoping to have with Caroline this morning.

"The Spine Chiller," Dawson says, noticing my frozen coffee. "I get the same."

"It's all he ever gets." Cole laughs. "He likes his milk and sugar with a little coffee."

"Yes, Sage too!" Caroline giggles.

"It's delicious. I don't know what you want from me," Dawson says.

"They just don't like good things, apparently," I say, catching his eye. He laughs, and a feeling very similar to pride creeps through me at the sight of his squinted eyes and perfect teeth.

I rack my brain for some follow-up that'll press his buttons, but Caroline interrupts my train of thought.

"Congrats on the guide job," she tells Dawson.

"Yeah, I hear Sunny Spirits is *very* exclusive." Cole winks at me.

"Oh, we are," I say, taking on a serious tone. "It's a very grueling, scary job. I hope you're ready."

"Funny, your mom didn't use the words 'grueling' or 'scary' during our interview."

"She never does, not with new employees. It's usually best to let them learn from experience. Organically, ya know?" I suck the last of my coffee up, pretending to be bored.

Across the room, Ed raises a hand, beckoning Dawson to come over. He sighs next to me and slowly pushes his chair away from the table.

"Whatever you say, Ghost Girl. Luckily I'll have you to protect me." He stands and looks down at me, his hazel eyes darkening. "I've gotta head out, though. Caroline, Cole, see ya later. G.G., I'll see *you* at 4:30."

Then he's gone, his presence somehow still lingering in the air with his cologne.

Cole and Caroline look at each other, then at me.

"What?" I ask, defensive.

"Nothing!" they chime together.

CHAPTER 6

PRESENT DAY, SEPTEMBER 2022

D*on't think of him, he's in the past. Don't think of him, he's in the past. Don't think of him, he's in the past.*

I'm going to have to find a new mantra. Because how can a person remain in the past when they're about to walk right back into your present?

It's noon on a Saturday, so Main Street is at peak busyness. Post-summer peak busyness, anyway, which can still be a tad overwhelming. Most of the island's restaurants and shops are packed into the historic district, so it's where everyone wants to be. Beans N' Boos has a line out the door for lunch, which I have to squeeze through on the sidewalk. The Phantom Eatery is also packed, and as I pass by, I wonder if Whitley and Sawyer are inside.

If I wasn't feeling so frazzled, I'd stop in and check. At the moment though, I need to be alone. I can feel the emotional breakdown building in my chest and rising up through my throat. Luckily one of our part-time employees is handling the day tours, so I still have a couple of hours before I need to report for duty. I don't know where I'm going yet. All I know is I need to get to my car.

Keeping my head down, I press forward, toward the end of the street where I parked. I only need to make it past Ghost to Coast and the tourist shop that sells Larkspur T-shirts and other novelties. The individual cobblestones on the street remain my point of focus. I inhale the salty air, depending on its comfort to keep me grounded. A public breakdown isn't on my agenda today.

"Sage!"

I recognize the voice immediately and consider pretending like I didn't hear her, but I've already stopped in my tracks so it's too late. Ms. Knox is crossing the street, looking left and right as she goes. She's carrying her daily to-go bag of lunch from Phantom, her brightly colored bohemian sundress billowing in the breeze. I attempt a smile, but in her comforting presence, a tear sneaks out of my right eye.

"Sage, love, what's the matter?" Ms. Knox places her free hand on my shoulder and guides me beneath the awning of the bookstore, out of the borderline intolerable September sun. Her brow furrows in concern as she studies my face, which is now covered in a few more tears.

"It's...nothing. Sorry, I can't really talk about it right now. I was just heading to have a bit of alone time before the evening tours."

She squeezes my shoulder, sympathy tears pooling in her own eyes. I never had the privilege of knowing any of my grandparents, but thanks to Ms. Knox, the grandparent-shaped hole in my heart has always been filled anyway. These days, her hair seems grayer and grayer every time I see her, and though she's still healthy and thriving and refuses to retire, I already dread the day I'll have to say goodbye to her in any way.

"Go do what you need to do. Have you eaten?" she asks.

"I had a coffee earlier, so I'm fine."

"Hell no," she says, her voice growing sparky. "You still have a long day ahead. You need something in your stomach."

She opens her take-out bag and rummages around before pulling out a smaller, folded paper bag, which she passes to me with a smile.

"Is this—?" I start to ask.

"You already know." She reaches out to wipe a tear from my cheek and pushes my ponytail behind my shoulder. "I'll see you later. You look exquisite in that dress, by the way."

"Thank you," I say, but she's already opening the shop's front door, brushing my gratitude away as she goes.

The inside of my car is a stifling six million degrees. I sit my things in the passenger seat, taking extra care with the goods Ms. Knox just passed to me. If those spilled out onto the floorboard, it would be the cherry on top of my Saturday shitshow sundae.

I'm driving toward home when a better idea hits me. At the fork just before the Aikens' house, I veer my steering wheel to the left and make for the island's north coast. It's been a few years since I've been where I'm heading, but with everything that has happened so far today, it seems like the right place to be.

On the right side of the road, about a quarter mile before the turn to Primera Beach, there's a tiny, overgrown gravel parking lot with just enough space for two or three cars. Beyond it is a short, narrow trail that snakes through the tepid woods and empties out onto one of Larkspur's hidden gems— a slender stretch of driftwood-covered beach.

Dad first showed it to me when I was a kid. Skeleton Beach, he nicknamed it, because the driftwood looked like distorted skeletons scattered across the sand. Like most other places on Larkspur, he believes it to be haunted, thanks to the many territory battles that took place on the beaches throughout the 1500s and into the 1600s.

It quickly became my haven after that—a place to escape to when I needed a break from my family, or school, or responsibilities. Many sweaty bike rides led me to the "skeletons," where I would sit and read a book or throw seashells back into their original home. When I was a teenager, I would sit and listen to my music, looking out over the never-ending expanse of water, contemplating everything new I was learning about the world. When I still had the moped, it often seemed to lead me here on its own accord after late tours in the middle of the night. Even under a deep, velvet blue sky, I was never afraid to be alone on Skeleton Beach.

Alone was how I preferred it. I never did bring Caroline, or even Sawyer, to visit. Dad and I never came back together. I've never brought Whitley. There has always been something about knowing it was mine.

It was for a while, anyway. I eventually learned it was Dawson's, too. Then after that, it quickly became ours.

For a couple of years after the end of Dawson and I, I still drove out here almost every day. It felt like the only part of him I had left. It was the one place I could safely and privately allow myself to think about him, to cry openly over my mistakes and come to terms with losing the only aspect of Larkspur that gave me any hope.

Finally, one day, while sitting on the sand with moisture seeping through my shorts, a switch flipped. I went from desperately clinging to the memories to wanting absolutely nothing to do with them. I stood up, wiped myself off, and walked away, determined never to come back again.

Now it's today, and I feel like the only way to cope with the news Caroline gave me at the old ice cream parlor is to allow myself to remember. To let myself feel all of that old hurt once again, so it can be out of the way by the time I inevitably run into the man who at one point upended my entire world.

Dawson is moving back to Larkspur.

"But...why?" I'd asked Caroline after she dropped the bomb on me.

"I don't know," she'd answered with concern in her eyes. "He's moving back and wants to buy the building. Those are the only details Cole gave me after Daws called him a few days ago."

With my keys and the paper bag in hand, I clamber along the trail. The pathway is hugged tightly by trees and coastal plants, but opens up to reveal a blue sky and white sand just as I'm starting to feel claustrophobic. Upon first glance, the beach looks exactly the same as I remember. I walk along the water, searching for my favorite piece of driftwood, crossing my fingers that it's still there, but also kind of hoping it's gone.

It's exactly where it should be, perfectly smooth and curved into a shape made specifically for sitting. I squat and settle into the little makeshift chair. It's not quite as comfortable in my thirties as it was in my teens and twenties, but it will do. The bag Ms. Knox gave me is still warm in my lap. I didn't think I was hungry, but my stomach disagrees when I open the parcel to reveal five little spheres of The Phantom Eatery's fried cornbread.

I break one of the nuggets in half and crunch into it, nodding my approval of the crispy exterior and pillowy inside. Ms. Knox knows these are my favorite. She loves them too, and eats them almost every day, often sharing with me if I'm at the shop during lunch. The fact that she gave me her entire bag today shows how much she cares about me, as if I didn't already know it.

I'm reassured by the fact that she still gets to enjoy the lima beans and rice the cornbread is usually served with. Phantom has specialized in southern comfort food since they opened before I was born, and it only seems to get better every year.

Right now, it's giving an entirely new definition to the word "comfort."

I finish my lunch and wiggle deeper into the driftwood's nook, tears still silently falling down my face. The sky is virtually cloudless today, with the Florida sun a perfect orange circle in the center. There are a couple of cargo ships on the horizon, and I wish one of them would come pick me up and take me somewhere far, far away.

The thought is dramatic, but a lot of thoughts seem dramatic when you're a 32-year-old woman who is still completely shaken up by the boy she left behind in her early twenties. Wondering why you can't get past it, wanting to be able to commit to someone else, trying to figure out why you never can—the thoughts and regrets are excessive.

When Whitley was around two years old, I felt myself starting to heal. Dad had given me free rein of Sunny Spirits's rebrand, and working on the logo and marketing and setting us up on social media had me feeling excited and fulfilled. Dawson had been married for a year, I'd completely stopped following him on any form of social media, and had forbidden Caroline and Cole from mentioning him around me. It didn't matter how curious I was, it wasn't healthy for me.

Life has gone on in the same fashion since, though the acceptance of it still often feels forced. The one saving grace was that Dawson didn't return to Larkspur after college. He's visited off and on over the years, of course. But with my best friend married to his best friend, I've been able to avoid accidentally bumping into Dawson or his wife thanks to their help.

It's immature, I know. I guess I'll have no choice but to toughen up now that he'll be living here again.

I saw him from a distance once, as I was leading a tour group from the square in the center of Main Street to the bed and breakfast on the next street over. He was standing in front of Ghost to Coast, chatting to Ms. Knox. Later, I learned he'd been dropping off another stock of his stained glass sun catchers, which Ms. Knox has been carrying since he started making and selling them. He was the same, but different. Bulkier in that way men get as they age. Hair shaggier and less polished—in a good way. I'm pretty sure he saw me too, but I kept my attention on my tour group, afraid of what would happen if our eyes met for even a second.

"He'll be here tomorrow," Caroline told me earlier.

"Like for good? Or just as a prep for the move?" I'd asked.

"For good."

It isn't enough time. How am I supposed to mentally and emotionally prepare for Dawson Aiken to become a permanent Larkspur resident again in less than 24 hours? I regret forbidding Caroline and Cole to tell me things about him now. It's obvious they waited until they had no other choice.

It isn't *fair*.

I wipe my eyes with my forearm, not needing a mirror to know I've ruined the makeup I put on this morning. My orange dress is splattered with tear marks and cornbread crumbs and my knees are shaky as I unfurl myself from the safety of my driftwood nest. The waves seem less calming now...angrier. As my trusty "tough girl" mask slides back into place, I draw my shoulders back and use the energy from the ocean to harden myself, too.

Don't think of him, I tell myself. *He's no longer in the past, but he isn't your future, either.*

CHAPTER 7

SUMMER 2009

"First things first," I tell Dawson, scrutinizing his khaki shorts and polo shirt, "you need a uniform."

"Uniform?" he asks, following me into Ms. Knox's office.

I drop to my knees and flip open the cardboard box of guide T-shirts shoved into the corner. "What size are you?"

"Large." He hovers in the doorway, but I swear I can feel heat radiating from him as if he were standing right next to me. I've been feeling shaky since seeing him at Beans this morning. There was something about knowing I was going to be seeing him again in a few short hours—knowing I was going to have to spend the entire evening with him.

Caroline and Cole and their *hypotheses* haven't helped either.

Outside of a few classes together throughout the years, passing each other in the halls and courtyard, and running into each other around Larkspur, I haven't spent much time with Dawson. And I definitely haven't spent any one-on-one time with him. It's one thing to try to out-snark him when we're in a group of people. How am I supposed to be alone with him without any social barriers? I don't know what to expect.

He's Golden Boy, my inner monologue interrupts. *You know exactly who he is. Successful, smart, maddeningly perfect Golden Boy.*

I pull a large tee from the box and toss it to him. He snatches it from the air and unfolds it, holding it out in front of him. The front has a tiny ghost with sunglasses on the right side of the chest. A larger version of the ghost in a beach scene takes up the back of the shirt. *Sunny Spirits Ghost Tours* is scrawled in the middle of the sun in the top corner.

"Cute," he jokes, peeking at me over the top of the shirt.

"But wait, there's more! It glows in the dark." I turn to flip the flaps of the box closed again. "You can change in the bathroo—"

Apparently, Dawson doesn't need the bathroom. Because he's already standing shirtless in the office when I look back in his direction. He discards his polo across the back of a nearby chair, and I can't stand myself for letting my gaze linger on the way the corner of his chest flexes. Like most of us who live on the island, he's tan in most places, slightly sunburnt in others, even after only being back from college for a couple of weeks. There's a distinct tan line just below each of his biceps, and a smattering of dark brown hair across his chest.

He begins to pull the shirt over his head and I look away at a breakneck speed, my heart pounding. "I'll meet you at the check-in desk," I mutter, slipping around him to leave the office.

Wait a damn second, has Golden Boy always been hot?

This situation keeps getting weirder and weirder.

"All righty, Ghost Girl. Let's do this." Dawson appears beside me, cracking his knuckles and looking better in the branded shirt than anyone is supposed to. The knuckle cracking, however, grates against my nerves and makes me remember exactly who I'm dealing with.

"Are you going to call me that forever?" I ask.

"Only until you ask me not to." His eyes search mine, like he's looking for something. He's tall, but I'm tall too, so our gazes are nearly level.

"It would be that easy?"

He shrugs. "Yeah, why not?"

"Wait, wait, wait." I switch the computer on, then turn my entire body to face him. "So you're telling me, I let you call me that for the entirety of middle and high school, and all I would've had to do to get you to stop was simply *ask* you to?"

"Yup." He smiles. "I'm a man of my word, Sage."

I let him continue to search my eyes and search his in return, looking for any sign that he's waving the red flag of bullshit.

"I don't believe you," I say, even though I can't find the flag. He seems...sincere.

The computer continues to boot up, far too slowly. A thought hits me and I snort. "Now that you're working with Sunny Spirits, wouldn't that technically make you Ghost Boy?" I ask.

"I guess it would." One side of his mouth lifts. "It's better than being golden."

"Really?" I squint at him. "Doesn't everyone secretly want to be *golden*, though?"

The corner of his mouth falls again, and his voice drops an octave. "Not me. At least, I don't think I do."

There's an element of seriousness to his demeanor now. For some reason, it makes guilt twinge deep in my stomach. He breaks our eye contact and stares out across the bookshop with a faraway look on his face. Then, he catches Ms. Knox's attention and waves at her, grinning again like nothing ever happened.

Interesting.

"Guests will be here soon." I change the subject and open our booking system. "Most are pre-booked, but there were a couple of cancellations so we do have space for walk-ins this evening. Checking everyone in and confirming payment is how you'll start every tour."

We go through the basics with the first couple of guests, and by the third Dawson is navigating the booking system and making small talk with them like he's been doing this his entire life. His charm is one thing I've never been able to deny. His laugh is genuine, his smile is warm, and he makes each person he speaks to feel like they're the only one in the room. I watch as he checks in two middle-aged women—sisters, they tell him. They hang on his every word, cheeks growing pinker by the second.

"Hang tight and we'll get started soon." He passes each of them a tour map and they beam like he's given them an expensive piece of jewelry.

"What a nice, handsome young man!" I hear one of them say as they walk away from the desk.

He turns from the computer screen to find me staring at him. "What?" he asks.

"Are you good at *everything*?" I ask grumpily.

"I don't know." He taps the top of my head with one of the maps. "Am I?"

I snatch the map from him and use my hip to bump him away from the computer so I can shut it down, then hold a hand up in front of my face. "Well, you were class valedictorian." I lower a finger. "Never missed a field goal, everyone at school loved you, everyone in Larkspur in *general* loves you, and your hair is always weirdly perfectly in place."

I'm in the process of lowering my remaining fingers, but he pinches my pinky and holds it in place. "I did miss a field goal once, so that one doesn't count."

"Wow, a single field goal? That must have been difficult for you."

"For my dad more so than me." He makes a sound between a scoff and a laugh. "But, yeah, it did kind of suck."

"Let me guess, you made straight As during your first year of college, too?"

Instead of answering, he bites his bottom lip and shrugs. It tells me what I already knew. Honestly though, it's impressive. I'm about to swallow my pride and tell him so when the time catches my eye.

"Let's get this tour on the road." I grab the binder next to the computer and pass it to him. "There's a script in here. You don't have to follow it exactly, but it gives you an idea of what to talk about at each stop, how to answer questions and keep things interactive...all that fun stuff. You can follow along while I'm guiding tonight."

"Cool." He flips the binder open and studies the first page. "Is all of this stuff true?"

"Everything is historically accurate. Dad's done a lot of Larkspur research over the years and takes pride in that."

"Have you ever seen, well, you know, an actual *ghost*?" He whispers the last word like it's a secret.

I shake my head curtly. We don't have time to get into my personal opinions on the paranormal at the moment. Especially not in front of guests.

Thirty minutes later, our group is standing in front of Larkspur's only bed and breakfast. The historic mansion is perfectly upkept, surrounded by small gardens of vibrant summer flowers. In the daytime, the home always looks like the dreamhouse of some early twentieth-century Barbie. The front porch swing sways gently in the evening breeze, and the sun sets somewhere behind the home, giving the soft yellow exterior a golden glimmer.

When our late tours start in a couple of hours, the B&B

will give off a completely different vibe. With its shadowy exterior and dimly glowing windows which seem to enhance every little movement inside, it transforms from idyllic to downright creepy.

"Welcome to McBride Mansion!" I turn to face the group as they circle around me on the sidewalk. "Can anyone tell me what architectural style the mansion is?"

An elderly man in a plaid shirt raises his hand and I motion to him, smiling.

"Victorian," he says confidently.

"Exactly!" I say just as Dawson says, "Ding, ding, ding!"

The group laughs, and I find myself chuckling with them. Dawson's been making little jokes since we started the tour and the group loves it. Sunny Spirits aims to keep tours light-heartedly spooky, so his surprisingly goofy humor is an unexpected but perfect addition. His hazel eyes find mine and his grin doubles in size. I realize I'm having...fun. It's been a long time since I've had fun giving a tour.

Maybe this summer won't be so bad after all. Maybe Dawson and I can be...friends.

"Y'all didn't know this was a game show too, huh?" I ask, playing off Dawson's joke. "The mansion was built in 1899 by David McBride. He was Larkspur's fourth residing mayor, and lived here with his wife until he died of old age in 1952. The current owners purchased the home in 1983 and turned it into a bed and breakfast, but before that the mansion was home to a few different things, including a restaurant, a temporary town hall, and even a funeral home."

Murmurs pass through the crowd at the first mention of something scary. Dawson touches my elbow and I jump, turning to find his face just inches from mine. "Can I take over?" he asks quietly, closing his binder and tucking it under his arm.

"Sure?" It comes out as a question. I've never had a trainee offer to take over before, especially on the first tour. Then again, none of them have ever had the confidence that Gold— I mean, Ghost Boy, exudes.

"So, let me tell you all something about Mayor McBride." Dawson begins to address the group. "He loved a good cake."

"Who doesn't?" the wife of the man in plaid asks.

"True," Dawson agrees. "He loved cake so much that he instituted an annual cake baking contest during his time as Larkspur's mayor. He was the head judge, of course, and tried hundreds of cakes during those years. But..." He pauses for effect, then lowers his voice so they all have to lean in slightly. "None of the cakes quite held up to his own wife's lemon pound cake."

He gestures to the house, looking to me for reassurance before he continues. I nod my approval. "Mayor McBride has been gone for many years now, but there's one thing all of the owners throughout the mansion's history can agree on— there's very much still a part of him here. Guests of the B&B have reported sounds of footsteps going from his old bedroom at the end of the upstairs hallway, down to the kitchen in the middle of the night, where drawers and cabinets would open and close and silverware would rattle. Whenever someone would go to investigate the source of the ruckus, the hallway and kitchen were always empty. Many believe this recurring phenomenon is Mayor McBride, going for a midnight snack of his wife's award-winning lemon pound cake."

"We're staying here," one of the sisters Dawson checked in earlier says excitedly. "Maybe we'll hear him tonight!"

"No thanks," the other sister says, crossing her arms and looking skeptically at the B&B. "You won't find *me* going out to investigate."

"Fun fact," I say, jumping back into the conversation. "The lemon pound cake at Beans N' Boos Coffee House is inspired by Mrs. McBride's famous recipe. I recommend giving it a try during your visit."

I let Dawson finish telling stories of the other spirits rumored to dwell at the bed and breakfast, then we give the group time to take photos and walk around the home's grounds and wraparound porch.

"How did you memorize that so quickly?" I ask, nodding to the binder under his arm as we walk to the rose garden that sits on one side of the house.

"Magic," he jokes, gently elbowing me in the side. "Plus, I've taken the tour a few times over the years."

"You have?"

"Yep, just never with you. Once with your mom, and a couple of times with your dad. I didn't think you would let me join if I showed up for one of yours." He shrugs.

My first reaction is to get defensive, but I stop myself, thinking about the past couple of days. About how angry and frazzled I've been over Dawson getting the job. About diving beneath Ms. Knox's desk yesterday to avoid him. High school Sage was even worse, so I'm having a difficult time coming up with a counter argument. I *would* have found a way to make sure he didn't tag along.

"I want to say you're wrong, but you're probably right," I confess.

"I know I am." He stops in the middle of the sidewalk and turns to face me. The sun is disappearing rapidly, taking the rays that amplify the green flecks in his hazel eyes with it. "You've never liked me very much."

I consider his honesty, wishing I could successfully put what I'm thinking into words. It's not that I don't like him, per say. Rather, I don't like that he challenges me. I don't like that he intimidates me in a way no one else does. I don't like that he seems to have everything a person needs to make them successful and fulfilled, and I have none of it. I don't like that he seems to know exactly who he is and what he wants, and I don't.

Then, there's the nickname thing. And the constant picking on each other, but was any of that really so bad?

These are all things my pride will never allow me to tell him. So instead, I cross my arms, take a step away from him, and ask, "Why are you here now, then?"

He furrows his brow. "Being away from Larkspur for a year has made me realize a lot of things. I won't bore you with the details, but the thought of working even one more summer for my dad makes me want to scream."

I take the binder from him and fan myself with it. "I guess I wouldn't want to work on a boat in the sun every day either. Especially with fish."

He laughs. "It's not necessarily the sun or the fish that are the issue. It's, well…never mind. Should we get moving?"

"We should," I say, pulling my phone from my pocket to check the time. Disappointment nags me, trying to get me to succumb to it. Each time Dawson and I have had a personal conversation today, I've found myself not wanting it to end. It's strange. I should be wanting our shift to go as quickly as possible, but instead I'm happy that we still have two more tours to get through.

"I'll gather the group." He walks around me, brushing my shoulder as he passes.

"Round 'em up, Ghost Boy."

CHAPTER 8

PRESENT DAY, SEPTEMBER 2022

I ask Dad to meet me downstairs with Whitley after the late tours.

There are a couple of reasons I don't want to go up to his apartment and get caught up in conversation. The first being I'm physically and emotionally exhausted. The second: I don't want to talk to him about my meeting with Caroline today.

It will simply have to wait until I don't want to pluck my brain out of my head.

"Thanks, Dad," I tell him as he opens the back door for Whitley to climb in. "I'm beat, so we're gonna get home and crash. See you tomorrow. Thanks as always."

"You're welcome, as always." He bends to look at me through the window. "Drive safe. Love y'all."

I pull away from the curb, watching in my rearview mirror to make sure he gets safely back inside his building. Since it's Saturday, The Phantom Eatery's bar is still teeming with patrons, and I have to wheel into the opposite lane to avoid a few who slip off of the sidewalk and into the street. Laying on the horn seems appealing, but it would only piss people off and that's something I don't want to deal with right now.

"How was your day with Uncle Sawyer?" I ask Whitley once we get away from downtown and onto the quiet highway.

"It was great," she says excitedly. "He bought us new boogie boards and we shredded waves for hours."

"Shredded, huh?" I laugh. "Sounds gnarly."

"Gnarly?" she asks.

"It means, like, exciting. But in a dangerous way. It's surfer slang."

"Oh, cool." I hear her adjust in her seat. "Gnarly. I like that word."

"What else did you do?"

"We made a sand castle. I saw Penelope from school and she helped us! Uncle Sawyer let me have *two* sodas at the beach, but told me not to tell you. I forgot that until I just said it though..."

"I can forgive him," I say, smiling.

"He did make me wear sunblock." Her voice takes on a disappointed tone.

"Good!"

A little ways ahead of me, a black sedan pulls onto the road from the highway that leads to the mainland. I slow down to avoid coming up on it too quickly, noticing the Audi symbol as we get closer. It doesn't have a Florida license plate, but that's not uncommon considering the amount of visitors our small island attracts every year.

All of a sudden, the car slams on its brakes. I do the same, but not quickly enough. My tires slide across the asphalt and we bump into the back of the Audi with a thud that leaves both vehicles rocking.

I take a deep breath, trying to comprehend what just happened. My heart thunders in my ears and my hands shake against the steering wheel. "You have *got* to be fucking kidding me," I growl.

"Mama, you're not supposed to say that..." Whitley says timidly from the backseat.

"I know, I know." I want to beat my head against the window. "Are you okay?"

"Yep! Lucky I had my seat belt on."

I peek at the time on the dashboard. It's nearing 1:00 A.M. There are no streetlights or homes on this part of the drive, so the headlights of the two cars are the only source of light. No one has gotten out of the car in front of me, and I'm afraid to make the first move. I'm a woman traveling in a car with her daughter late at night. Larkspur's crime rate is almost non-existent, but what if this is some type of setup? I take a deep breath and unbuckle my seat belt.

"Stay in the car," I say firmly, making eye contact with Whitley in the rearview mirror.

Night air, sticky with salt and humidity, greets me as I climb out. I leave the engine on and my door open, just in case we need to make a quick getaway, and wish I had some pepper spray or something. I walk to the front of my aging Chevy Cruze to inspect the accident. My red car looks cheap against the sleek Audi, but the damage doesn't look too bad.

The Audi's driver's-side door finally cracks open and a tall figure steps into the dark. "I'm so, so sorry," a face covered in shadows says. "There was a rabbit. I didn't want to hit it."

A decade later, I still recognize the voice immediately.

Please, please no.

Panic flows into every nook and cranny of my body, making my knees weak and my hands tremor. The man walks closer, and my headlights reveal him bit by bit—Converse sneakers, dark jeans, tan arms and a broad chest wrapped in a plain black T-shirt, and finally, a face stricken with stress. *His* face, which only grows more concerned when he realizes who just ran into the back of his car.

"Sage?" His voice is low, barely audible above the car

engines. His cheeks and chin are stubbly, and his hair is tousled and unstyled. Silver-rimmed glasses frame eyes that look black in the shadows, but I know are actually the most glorious combination of brown and green, flecked with gold.

Dawson.

He's different. Older. Wiser-looking. Messier.

But still beautiful. Still perfect, only not in the way he used to be. And here I am in a Sunny Spirits tee layered over my orange dress, tired and disheveled, looking exactly like I used to in a not-so-perfect way.

"I didn't see a rabbit." It's all I can think to say.

"Are you okay?" He takes a step closer, lifting and lowering his arms like he's trying to decide whether or not to hug me or shake my hand.

"Yeah, we're fine. You?" I stare at his forehead to avoid his eyes.

He nods, and we continue to gawk at each other, sand gnats swarming around us in the glow of the headlights. "We?" he eventually asks.

Whitley's door flies open and before I know it, she's standing between us on the asphalt, which is still warm from a day of being baked in the sun. She stares at our battered bumpers and claps a hand over her mouth like it's the worst thing she's ever seen.

"Whoa! *Gnarly!*" she gasps through her fingers.

"I thought I told you to stay in the car?"

"Sorry, Mama," she says, coming to stand beside me and peering curiously at Dawson. "I couldn't."

"Gnarly?" Dawson repeats, one side of his mouth lifting.

"It's surfer slang," Whitley tells him, like she didn't learn the meaning of the word less than three minutes ago.

"This is Whitley," I tell Dawson, finding my voice. "My daughter."

"Hey there, Whitley. I'm Dawson." Instead of bending to

her level like most adults would, he extends a hand for her to shake. She takes it lightly, her small fingers disappearing into his large palm.

"Do you know my mom?" she asks him.

He looks to me for guidance.

"He does," I tell Whitley, running my hand down one of her pigtails. "Dawson and I were really good friends once upon a time."

"Why aren't you friends now?" she asks.

Now I'm looking to him for guidance. This definitely isn't the way I expected to run into him (literally) after more than ten years. I'm sure he would say the same, if given the opportunity. Strangely, I'm thankful for the distractions of Whitley and our cars. It takes the pressure off of the pleasantries and other topics of small talk we would inevitably have to succumb to otherwise. The pleasantries I'm sure we'll eventually have to push through.

"Sometimes adults can't be friends forever," I tell her, looking at Dawson over the top of her head. His eyes looked tired before, but now there's a hint of sadness in them too. I wish they were blank and soulless. It would be easier to have the immediate satisfaction of knowing he could care less about our past.

"Sorry my mom ran into you," Whitley says. "She's very tired."

"It's okay." He smiles gently. "I'm very tired too. I've been driving for eight hours. Can you believe that?"

Her eyes widen. "I've never been in a car that long in my life. Not even when we went to Disney World!"

Dawson laughs, and the sound of it is as delightful as it always was. Except now it's deeper and more contained—like he's perfected it throughout the years. It transports me back to 2010. To us crammed together on the teensy seat of my moped, driving over the bridge to the mainland in the middle of the night, his hands on my hips and his laughter a song in my ear.

The memory jars me so hard it ejects me right back into the present, to us standing in the middle of the road at an ungodly hour, chatting while our cars run in the background. He's always had this effect on me. He makes me forget where I should be or what I should be doing. Time hasn't changed that, apparently.

Which is nice and all, but I have to shut it down.

"Should we call the cops, orrr...?" I reset the standoffish circuit breaker in my brain. "We can't stay here all night."

"Oh, um..." The warmth drains from Dawson's demeanor, and he turns his attention back to our cars. "It doesn't look bad. It's late and we're all tired. This was my fault so I'll cover any damages."

"You don't have to do that."

"Just let me take care of it, Sage. I want to. Do you trust me?"

It's not the first time he's asked me that.

"Yeah." I sigh. "Sure."

Bored with the situation, Whitley gets back into the car and slams the door behind her.

"Here." Dawson pulls his phone from his pocket, unlocking it and passing it to me. "Put your number in. I'll reach out tomorrow and we'll figure out the next steps."

I stare at the phone. Is it really going to be this simple? After a decade of breaking ties, blocking old phone numbers, threatening my friends to never speak his name in front of me, and fighting memories, a stupid car accident is going to be the thing that forces me to have open communication with the one person I've spent my adult life trying to forget?

"Sage?" he prods again, and I wonder how long I've been

staring at his iPhone. The last time I gave him my number, his cell still had actual buttons.

"Sorry." I grab it from him and start entering my information. His gaze is hot on my face.

"It's good to see you," he says. "Your daughter looks just like you."

"That's what everyone says." I keep my focus on the screen. "Minus the hair color. She got that from her dad."

I pass the phone back to him and my fingers brush his. Our hands linger there for a moment, wrapped together around the phone. I force myself to let go first.

"Are you okay to make it home?" he asks.

"I'm not the one who's been driving for a day straight. I should be asking *you* that question."

"Yeah, I'll be fine." He runs a hand through his hair and his glasses go lopsided. "I am sorry about all of this. I hope it didn't ruin your night."

Don't worry, you don't know it but you've been ruining my life all day today.

"It could have been worse," I say. "Watch for rabbits. I'll talk to you soon."

He backs toward his car, lifting a hand in an awkward farewell. I'm about to slide into my seat when he calls my name. "Sage?" "Yeah?" I grip the top of the door so hard my knuckles crack.

"Did you know I was moving back?"

The mean side of me wants to tell him no.

"I learned today." The truth seems better.

"Cole and Caroline?" he guesses.

I smile, knowing he won't be able to see it through the dark. "Who else?"

He chuckles and climbs into his car. I put my seat belt on and wait for him to pull away before shifting into drive. Whitley is sound asleep in the back seat.

At the fork near his parents' house, he turns left before I turn right. I drive slowly, glancing into the rearview mirror to watch him disappear in the opposite direction. It's only when his headlights have completely faded into the night that I realize no one else was in the car with him.

CHAPTER 9

SUMMER 2009

"Special delivery."

I look up from the booking system to see Dawson in front of the desk with two large Spine Chillers from Beans in his hands. He passes the fuller one to me, along with an unopened straw. I accept it with a goofy grin, then return to my usual poker face the second I realize what's happening.

"What's this for?" I ask.

"To celebrate my last day of training," he says. "Plus, I know it's your favorite."

"It is." I unwrap my straw. "Thanks, Ghost Boy."

"Anytime." He joins me behind the desk and discards his backpack beneath it. His smell, which has become quite familiar over the past week, fills the space. He looks freshly showered, his damp hair combed carefully into its usual style.

The computer pings with a cancellation notification, and I return my attention to what I was doing. Out of the corner of my eye, I watch as Dawson fidgets with the office supplies and other objects on top of the desk, straightening and rearranging them. It's a habit of his that I've noticed a lot over the past few days—he's adjusted books and other merchandise in Ghost to

Coast, re-organized the training binder, and several times, like right now, given the desk a once-over.

"Sorry my organizational skills aren't up to your standards." It's meant to be a joke, but he swiftly shoves his hands in his pockets with a guilty look on his face.

"Oh, uh...no, it's not that. Just a stupid thing I do. My bad."

"Cleaning is your bad habit?" I laugh. "Just when I thought you couldn't get any more perfect."

He doesn't laugh with me. He doesn't say anything at all for a minute or two, and I'm on the verge of worrying I've fucked something up when he finally speaks again.

"Cole and I are having a fire on the beach behind my house tonight, after our shift."

"That sounds fun."

"Caroline is coming," he adds.

"Is she?" She didn't tell *me* that.

"Yep." He pauses, pulling a piece of non-existent lint off his T-shirt. "You should come."

I click the mouse around the screen a few times, pretending to be focused on a task.

"Will anyone else be there?" I ask, worried other people from high school might be a part of the plan.

"No, just the three of us." He steps closer, forcing me to look at him. "You would be the fourth, obviously."

"I'll text my parents and make sure they don't need me at home for any reason." I already know they don't, but I feel better having an excuse to potentially get me out of the situation.

Although, I'm surprised to find myself wanting to go.

"Cool." Dawson grins, and his eyes crinkle at the corners. I used to hate that about him. After spending some time with him, I'm learning that I actually really, *really* like it.

You're getting soft, Sage.

79

Three tours later—three tours that Dawson absolutely crushes—our final shift together is finished. Starting tomorrow, he'll lead the evening and late tours three days a week, and I'll have more free time than I've had in months. Normally I would be jumping for joy. One thing I can't deny though, is how much fun Dawson has made my job over the past week.

"Like everything else," I tell him later as we're locking up, "you're super good at this."

"From you, I'll take that as a compliment." He opens the door to let me exit first.

"You should."

We linger on the sidewalk, me waiting to see if he mentions the fire again so I'll know he really wants me there, and him probably assuming I'll give him an answer regardless. So many of our conversations feel like this: like a competition to see who can go the longest without broaching a subject.

"Soooo, are you going to come?" He breaks first, which means I win this round.

"I'll come. But I'm gonna go home and change first."

His face lights up, like he was expecting me to say no and I surprised him by saying yes.

"You can park at my house," he says. "But we should probably exchange phone numbers, in case you have any issues getting through the gate. It's been having some electrical issues lately."

"Okay?" I don't mean for it to come out as a question.

He hands me his BlackBerry and I pull my phone out of my back pocket, trading him. Putting my name in his contacts feels forbidden, but also exciting. I've always been the kind of girl to keep my social circle small. Besides Caroline, I had a few other friends in high school, but most of them moved away for college. I occasionally see their posts on Facebook, but have lost contact besides that. Dawson's number is now one of the handful I have.

A year ago, I would have thrown my phone into the ocean before giving him my number.

"You know where I live, right?" He backs down the sidewalk, toward his truck.

"Everyone on this island knows where you live, Dawson."

The Cape Cod–style mansion isn't exactly difficult to miss. You can drive around the entirety of Larkspur in less than thirty minutes, and the Aikens' house will most likely be the one landmark you remember, thanks to its grandeur. Sawyer has been calling it "the castle" since he was old enough to talk.

"See you soon. Caroline and Cole are bringing snacks and drinks, so come hungry!"

When it's dark, I drive the moped through all of the back streets to avoid the highway. It takes an extra five minutes, but I promised Mom and Dad (and Ms. Knox) that I would do it this way. As I pass by, homes are quiet and the night is still, with less breeze than usual. The moon is full in the sky above, helping my tiny headlight lead the way home, and I find myself in a rare moment of peace.

Then I park in front of the cottage, and I can hear Mom and Dad's raised voices coming from inside before I've even turned the moped's engine off. I remove my helmet slowly and listen, trying to get an idea of what I'm about to walk into. The curtain in the living room window moves, catching my attention. Sawyer looks at me through the foggy glass, a worried expression on his face. He waves at me and I wave back before swinging off the seat to go inside.

"Something has to change, Gerald!" Mom yells as I try to slip unseen through the front door. Her voice sounds thick, like it's barely squeezing through a throat constricted with unshed tears.

"It will change!" Dad sounds slightly less flustered. "You just have to be patient."

There's a moment of silence.

"Patient?" Mom hisses. "I've been patient for years. Your *daughter* has been patient for years!"

They're in the sunroom, but I might be able to slip by undetected if I'm lucky. I tiptoe down the hallway, poking my head into the living room on the way and motioning for Sawyer to follow me. We slip through the sheet and into my bedroom, and I breathe a sigh of relief.

"How long have they been doing this?" I ask Sawyer.

"I don't know," he says, tears swimming in his eyes. "The yelling woke me up."

I sit on the edge of my bed and pat the space next to me. Sawyer falls onto it and buries his face beneath my shoulder. I wrap an arm around him and rest my cheek on top of his head.

"It'll be over soon, like always," I murmur.

"Mom's going to leave," he says into my armpit.

Poor kid. I've been wearing this shirt in the heat all day.

"She said that?" I ask, surprised.

"Y-yes." He doesn't elaborate, but starts sobbing. I can feel his tears soaking through my shirt.

Mom has been getting upset with Dad more and more lately, but she's never threatened to leave us.

Maybe I won't be going to the beach after all.

My mood sinks with the realization. How did my tranquil drive home lead me to this?

I rub Sawyer's back for several minutes. His sobs turn to hiccups, then eventually, silence. I look down at his sleeping face streaked with tears and, unfortunately for my shirt, a little snot. Carefully, I stand and cradle the back of his neck to lower him onto the bed. I switch the window unit on for some white noise and cover him with my blanket. He rolls onto his side, settling deeper into my pillow.

Finding the courage to go tell my parents to get it together, I stomp into the hallway. Mom flies out of the sunroom just before I reach the door, nearly colliding with me.

"Sage." Her face softens and her voice is hoarse. "We didn't hear you come in."

"Not surprising. It's hard to hear things over the screaming." I narrow my eyes.

"We were just talking."

"Tell that to your son who just cried himself to sleep in my bed!"

She backs away like I slapped her across the face. *Good*, I think.

Dad joins us in the hallway. "Wedgie, you're home."

"And I'm about to leave again." I hastily make the decision and walk back toward my room, silently ducking in to grab a pair of shorts and a fresh shirt.

They catch me the second I step back into the hallway. "To go where?" Mom asks.

"It's the middle of the night," Dad adds.

"To hang out with friends." I walk into the bathroom and look them directly in their eyes before slamming the door in their faces.

"Sage, it's too late," Mom pleads from the other side.

"I'm nineteen and work every single day to keep Sunny Spirits alive, so I think I'm adult enough to make my own decisions!" I yell through the door before turning the shower on.

If they say anything else, I don't hear it. I let the water drown them out.

By the time I'm out of the bathroom, they've retreated to their respective burrows—Mom to her bedroom and Dad back to the sunroom. I poke my feet into my Vans and grab my phone and the key to the moped before leaving, making no special attempt to do it quietly after I'm out of Sawyer's earshot.

Back on the moped, I'm sliding my phone into my pocket when I notice I have a text from Dawson.

DAWSON

Park behind Cole in the driveway and follow the path on the left side of the house.

I make the five-minute drive and successfully get through the gate, then follow his instructions. From the road, you can tell the house is massive, but standing next to it, I feel even smaller. There are more windows than I can count, and between the detached garage, the screened-in gazebo, the guest house, and the main house, it feels more like a compound than a single-family home. You could fit ten of our cottages inside.

The path to the beach is marked by a trellis covered in thick ivy, and stepping through it makes me feel like I'm entering a secret garden of some kind. The sand is warm and thick, and I take my Vans off to carry them the rest of the way. Above the dunes a hundred feet ahead, the orange glow of a fire dances against the star-laden sky.

"Sage!" Caroline calls when she sees me emerge onto the beach. "Hi!"

She runs and meets me halfway, her energy faltering when she reaches my side. "Are you okay?" she asks.

"It's a long story." I've kept my parents' issues a secret from her and don't feel like getting into it now. "I'm good."

"If you're sure…" She links her arm through mine and we trudge the rest of the way through the sand.

"Why didn't you tell me about tonight?" I ask her.

"I was going to, but Dawson said he wanted to invite you." She winks at me.

"Don't do that," I say.

"Do what?" she asks innocently, fluttering her eyelashes.

Caroline falls back into the beach chair next to Cole,

leaving only one available seat, and it's next to Dawson, of course.

"Long time no see," he jokes. The fire dances in his eyes and glints against his hair.

Honestly, it's unfair that he always looks like the main character in any situation. He's still wearing his work shirt but his khakis have been replaced with gym shorts and his feet are bare. He's more relaxed, and I like it.

"Look at you two, being friends and stuff," Cole says, leaning forward to hold a marshmallow over the fire.

"S'more?" Dawson holds the sharpened stem of a palm frond out to me.

"Absolutely." I take the stick from him and Caroline tosses the bag of marshmallows my way.

"Do you like leading the tours, Daws?" Caroline asks.

"It's great." He finishes building his s'more and takes a bite. "Although, Screaming Lady did give us a hard time tonight."

"Screaming Lady?" I ask, confused.

"It's the nickname I secretly give the most nervous person on each tour," he explains. "Tonight, it was the lady with the short black hair and big necklace."

I think back to our last tour. The woman in question refused to go into Phantom's wine cellar, so I had to wait outside with her on the sidewalk. Then at Ghost to Coast and every other stop, you could hardly hear Dawson speak over her anxious commentary.

I smile. "Do you nickname every guest on every tour?"

"Most of them," he says around a mouthful of graham crackers. "Tonight, we had Screaming Lady, Messenger Bag Dude, Grumpy Teenagers one and two...I can keep going if you'd like. Obviously the nicknames are just for myself."

Cole and Caroline laugh as he continues to recite his list.

"Fascinating," I say, pulling my flaming marshmallow from the fire. "Maybe I'll start doing that, too."

We pass the bag of marshmallows around, making s'mores until it's empty. My stomach hurts from the sugar and it's technically too hot for a fire, so I'm sweaty, but those things combined with my current company help me forget everything that happened with my parents only an hour ago. I think of Sawyer asleep in my bed, and cross my fingers that he doesn't wake up to more yelling and find me gone again.

"I have an idea." Cole suddenly stands, pulling his T-shirt over his head at the same time. "How about a swim?"

He holds his hand out to Caroline, but she ignores it, her eyes glued to his strong arms.

"It's too dark!" She laughs.

I stare out at the inky expanse of sea, at the waves capped white in the bright, full moon.

It looks dangerous and inviting all at the same time. Maybe it's the s'more-based sugar coursing through my veins, or the feeling of laughing with friends after having to be a parent to your own parents, or the constant need to prove myself to the boy sitting next to me, but I want to be out there.

Before I know it, I'm on my feet, standing in nothing but my sports bra and panties.

"Let's do it," I say.

Cole comes over to give me a high five. "YES, Sage!"

Caroline stares at me in shock. I look at Dawson, and when I do, he slowly trails his gaze from my ankles all the way to my eyes, making me question my sanity, but only momentarily. I turn my back to him and begin sprinting for the edge of the water.

"Last one in owes everyone else a coffee!" I yell over my shoulder.

Cole's footsteps thunder across the sand, eventually

catching up to me and breezing by at twice my speed. He crashes into the waves, whooping as the Atlantic chills his body. I follow his lead before I can talk myself out of it, running until the water gets too deep, then diving into a cresting wave.

I surface to find Cole laughing and Dawson and Caroline standing at the edge of the water.

"Come on, chickens!" Cole walks toward them, using his hands and feet to splash water

in their direction. "Sage, help me get these two."

High stepping through the knee-deep water, I join Cole in sending armfuls of salty water toward them. They run along the beach, dodging each splash, laughing and begging us to stop at the same time. Eventually, one of my splashes hits Dawson directly in the face and he makes an uncharacteristic noise between a screech and a guffaw.

"Now who's the Screaming Lady?" I ask, snorting in an attempt not to laugh at my own joke. He somehow manages to smirk and let his mouth fall open at the same time.

"That's it." He rips his shirt over his head. "I'm gonna get you back for that one."

Then he's running at me. I'm so awestruck by the image of him shirtless again, and by the lock of hair that has come free and stuck to the top of his forehead, that I forget how to run and my feet remain rooted in the shifting sand. One second I'm mesmerized by the droplets of water running down his chest and the next, that chest is pressed against mine and we're completely submerged beneath the water, skin to skin and floating gently to the rough ocean floor.

We hit the bottom and separate to push ourselves back to the surface. I pop up, wiping the hair out of my eyes and the briny water from my nose and mouth. A foot away, Dawson does the same, still unable to stop laughing. My skin where it touched his feels like it's on fire, and he runs a hand across his chest like he feels it too. He doesn't look away from me, and my stomach does a flip over the way he seems to glow against the dark water. On the shore, Cole successfully drags Caroline into the waves. She continues to protest through her screams and giggles, but I barely notice the noise.

Right now, my senses only detect the brightness of the moon, the salt on my lips, the sounds of the ocean, and Dawson Aiken.

CHAPTER 10

SUMMER 2009

W hen I wake up, my hair is tangled and stiff with dried, salty water.

The cottage is eerily quiet. Absent are the sounds of coffee splattering into our ancient carafe, or Sawyer's favorite cartoons blaring from the living room television. There are no footsteps on the creaky board in the hallway, or squeals from the leaky shower head in the bathroom. I fling an arm over my eyes and listen for the muffled sounds of Dad typing, but even those are nowhere to be found.

Sitting up slowly, I squint into the sun streaming through my open curtains. It feels like I've slept for many hours and mere minutes all at once. I'm not sure how long I spent on the beach with Dawson, Cole, and Caroline last night. All I know is I was in the rare mindset of enjoying myself—of never wanting a moment to end. The sun was peeking over the horizon by the time I got back on my moped to drive home in the pink glow of an early Larkspur morning.

My feet land on something wet and sandy when I swing my legs over the edge of the bed, and I look down to see my clothes from last night, discarded in a damp little pile. My stomach growls hungrily. Apparently s'mores aren't a filling, nutritious dinner. I try to remember how many I ate last night, smiling at the memory of laughing with my friends around a much-too-hot summer fire.

Swiftly, a different memory slides into place. Dawson rushing through the water toward me. His arms wrapped around my shoulders, his body pressed against mine and barely an inch of space between our faces. The way he looked at me as waves crashed around us. The way I looked at *him*. How our eyes seemed both desperate and nervous to take in every inch of each other. I touch the corner of my mouth, needing reassurance that the expression on my face is a happy one.

Stop it, my brain reprimands. I feel my lips tilt down beneath the tip of my finger.

So Dawson Aiken isn't shaping up to be the annoying, completely spoiled rich boy I've always assumed him to be. This changes nothing. Can we enjoy working together? Sure. Can I call him a new friend? Yeah, no worries. Am I allowed to fantasize about what could have potentially happened between us if Caroline and Cole hadn't been around? Absolutely fucking not.

We're not the same. He will always be Golden Boy, regardless of whether or not he wants to be. And I will always be Ghost Girl, destined to be less than him.

I venture into the kitchen and find a note from Mom on the kitchen counter, telling me she's working and Dad took Sawyer to Hayworth, the closest mainland town, to see a movie. The fact that I wasn't invited miffs me a little, but after the way I stormed out of the house last night he probably assumed I wouldn't want to go anyway. Not to mention, Sawyer could use the alone time with Dad, and I have to work. I think about my baby brother's tear-streaked face. I didn't get a chance to talk to him this morning. He was back in his own room by the time I got home.

Would Mom really leave us?

Dawson becomes a blip on my radar, replaced by more pressing worries. It's no secret that Mom has become borderline miserable over the past several years. She's never threatened to do something like leave, though.

What would that mean for the rest of us?

Feeling dizzy, I place a hand on the kitchen counter to steady myself. My stomach feels like it's flipping itself inside out, and sweat is rapidly forming in droplets across my forehead. The sink is full of dirty dishes, but it's either that or the floor, so I have no choice but to add a handful of partially digested s'mores to a bowl holding the remnants of Sawyer's morning Frosted Flakes. I breathe deeply through my nose and turn the faucet on, rinsing out my mouth then sticking my entire face beneath the cold stream of water. The ringing in my ears subsides as I push away from the sink, taking deep breaths.

This is new. Same as all humans, I worry about things sometimes. But this felt different; overwhelming. Like I would never escape the sense of dread that decided to swaddle itself around me like a boa constrictor. It was like lying at the bottom of a swimming pool, staring up at the rays of sunlight streaming through the water, but already knowing I was never going to make it back to the surface.

Fuck.

I lean against the refrigerator and rest my forehead on its cool exterior. My brain is foggy from riding a rollercoaster of emotions in a short period of time. The confusing thoughts about Dawson, the s'more hangover, the panic over Mom— it's all way too much to deal with within ten minutes of opening my eyes.

Then the clock on the stove catches my attention and gives me something else to add to the list. 2:43 p.m. glows green and angry on the display, and a yelp pushes itself up my throat and out of my mouth. I sprint back to my bedroom and begin digging through my dresser, throwing various clothing items around the room like confetti until I find one of my many Sunny Spirits tops and a pair of denim shorts I don't completely hate. I wash my face and brush my teeth, but there's absolutely no chance of getting a comb through my tangled hair, so I throw it up into a ponytail and hope I don't look completely horrifying.

Tonight's guests will think *I'm* one of Larkspur's undead. How the hell did I sleep so long? Even after not going to bed until the sun was up.

One of my Vans is next to last night's pile of dirty clothes, but the other is nowhere to be found. "Dammit, Buster!" I yell as I search every nook and cranny of my room, desperate to find the missing shoe. Dad's idea of our cottage having a ghost dog is ridiculous, but sometimes it's easier than admitting I suck at keeping track of my things. I finally find the other shoe underneath the wet clothes, grimacing as I slide my foot into the damp canvas.

If you ever need to be somewhere in a hurry, a moped isn't the best form of transportation. The handle is twisted as far as it will go beneath my palm, and I'm still crawling along at a pace that is massively underwhelming compared to my sense of urgency. My phone vibrates in my pocket, but I can't stop to answer it. It's probably just Mom calling to see where I am. Or Dawson.

My stomach lurches again at the thought of him, and I cross my fingers that there are no more s'mores hanging out to make a reappearance.

Mom is behind the check-in desk with Dawson when I burst into Ghost to Coast. The bell on the door slams forcefully into the glass and Ms. Knox looks away from the stack of books she's pricing with a frown. Her forehead relaxes when she sees it's me. "Where's the fire, love?" she asks.

"Sorry..." I mutter before booking it (no pun intended) toward Mom and Dawson. They stare at me with matching confused expressions.

"What are you doing here?" Dawson asks, his eyes softening the closer I get to them.

"What do you mean?" I snap. "Working."

"Sage, you're..." Mom starts to say.

"I'm late, I know."

Mom changes her tone to match mine. "*No*. What I was going to say was, it's not your night, remember? You're off."

Huh?

I look back and forth between the two of them, realization dawning over me. Dawson's training is finished. He doesn't need me anymore. Embarrassment paints my cheeks pink. The events of my day so far crash down around me, and anger joins the embarrassment to take my face from pink to bright red.

"Right." I swallow the lump that's forming in my throat.

"You can still do the tours with me. If you want?" Dawson jokes. His face is hopeful, though.

Mom observes us silently. My first instinct is to say yes. I mean, I am already here. But...

"Why would I want to do that?" I ask. His shoulders fall and his eyes darken. It's exactly the reaction I was fishing for. What I don't expect is the guilt that comes along with it.

"Whatever. I was just trying to be nice, anyway." His reply stings. The lump in my throat doubles in size.

Mom continues to observe us silently. She's probably upset with me. I don't really care though, because what she doesn't know yet is that I'm more upset with her.

"Well then." I toss my moped key into the air and catch it, plastering a smug grin to my face. "I'm gonna go enjoy my day off."

Dawson and I exchange one more stony glance before I turn on my heel and weave back through the tables of books. My hip catches the corner of one of them and I hold back a cry of pain, limping the rest of the way to the front door. That's definitely going to leave a bruise.

Back outside in the heat, I slump against the bookshop's brick exterior. "Ow," I whimper, pressing my palm to my hip. I stare out across Main Street, trying to tame the chaos of my brain. And now I have a whole evening to do nothing but continue to overthink.

"Do you wanna talk about it?"

Mom's voice startles me. She's walking toward me with her purse thrown over her shoulder. Her sunglasses sit on top of her head, and I can see my reflection in them, crazy beach hair and all.

"Talk about what?" I growl.

"Whatever is making you mean," she says. "You're always grumpy, but when you're mean it's because something is wrong."

Rude.

"I'm fine." It's my go-to answer in situations involving too many emotions.

"Sage."

I stare at her, jutting my lower jaw out. "Sawyer told me something last night. Something you said. When you and Dad were fighting."

She sighs and looks up at the sky, like she's been caught. "Can we at least talk about this over some lunch?"

"It's 3:30, Mom."

"Okay, early dinner then." She takes my hand and pulls me away from the wall.

"I am kind of hungry…"

I let her put her arm around my shoulders and lead me

down the street toward The Phantom Eatery. "Let's split some beans and cornbread. I'll tell you everything," she says.

Later that night, I toss and turn in my too-small bed. Who knew a day could still feel so long after sleeping most of it away? Thanks to Sunny Spirits's rogue hours of operation, all of us in the Murray household struggle with a regular sleep schedule, but tonight is one of the rare nights where everyone is snoring before 1:00 A.M. Everyone except for me. I lie on my side, watching the minutes tick by on my alarm clock.

Things are going to change soon, Sage.

I can't stop thinking about my conversation with Mom. And it's the biggest thing I *don't* want to ponder right now. Looking for a distraction, I grab my cell phone and open my text messages. Dawson's name sits just below Caroline's in the list, and I scroll down to click on it.

DAWSON

Wish me luck on my first night working alone! I might miss you, Ghost Girl. ;)

It wasn't a call that came through on my drive to town earlier today. It was this text from Dawson. He'd told me he was going to miss me, then shortly after I'd rushed in and acted like an ass. Now I can't bring myself to respond to him and apologize.

Climbing out of bed, I use the light of the moon to find my shoes and my moped key. Still in the tank top and shorts I wear for pajamas, I creep through the sheet and into the hallway, being careful to avoid the loudest floorboards as I head to the front door.

Outside of the sunroom, I freeze. Dad's lamp is on, but when

I peek around the corner, he's sound asleep on the couch. Tiptoeing to his desk, I switch the lamp off, submerging the room in darkness. Then I leave the cottage, pushing the moped to the end of the driveway before I start it up to avoid waking someone.

It's not the first time I've snuck off to Skeleton Beach in the middle of the night. And as I park and jog through the woods and onto the driftwood-infested beach, I know it won't be the last. The water is still tonight; small waves crawl slowly up the shore, like they're competing with each other to see who can make it the farthest. I forgo sitting on my favorite piece of driftwood and plop directly onto the sand instead. It's cold against my legs. Goosebumps pop up all over my body, matching the pattern of the stars in the clear sky above.

Here, I can allow myself to think. Here, I can feel what I need to feel. For the first time all day, the tension in my temples eases up.

"Hello?" A voice cuts through the dark and I jump to my feet, turning to search the maze of driftwood behind me. My eyes find him immediately. Even in the dark, he's easily recognizable. Dawson stands about ten feet away, frozen in place like he's afraid to come any closer.

"I thought that was you." He takes a timid step forward. "I saw your moped in the parking lot."

I cross my arms over my chest, wishing I had put some real clothes on. "Are you following me or something?"

"No, Sage. I'm not." He sounds offended. "Isn't this a public beach?"

"Yes," I hiss, turning my back on him to stare at the black horizon. "I never see anyone else here though. Especially at this time of night."

The hair on the back of my neck raises as he walks closer, stopping next to me. "I come here a lot," he says quietly, like he's trying not to spook me. "Mainly when I need to get...away."

"Same," I say. Then, "Away from where?"

He takes a seat on the sand and looks up at me. "Home."

I think about his dream mansion on the coast. Why would anyone ever want to get away from there?

Uncrossing my arms, I lower myself down next to him. My bare shoulder brushes the sleeve of his T-shirt and I shiver. We sit in silence for what feels like forever, playing our usual game of "who will speak first?"

His eyes heat the side of my face, and I cautiously turn to look at him. "What was that about earlier? At Ghost to Coast?" he asks.

"What do you mean?" Truthfully, I already know.

He shrugs, his gaze briefly flitting to my mouth. "I don't know. I thought we were getting along. But today made me second-guess everything."

"It had nothing to do with you," I tell him. *For the most part, anyway*, I think.

"You sure about that?" There's a bit of fire in his voice, and the flames tease my temper.

"I think you secretly just can't stand the idea of anyone not bowing at your feet."

He turns his body to fully face me, kicking sand across my legs as he does so.

"Well, I think *you* judge people too quickly, and use that as an excuse to avoid letting anyone get too close to you," he says.

"And you've learned this after a week of working with me? Seems like a rushed opinion."

"No," he argues. "I've learned this after years of growing up with you. After years of trying and failing to be your friend."

We're now fully facing each other, our eyes shadowed and our shoulders rigid with defense.

"Have you made all of your friends by giving them stupid nicknames and being generally obnoxious?" I ask.

97

"You caught me." He holds his hands up in mock surrender.

"Why would you want to be my friend anyway?"

Dawson looks over my shoulder, then slowly lies back onto the sand to stare up at the stars. "Because you're one of the only people in Larkspur who *doesn't* pretend to bow at my feet."

I look down at him, at his perfect face and dark hair that is now flecked with white sand. His eyes hold mine and he licks his lower lip. He looks sincere, and I wonder what I've done to deserve the nugget of honesty he just threw my way.

"Do you want to know why I don't do that?" I ask quietly, lying down next to him.

"Maybe. Maybe not."

"It's because..." I hesitate, filling my lungs with air. "It's because I'm jealous of you."

He rolls his head along the sand to look at me. I keep my eyes on the sky, afraid I'll find smugness written all over his face. When I finally get the courage to look at him, it's not what I see. It's sadness. He doesn't say anything, so I keep going.

"You have...everything, and you always have. Perfect grades, everyone loves you, you're going to college...I look at myself in comparison and feel behind. My dad is the local ghost freak, every spare second I've had since I've been old enough to work has been devoted to Sunny Spirits, and I'm stuck here on this island, with no sign of change in sight."

Dawson's arm twitches and his pinky settles against mine, sending sparks up my arm. Neither of us attempts to move. "Would it help if I told you a life like mine isn't all it's cracked up to be?" he asks. "Not really." I laugh. "Well, it's not. My dad got to where he is by setting stressful, almost unrealistic standards. He's always expected the same of me, too. I'm not even twenty and my brain rarely gets a break. I can't be great at just one thing; I have to be great at everything. And if I'm not, I'm a lazy failure."

"He tells you that?" My brows arch.

"I tell myself that." He swallows hard. "But I know he thinks it."

I focus on the red, blinking light of a passing airplane, working through my thoughts. Dawson isn't the only person I've ever judged unfairly, but hearing how wrong I've been about certain things makes me set a goal to make him the last person I make assumptions about.

"It sounds like we both have a case of wanting what we don't have," I say. "I'm sorry, for making things harder for you."

"Don't be. While we're at it though, I'm sorry too. For all of the times I may have made you feel less. You're not. You know that, right, Sage? You're far more than you think." His voice is so warm I have no choice but to believe it.

We fall into another silence, alone on Skeleton Beach, nothing but the waves and the stars to keep us company. Between us, Dawson flips his palm to the sky. Without thinking about it, I place my hand fully in his.

CHAPTER 11
PRESENT DAY, SEPTEMBER 2022

On the last day of September, Whitley and I walk outside to heat and humidity levels that don't make me want to die quite as much as usual.

It's the first sign of a Florida fall—if you can call it that. Fall in Florida is really just a "lesser summer," but I look forward to it all year anyway. We may not have chilly weather or changing leaves, but there's still always the much-needed reset that seems to come with each new season.

Currently, I'm needing that reset more than usual.

Whitley jogs ahead of me to the car, squatting to pat the "gnarly" front bumper. "You're getting fixed today!" she tells it.

Laughing, I open the back door and wait for her to climb in. "Do you think the car will be happy?"

She pauses buckling her seat belt to stare at me like I'm the dumbest person on the planet. "I don't actually believe it's alive, Mama."

I can already imagine the teenage eye rolls to come.

"Hey, Whit." I look at her in the rearview mirror as we pull up to Larkspur's elementary-middle school a few minutes later. "What did I say you're supposed to work on at Grampa's after school today?"

"Deciding what I want to be for the Halloween costume contest!" she says.

"And what are the rules?" I ask, stopping at the back of the drop-off line.

"No clowns. Nothing bloody." She stops and sighs forlornly before listing the last one. "And nothing with glitter."

"Sorry, Whitty Bitty. Our house is messy enough without it."

"BO-RING. Penelope's mom is letting her use glitter. She's going to be a butterfly."

We creep up a few spaces in the line. "Butterflies aren't glittery, though," I joke.

"You only think that because you're a grown-up and you don't have any more imagination left." She says it like it's a verified fact.

"Hm, I didn't realize it worked like that..."

At the front of the line, Whitley hops out of the car with a quick "Love you." I watch to make sure she gets through the front gate, then wave at Principal Sutton before I pull away. The inside of the car feels deathly silent now, and I fumble for the scan button, turning up the volume on the first talk radio station that comes through clearly. I don't really care what the two hosts are speaking about, I just need a distraction before my thoughts become too loud.

I have to see Dawson again today. It's been almost a week since our fender bender, and other than the abrupt texts we've exchanged to set up an appointment at the auto shop (which basically consisted of him telling me where and when and me replying *You really don't have to do this* every time until he was probably screaming at his phone screen along with me), I've been extra vigilant about not speaking to or bumping into him again.

Hopefully the process of dropping off my car will only take a few minutes. Dawson is picking his up today, and insisted on meeting me so he can ensure everything is in line with the services and payment for mine.

A phone call comes through my car's Bluetooth, and Caroline's name pops up on the tiny display screen. "Hi," I say once the connection clears up. On her end, kids argue in the background and air rushes through a cracked window.

"Don't be mad at me," she says right away.

"Okay?"

"I can't pick you up from the auto shop. Cam, Maddie, will you two *stop* with the pinching, please!" Giggles fill the air and I can envision Caroline giving her kids the evil eye in the rearview mirror. "Sorry, Sage...these two are pressing my buttons this morning. Anyway, I'm really sorry but I'm pulling into the drop-off line now, then I have a paperwork emergency I have to go deal with. If you want, I can see if Cole can come get you and take you to Main Street?"

"No, no, that's okay." I'm already trying to solve the problem. "Dad should be able to give me a ride."

"Are you sure?" Her voice is laced with stress.

"Positive. If nothing else, I can walk. It's not that far." I turn my blinker on and take a left.

"Okay." She sighs. "I'm just realizing how much of a challenge this is going to be..."

"What's going to be a challenge?" I ask, confused.

"Keeping you and Daws away from each other," she says. "I should have told him to stay in Virginia."

A wave of panicked guilt rolls through me.

"Stop it, Care. Don't add that worry to your plate. You've gone above and beyond to help me over the years and it's time for me to be an adult and face things head-on," I say quickly, then change the subject because it's making me nauseous. "Are we still good for lunch?"

"Yes!" she yells. "Lunch is a must in what is shaping up to be a crazy day otherwise."

"I wanna go to lunch with you!" Maddie whines in the background.

"I'll let you go." I laugh. "And Caroline?"

"Hm?"

"At least it's Friday."

"Fucking finally," she mutters quietly. Cam overhears and starts reprimanding her.

"See you in a few hours." Smiling, I end the call. Cam is Whitley's age and Maddie is two years younger. Sometimes it's hard to believe that Caroline and I have been moms for 11 years of our almost-lifelong friendship, especially when talking to or being with Caroline always makes me feel like I'm an eternal teenager.

There's one other person who makes me feel frozen in time. In a different world, maybe I would be excited about seeing him in a few minutes.

Larkspur's only auto shop is one of the island's newer establishments. Until it was built a few years ago, you had to cross over into Hayworth for oil changes and other car maintenance. I recognize Dawson's Audi as soon as I pull into the parking lot. It's front and center outside of the office, looking shiny and brand-new like I never accidentally drove into the back of it. Claiming the spot next to it, I take a deep breath before climbing out of the car to walk inside.

The first thing I see is the back of his head. His elbows are propped on the service counter and he's leaning forward, chatting animatedly to the young, red-haired mechanic sitting behind the desk. They both turn to look at me when I walk inside, and he gives me a smile so much like the ones he used to give me that my knees buckle with the first step I take and I trip over the rug in the entryway.

Before I can hit the floor, he's next to me, one hand on my lower back and the other on my elbow. He steadies me, his face so close I feel claustrophobic. His smell is different but the same—it's not the cologne I remember, but the underlying scent is still him. Still Dawson Aiken.

"You okay?" he asks. His hair is slightly overgrown and has a bit of wave to it, like the night of our accident. At that time, I assumed it was the result of a long day of driving, but maybe this is just how he wears it now. He's also wearing the same silver-rimmed glasses, which emphasize the fine lines at the corners of his eyes.

"Yeah, I forgot how to walk apparently." I squirm away from his touch, which may as well be burning holes through my shirt and skin.

"Sorry about that," the mechanic behind the desk says. His name tag says Dave. Surprisingly, he's a Larkspur resident I don't know. "We need to replace the rug. The corners are always tripping people."

It wasn't solely the rug, I think, walking to the desk. I can feel Dawson's eyes following me.

"Dropping off the Chevy Cruze?" Dave asks.

"Yep." I place the keys on the counter and move slightly to the right when Dawson comes to stand beside me.

"And I understand Mr. Aiken will be taking care of payment?"

"It's Dawson," Dawson corrects politely.

"He is," I confirm. Then, under my breath, I add, "Slightly against my will."

"Considering it took three days of texting for you to accept my offer, I would say it's fully against your will," Dawson jokes, keeping his eyes focused on Dave and his computer.

"It would have been less than three days, but I forgot you're almost as stubborn as I am." I also keep my gaze on Dave, as if I'm speaking directly to him.

"Good to see your willfulness hasn't changed."

"Nope. And it never will."

"Same here."

Dave's eyes bounce between us, trying to keep up with our verbal tennis match.

"So, uh...should we take a quick peek at the bumper?" he asks hesitantly.

Back outside, Dave gets down on his knees and runs a hand over the front of my car. "It's not bad at all. Should be a pretty quick fix. How does picking it up tomorrow afternoon sound?"

"That works for me," I say.

"Great, I'll call you when it's ready. Dawson, I'll let you know too. See ya tomorrow." Dave goes back inside, leaving Dawson and me standing awkwardly in front of our cars. It's only now that I realize I never called Dad about a ride. I pull my phone out of my bag.

"Calling an Uber?" Dawson asks.

I snort. "Larkspur hasn't made it *that* far into the 21st century yet. Caroline was going to give me a ride downtown but she had an emergency with work. I'm gonna call Dad."

He pulls his keys out of his pocket and unlocks the Audi. "I can give you a ride if you want. It would save your dad the trip."

Absolutely not.

"It's okay. If he can't come, I'll walk." I try to sound nonchalant—unbothered.

"Sage."

"Hm?" I look away from my phone, biting my tongue when our eyes meet. He's still too gorgeous for his own good. And it still makes me squirm.

Get it together, Sage. We don't admire married people.

But speaking of...where is his wife? Maybe she's meeting him down here in a couple of days or something.

"I'm going to Beans, anyway. Let me drive you to work. You can't walk." There's a hint of a scoff in his voice and it irritates me.

"It's not that far," I snap. "Plus, the weather is nice."

The second part is a bit of a lie, as the fake Florida chill is rapidly dissipating and a sheen of sweat is already working its way across my back.

"It's at least a mile and a half." He looks up at the sky, and the sun glints off the frames of his glasses. "Is this really how we're going to do this?"

"Do what?" I ask.

"Treat each other after this long? Use the past to skirt around each other uncomfortably? Because this is a small island, and I'm here to stay again. It's going to get tiring for both of us really quickly, Ghost Girl." The nickname rolls off his tongue like it's 2009 and my protective outer shell chips in a few places.

I look down at my cell phone and navigate away from Dad's contact info. "I haven't been called that in...well, a long time," I say.

"Sorry." He runs a hand through his hair, and a few early grays shine in the morning light. "It slipped out before I could catch it."

"It's okay." And I mean it. "But, it's Ghost Woman, now. Though that doesn't quite have the same ring to it."

He laughs and walks to his driver's-side door, looking at me over the top of the Audi. "Will you please get in the car, Ghost Woman?"

My feet are filled with concrete, but I drag them to the passenger seat anyway. "If you insist."

The car's black leather interior is spotless and has that

new-car smell. The nosey side of me wants to open all of the compartments and see if they're as spotlessly clean, or if they're filled to the brim with old sunglasses and tag registrations like my car is. There are no crumbs, no extra shoes or clothes, and no layers of dust covering the screens and buttons.

Messy Hair Dawson may be different from the version of him I remember, but Spotless Car Dawson is definitely the same.

"So," he says as he backs out of the auto shop's parking lot. "What have you been up to for the past decade?"

"Livin' it up," I joke. "Being a mom. Running Sunny Spirits. Drinking lots of Spine Chillers. Hanging out with the rich and famous. The usual."

The right side of his mouth lifts. "I've had at least ten Spine Chillers over the past week. They're just as good as they always were."

"Maybe even better! Pro tip, have them add an extra shot of espresso. It makes it feel more 'adult.'"

"I'll try that next time." He momentarily shifts his focus from the road to me.

"How about you?" I ask.

"Well, no kids for me." He shifts his arm on the center console, brushing mine and causing both of us to jump away from each other. "I've been working in finance since after college, but I quit some months ago to start my own business."

"Really?" I think about the old ice cream parlor, and a few puzzle pieces begin to click into place. "What kind of business?"

"It always sounds a little silly when I explain it." A pink flush takes over his face.

"Dawson, I run ghost tours on a tiny island off northeast Florida that started because my dad is addicted to the paranormal. It can't be any sillier than that."

He tilts his head against the back of his seat and laughs. "Hey, first of all, Sunny Spirits is cool. Anyway, I'm sure you know about my stained glass? Ms. Knox sells it at her shop."

"The suncatchers? Yeah," I confirm. "They're really pretty. And they sell like hot cakes."

"Thank you, I appreciate that. Anyway, I'll still be making the suncatchers, but I'm also shifting things to a larger scale— stained glass contracting. Windows and pieces in homes and businesses. It's something I've been practicing and perfecting for years in my free time."

"Wow." I shift in my seat to look at him. "That's awesome. So...creative!"

"I have some photos, if you want to see?"

"Of course."

He grabs his phone from the space beneath the radio and opens a photo album before passing it to me. "This was the first window I did for a coffee shop in Richmond. If you scroll through, you'll see the newer stuff."

I swipe through the pictures of colorful art pieces, each one becoming more detailed and unique. Some stick to a scheme of a few different colors, and others are crafted with every color imaginable. In a few of the photos, sun streams through the pieces from the outside, casting rainbow rays across the walls, wooden floors, and furniture of the interiors. It's magical.

"These are beautiful. I have no words." I stop on a blue and green mosaic window, locking the phone and passing it back to him. "You're talented."

"Eh." He takes the phone from me. "It's not talent. Just a lot of practice."

"You never were good at accepting compliments," I say.

He rolls his eyes at me. "I'm working on it."

"How did you get started? With the stained glass, I mean."

"I was miserable during my first year of work," he says.

"Richmond is a cool city, but settling down there was just... different. I needed some type of outlet. One day I was grabbing coffee at the shop near our apartment and I saw a flyer on the door for a beginner's stained glass class at the YMCA. I went on a whim, and loved it. Then I started making the suncatchers, and when Eliza moved out a couple of years ago, I really went all in on planning and turning it into a business."

Eliza. His wife's name makes my throat constrict. I've heard it once or twice over the years, but that's all I know about her. I've never wanted to know more—what she looks like, what she does for a living—nothing. In my opinion, it was none of my business. And it was bad for me to know too much.

"Moved out?" I ask before I can stop myself.

"Yeah." Dawson's grip on the steering wheel tightens as he turns us onto Main. "We divorced not long after we separated. I assumed you knew that, because of Cole and Caroline."

"No." I rub my throat. "We don't talk about you. I don't... let them."

"Oh." The energy in the car shifts, taking our positive conversation with it. Dawson parks, and I gather my things from the floorboard.

"Thanks for the ride!" I say, voice squeaky as I reach for the door handle.

"Sage, wait." He touches my forearm and I turn to stone. "I was hoping we could talk about the old ice cream parlor. I know you're looking at it for Sunny Spirits."

"What's there to talk about?" I ask, staring him in the face. "Now I know you have a business to house, too. And you're probably in a better position to buy the building than Dad and me. So, that's that."

"It doesn't have to work that way. I have—"

"*I* have to go." I open the door and step out. I don't want to talk about this right now. I *won't* talk about this right now.

We've discussed too much already. Learning personal things about who this version of Dawson is wasn't and isn't on my list of things to do.

"Okay, another time, then." He smiles sadly, looking slightly confused, probably trying to figure out the sudden swing in my mood.

"Sure. Thanks again." I shut the door and hustle into Ghost to Coast.

Ms. Knox bombards me at the door. "Did you just get dropped off by Dawson Aiken?" she asks, her eyes lighting up. "I recognize the car."

"It's a muddled story." I skirt around her, trying to shake her off by weaving through the maze of book-covered tables.

She follows me step for step. "It's been a long time since I've seen the two of you together," she sing-songs to the back of my head.

"And you never will again."

"Says who?" She stands in the door of the office, her dozens of tiny bracelets clinking together as she clasps her hands together at her chest.

"Says me!" I turn to face her, and she looks so sweet and hopeful that I feel bad for snapping at her. I walk over and pull her into a quick hug. Her head hits the same spot Whitley's does. "I'm sorry. I can't talk about things like that, though. It's for the best."

"Whatever you say, love." She pats me on the back then reaches up to tap the tip of my nose before going back to her post.

I close the office door and press my forehead against it. I should have walked the mile and a half in the sun.

CHAPTER 12

SUMMER 2009

The summer passes quickly, as every summer seems to do, and the second week of August marks Dawson's final week of working with Sunny Spirits.

"Are you excited to go back to school?" I ask him as we're heading out at the end of our Monday night tours. Over the past weeks, we've started doing most of our evening tours together, even though there's only one of us on the schedule. Since that night on Skeleton Beach, there's been a shift between Dawson and me—like knowing a little more about each other has allowed us to finally become real friends instead of fake enemies.

"Yes and no." He lets me exit first then locks up behind us. "It's complicated."

"I have time." We fall into step beside each other on the sidewalk, heading to the end of the street where my moped is parked behind his truck.

"Oh, you do?" He grins at me. "The old Ghost Girl would have never willingly spent more time than needed with me."

"You're the one who's been hanging out with *me* for six unpaid hours. So technically, you started it."

111

"Touché." He laughs.

We stop beside his truck and he leans against the front fender, folding his arms across his chest. For the most part, he looks the same as he always has, but in this moment, submerged in shadows just outside of the street lights, I notice all of the little things that are different about him. The Converse sneakers that have replaced his Sperry boat shoes most days of the week. The stray piece of hair that has become a permanent fixture on his forehead, like he's not spending quite as much time styling it every day. The Sunny Spirits T-shirt, which now seems like the only item of clothing he belongs in.

Maybe none of these things are true changes. Maybe they're all just the result of me seeing him in a new light...of learning to appreciate him instead of writing everything about him off immediately.

"So what's complicated about going back to school?" I ask. "You're good at it."

He breathes deeply and looks up at the sky, which is black and starless on this particular night. "Being good at something doesn't always mean it's enjoyable. Business isn't exactly the most exciting subject to major in."

"How did I not know what you're studying until now?" I ask.

He shrugs. "I guess we've never talked about it."

"Could you change your major?"

"As long as Dad is paying for my education...no. He says a business degree is the smartest degree you can get. That it can take you anywhere. The funny thing is, he only wants it to take me one place—and that's under his thumb, working for Aiken Incorporated. Managing our properties and the fishing charters and all of the other useless extra streams of income that my family doesn't even need. But I'm an only child, which apparently makes taking over the family business mandatory."

His face darkens as he speaks. He doesn't willingly talk about his dad much, but when he does, it's always with an expression of near disgust, like he's just bitten into something rotten.

"What would you do if you could do what *you* wanted?" I ask gently.

"It's hard to answer that, because I don't know." He grabs my forearm and pulls me closer, inviting me to lean next to him. "For a long time, I thought making my family happy was what I wanted. Every year it becomes more and more obvious that's not the case."

"Let me rephrase the question then." I sit my bag on the hood of the truck and turn to face him, propping myself up on my elbow. "What do you *like* to do?"

Twisting his mouth to one side, he looks at me, then back up to the sky. "Nothing worthy of a career."

"Hey, I'm supposed to be the pessimist here." I flatten my mouth into a line and narrow my eyes at him.

"I don't know how to think any other way." He looks down and traces the outline of the ghost on his shirt. "I've been taught that everything you do in life should be the end result of a goal—that everything should have a purpose."

"Everything?"

"Everything." A breeze blows a strand of hair into my face and he reaches out like he wants to smooth it away, but drops his hand at the last second. "That's a big reason I decided to work for Sunny Spirits this summer. I wanted to do something different, something that seemed like fun, and not like another responsibility."

For the millionth time I think about how vastly different my life is from Dawson's. Because Sunny Spirits is *my* responsibility—my version of school and career development and football and success, and all of the other things Dawson has worked hard at and depended on to move him forward. It makes me realize that we're all out here trying to find the meaning of life—trying to make it all make sense.

"Was your dad upset that you didn't work for him this summer?" I ask.

"That's an understatement." He laughs nervously. "My mom is the only reason he finally stopped complaining about it."

"What about next summer?" I ask. "Will you go back to working with him?"

He scoots a half inch closer to me, his nervous laugh becoming a devious smile. "Is that your way of giving me an advanced job offer?"

I bit my bottom lip to avoid grinning too big, and make a note to tell Mom to save room for Dawson on staff next summer...just in case he wants to come back. Then I remember that I'll most likely be the one making those types of decisions this time next year. My mood falls slightly, but it doesn't stop me from telling Dawson, "Yes."

"Offer accepted." He holds his hand out to me and we shake. It reminds me of a moment we shared on our last day of senior year—the moment we touched for the first time ever. Even then, his touch gave me chills.

"What if your dad is still mad about it a year from now?" I ask, our hands still clasped together.

He loosens his grip and runs his thumb across the top of mine a couple of times before letting go. "He will just have to deal with it."

The day before Dawson leaves, Mom gives us both the evening off to hang out with Cole and Caroline.

Caroline picks me up around 5 o'clock and we meet the boys at Larkspur Marina for a boat ride to the sandbar. They're loading the cooler and life jackets onto the small deck boat when we arrive, Dawson in a pair of teal swimming trunks, shirtless and barefoot. As we approach, I don't realize how focused I am on the pale line of skin peeking over the top of his shorts until Caroline grabs my wrist to pull me away from the edge of the dock I'm veering closer and closer to.

"That's not where his eyes are…" Caroline whisper-giggles into my ear.

"I don't know what you're talking about," I say.

"You do. And one day you'll admit what I've already figured out."

"I'm going to push you off this dock." I give her shoulder a little shake.

"Good thing I know how to swim."

"Ladies," Cole greets us, bending to give Caroline a kiss on the forehead before he looks to me. "And…Sage."

"So funny." I lift my middle finger in his direction then turn to the boat, where Dawson is already boarded and holding a hand out to help me in. I take it, stepping onto the side of the boat to hop inside. A stray wave rocks the vessel as I land, knocking me off-balance. Dawson catches me and pins me against his sun-warmed chest.

By the time he's released me, I've already added the moment to my list of all the times Dawson has set me on fire with his touch—the night we had s'mores, holding hands on Skeleton Beach, this accidental hug—the list is growing rapidly. The moments themselves have been brief, but the memories of them linger for what seems like an eternity.

Cole jumps in behind me, then turns to place his hands on Caroline's hips, lifting her off the dock. After claiming one of the seats at the back, I pull my sundress off and spray some sunblock over my shoulders before helping Caroline do the same. Her red bikini is the same shade of Cole's swimsuit. They've been dating less than three months and they're already the matching married couple.

"I can't believe your dad is letting you take the boat," Dawson tells Cole.

"Oh, it took days to talk him into it," Cole says, untying us from the dock. "I practically had to sign a contract."

"What made him change his mind?" Caroline asks.

"I have to mow the lawn for the next year. Literally," he grumbles.

"Aw..." Caroline steps behind him and wraps her arms around his waist. "You did that for your friends?"

He visibly melts beneath her touch, a goofy lopsided grin taking over his face. Feeling like I'm intruding on a personal moment, I sneak a peek in Dawson's direction. He's staring straight at me, and his cheeks turn pink when our eyes meet. He busies himself with pushing us away from the dock, and Cole takes his spot behind the steering wheel and starts the motor.

"I can't find my Dramamine!" Caroline says, digging through her bag. "I know it was in here. I'll get seasick without it."

We putter away from the marina and Dawson and I help Caroline search the boat for her medicine. I'm about to suggest she forgot it at home when Dawson plucks the box of pills out from beneath the captain's chair. "Got it!" He tosses it to Caroline.

"How the hell did it get down there?" She furrows her brow, confused.

Dawson and I exchange a glance. "Captain Crook!" we say at the same time.

"Who?" Cole and Caroline parrot back to us.

"The marina ghost," I explain, forming quotation marks with my fingers. "Allegedly."

"He likes to hide things," Dawson adds. "The marina isn't part of the tour, but we always find a way to mention Captain Crook."

"Are there any ghost-free places on this damn island?" Cole yells as he picks up speed. The rest of us fall into our seats, grabbing stray items and tucking them away so they aren't swept up by the wind.

Technically every place is ghost-free, I think. The Dramamine probably fell out of her bag when she got on the boat.

"Not many." Dawson laughs.

The water is calm and the sky is quickly transforming from a clear blue to varying shades of orange and pink. Wispy clouds hover just above the horizon, becoming thinner and thinner as the sun sinks lower. Next to me, Dawson stretches his arms across the ledge behind us, and his hand brushes my shoulder. He plucks a strand of my ponytail from the breeze and tugs it gently.

"Your blue tips are almost gone," he yells over the rush of wind and water, then releases it.

"That's what a summer of sun and salt water will do!"

"Too bad, I like the blue." He looks surprised after he says it, like he didn't mean to. "I mean, it looks nice either way! I mean, you look great! I mean..."

I reach over and press a finger to his lips. They're smooth and full, and I'm not sure who's more shocked at the gesture —him or me. I snatch my hand away and pretend to be interested in the scenery, although we're far enough away from the shore that there isn't much to see besides water. In my peripheral vision I can see Dawson still staring at me, then the wind blows my ponytail into my face and blocks my view. I don't move it.

These are the types of moments that make me question whether or not warming up to Dawson has been a good idea.

Being friends is one thing. The fact that I occasionally find myself wanting more seems borderline unthinkable.

Twenty minutes later, the boat slows and Cole kills the engine. The air stills and we're surrounded by quiet, nothing but waves lapping against the side of the boat as we float the remaining distance to the sandbar. I stand up and lean over the side, watching the water turn clearer as it shallows. At the edge of the bar, Dawson tosses the anchor over. This late in the day, there are only a few other boats hanging around.

Caroline finishes blowing up a lime green inner tube and tosses it into the water. "Dibs!" Cole says, standing on the side of the boat and jumping so his butt lands right in the center of the tube.

"No way, that's mine!" Caroline cannonballs after him, spraying all of us with cool water.

"There's another tube," Dawson tells me, pulling it out of one of the boat's many storage consoles. "I'll blow it up for you if you want?"

"Sure." I smile at him. "I'll share if you're nice."

"Am I not always nice?" He places the plastic mouthpiece between his teeth and starts blowing. My eyes follow his every move.

"That's debatable."

He rolls his eyes at me before letting them drop to my black bikini. I turn my back on him and follow Cole and Caroline into the water. A couple of minutes later, Dawson tosses the tube in, perfectly ringing it around my head.

"Thanks, Ghost Boy." My voice echoes in the tube and he jumps in next to me, holding the tube still while I shimmy onto it.

Caroline and I float near the boat, holding on to the anchor rope. We watch as the boys make their way across the sandbar, swimming then eventually standing in the knee-deep water at the shallowest point. It's getting darker, but there's enough light to make things feel safe and serene. Beneath the richness of the setting sun, it all feels surreal. It's just the four of us, a couple of remaining boats, and water as far as the eye can see.

"You're going to miss him," Caroline says, drawing my attention away from Dawson's figure in the distance.

"What are you talking about?" I spin in my float to face her.

"Come on, Sage. You can be honest with me. You like him. You *more* than like him."

"We're friends," I correct her. "He's cool. Working together has been fun."

"I see the way you've been looking at him all summer," she argues. "And the way he's been looking at you."

I crane my neck to look at the boys again. Dawson waves and I lift a hand.

"Even if there was...something." I lower my voice as if he can hear me. "There's not much I can do about it."

"Bullshit!" Caroline kicks water at me.

"He's going back to school *tomorrow*, Care. I won't see him again until at least the holidays. Regardless of whether he's interested or not, it's too late to do anything about it."

She sighs and tilts her face to the sky, which is now a marvelous shade of purple. "I guess there's always next summer?"

"Yeah..." I say, running my fingertips across the surface of the water, considering it. "Maybe next summer."

Too bad next summer feels lightyears away.

Fingers wrap around my wrist and I yelp, ingesting a mouthful of salt water as I'm pulled off of the tube. Spluttering, I surface and come face-to-face with Dawson, who's looking very proud of himself. "Gotcha." He laughs.

"What was that for?" I reach out and push his shoulder.

"Swim with me." To my surprise, he grabs my hand and

pulls, leading me toward the deeper water on the other side of the boat.

"Okay?" I say as the sand disappears from beneath my feet.

Here, we're hidden from the rest of the world. I can hear Cole and Caroline, but I can't see them. The water is black in the final hours of daylight and I find myself moving closer to Dawson, creeped out by the unknown of what could be floating beneath us. The boat shifts and the anchor rope comes into view. Dawson grabs it with the hand that isn't holding mine.

"What are we doing?" For some reason it feels appropriate to whisper.

"Talking." His hazel eyes do the crinkly thing, dark as the water around us. We're so close I can see tiny water droplets clinging to his lashes.

"About what?"

"I just wanted to say thanks." He lets go of my hand and grabs my waist instead, pulling me closer. Our stomachs touch, and the familiar heat is so intense I expect the entire Atlantic to evaporate.

"For what?" My voice is shaky.

"A great summer." Our feet bump together as we tread. Our breaths come faster. Whether it's from the exertion of staying afloat, or from the tension between us, I'm not sure. Probably both.

"Well, thank you, too. For helping my family out."

"Best job I've ever had," he says, licking his lips.

"Good thing your position for next summer is already saved." I smirk.

His eyes go to my mouth and his grip on my waist tightens. "There is one other reason I pulled you back here," he says.

"Okay?" My heart pounds in my chest because I hope I already know.

"Can I show you?" He grabs one of my hands and places it next to his on the rope, giving us more stability.

I inhale shakily. "Yes."

He leans in, and the last thing I see before my eyes close is the pesky strand of hair that always sticks to his forehead. His lips touch mine, softly at first. His hand moves from my lower back to the side of my neck, and when our lips part, my tongue explodes with the taste of salt water and Dawson Aiken.

We kiss hungrily, like we've been starved of each other for years. And who knows, maybe we secretly have? His teeth gently grab my lower lip, and I've decided there's no way I'm going to be the one to pull away first, when a splash of water meets our faces and makes the decision for us.

"What's going on back here?" Cole asks in a sing-song voice, swimming toward us and dragging Caroline behind him in her float. A grin the size of the boat next to us is plastered on her face.

Caught, I think as Dawson and I exchange a sheepish look. He releases my neck and brings his fingers to his lips. There's only one thing on my mind, even with my legs tired from kicking and our friends lurking in the background:

I can't wait to kiss Ghost Boy again.

CHAPTER 13

PRESENT DAY, OCTOBER 2022

"Mama, look!" Whitley tugs on my sleeve and points down the sidewalk. "It's fall!"

Up and down Main Street, business owners and volunteers are placing pumpkins, wrapping light poles in garlands of orange and yellow leaves, and setting their window displays with spooky scenes. The square is filled with bales of hay and scarecrows of all shapes and sizes, and fairy lights are being strung from building to building, creating a canopy over the street.

"Look at that," I say, running a hand over her hair. "That means the Halloween festival will be here before we know it."

"Good thing I have my costume figured out," she says with a sigh of relief.

"We need to work on that next weekend," I tell her.

"Don't worry, I'll remind you," she says.

And I know she will.

I pull the familiar door open and herd her inside, hearing the chime of the bell against the glass. "Why are we here if you don't have to work todayyyy?" she whines.

"Because I have to do a few things in the officeeee," I whine back. "Then we're going to Aunt Caroline's."

"Is someone not excited to see me?" Ms. Knox stands from her spot behind the desk, a fake pout on her face. "That hurts my feelings, Whit."

"And mine too!" Ms. Knox's partner, Eve, is beside her, her sandy, curly hair held back with a headband.

Whitley runs behind the desk and hugs them both around the waist. "Sorry," she says. "That's not what I meant. You know I like both of you."

They look at me and laugh. "Well, we sure hope so," Eve says.

"I need to do a couple of things in the office," I tell them. "Can she hang out up here for a few minutes?"

"Sure," Ms. Knox says. "Your dad is in there, though."

"He is?" She nods. I bite the inside of my cheek, trying to hide my disappointment. I've been avoiding him as much as possible, hoping to put off the conversation of the old ice cream parlor. I also can't remember the last time he came down here to work. He's been so hands-off with everything for so long.

No time like the present, I suppose.

"Guess what I'm being for Halloween?" I hear Whitley ask as I head for the office.

"Hmmm...a clown?" Eve guesses.

"No!" Whitley says sternly. "Mama hates clowns. And I don't like them very much either."

I crack the office door open quietly, and Dad spins in his chair. A grin spreads across his face when he sees it's me. "Wedgie," he says, removing his glasses and sitting them on top of his head. "I thought you were off today?"

"I am. I was just going to do a couple of things for payroll so I don't have to do it tomorrow. What are you doing here?"

"I needed a break from the writing cave. Thought I'd come

down and see if there's anything I can help you with." He pats the metal folding chair next to him. "I'm happy you're here. I've been wanting to talk to you."

Letting my shoulders relax, I slide into the chair. It's been a while since he's really helped me with anything. I'm not sure what to think of the gesture.

"About what?" I ask.

"The building, of course," he says. "What's the status?"

"Well...there's good news and bad news." I stick my hands under my thighs to avoid fidgeting.

He raises his eyebrows. "Proceed."

"Caroline said everything looks great from a financial aspect," I start.

"Don't you know you're always supposed to start with the bad news first?" Dad asks.

"What if the bad news has more influence than the good news?"

"Well, shit." He leans back in the rolling chair and laces his fingers behind his head. "Go ahead and rip the Band-Aid off."

I take a deep breath, then tell him all about Dawson's return to Larkspur. About Caroline saying he also wanted the building, then about our accident, him paying for my bumper repair, and about Dawson's new business.

"All of this has happened in a week?" Dad asks.

I nod, feeling guilty for being standoffish with him.

"I have to admit...I knew he was back," he says, concern in his eyes. "I ran into him at Phantom the other day. That's kind of why I'm down here to see if I can take anything off of your plate. I didn't know if you were okay or not."

I still don't know if I'm okay or not, is what I would say if I was honest.

"I'm fine," I say instead. Shortly and coldly, hoping to send the message that I don't want to talk about that part of things further.

"No, you're not," he says. "But I won't push you."

"Thanks for that," I mumble, then motion to the spreadsheet that's pulled up on the computer. "And for the help with this."

"I think we should still make an offer." He wastes no time giving me his opinion. "What's the worst that could happen?"

"We won't get it?" I state obviously.

"Exactly. If it doesn't happen, it just means it's not the time or place."

"Your optimism is *really* messing with my pessimism." I give him a half smile.

He takes one of my hands in his and gives it a squeeze, looking deeply into my eyes. "What's meant to be, will always be, Wedge."

For some reason, I don't think he's talking strictly about the old ice cream parlor.

I squeeze his hand back before letting it go and standing. "Whit and I are going to Caroline's for lunch today. I'm sure we'll talk about it more."

"Keep me updated please—good or bad."

"I will, I promise." I walk to the door.

"And Sage?" He stops me before I exit and I turn to look at him. "Try not to worry. About anything."

"I'll try."

Easier said than done, I think as I walk back to the front of the store, where Whitley is looking at a coffee table book full of photos of dogs underwater with Ms. Knox and Eve. My heart warms at the sight of them hunched over the book together. As I've gotten older, Ms. Knox has told me countless times that I can call her by her first name, Adrienne, if I would like to. The truth is, I've known her for so long, and she's always been so important to me, that Ms. Knox has become a term of endearment in my mind. Calling her anything else doesn't seem right.

"Ready to go?" I ask Whitley.

"Yep!" She wiggles out from between the two women, closing the book and taking it back to its place on one of the front tables.

"Thanks for keeping an eye on her," I say. "Good to see you, Eve."

"And me?" Ms. Knox raises an eyebrow.

"Of course, you too." I stick my tongue out at her. "But luckily I see you almost every day.

"Enjoy your Sunday!" Eve calls after us.

"I will." I grin at them. "I have the day off, and nothing is going to ruin it."

My day is ruined the second I turn onto Cole and Caroline's street.

The black Audi parked behind Cole's Jeep is a flame, and my attention is a moth. "You've gotta be kiddin' me," I growl.

"What?" Whitley sits taller in her seat, trying to look out the windshield.

"Nothing," I snap as I take the empty spot behind Caroline's minivan.

"Grumpy," Whitley says under her breath, then points out the window. "Hey! That looks like the car you hit! Is your friend here?"

"I hope not." I climb out of the car and open Whitley's door.

Caroline comes rushing out of the house, an apologetic look already apparent on her pretty face. I look at the car, then her, widening my eyes and hoping it conveys the *What the actual fuck?* that I can't say in front of my eleven-year-old.

"There's been a little communication error," she tells me before turning to Whitley. "Hey, Whit. Cam and Maddie are in the backyard playing on the Slip 'N Slide. Did you bring your bathing suit?"

"Yep!" Whitley proudly holds up the bag she packed this morning.

"Perfect! Go on inside and get changed." Caroline touches her shoulder as she runs by.

"Is he here?" I ask the second Whitley is gone.

"It's kind of a funny story, actually. You see, Cole invited Dawson for lunch and I invited you, and well, we forgot to tell each other. When the doorbell rang, I opened it expecting you, so it was quite the surprise for me too." She winces.

I sigh. I'm not mad at Caroline, but I'm also completely unprepared for this. We stare at each other for a few seconds, her with a hopeful smile, me with a poorly contained scowl. What I really want to do is hop back into my car and peel out of the driveway, tires screeching. But Whitley is already inside, and if I pull her away from a perfectly good Slip 'N Slide I'll never hear the end of it.

It's been ten years, Sage. This is fine.

"All right then." I take a deep breath, rolling my shoulders back. "I'm an adult. We're all adults. I can do this."

Caroline visibly relaxes. "Are you sure?"

Yes. No. Maybe?

I scrunch my nose and nod stiffly.

She links her arm through mine and guides me toward the front door. "Does it help to know that we're grilling steaks?" she asks.

"Why didn't you lead with that, lady?"

Cole and Caroline's house is a modest three-bedroom in one of the newer neighborhoods on Larkspur. It always looks perfectly lived in—never too messy and never spotlessly clean. It's the kind of home many dream of raising a family in, complete with plenty of throw blankets, lots of photographs, and a marvelous kitchen. The counter is covered with sides of garlic bread, roasted vegetables, and macaroni and cheese. My stomach growls as we pass through to the backyard, then growls even louder when Caroline cracks open the sliding glass door and the smell of steaks wafts inside.

"Look who I found," Caroline says brightly.

Dawson and Cole look over at me from their spot by the grill, and I ping-pong back and forth between their faces, unable to decide who to make eye contact with first. I settle on Cole, who seems to be pleading for forgiveness with his dark eyes. Apparently, he feels bad about the miscommunication too. I smile gently at him, letting him know I'm not going to come slam his hand in the grill. Not yet, anyway.

"Hey, guys," I say.

Dawson's glasses are missing today. He looks younger without them...more like the Dawson I used to know. Next to Cole, who hasn't changed much at all besides putting on a bit of dad weight, they're a scene straight from the past. I have to pry my eyes away to ground myself in the present.

"Aunt Sage!" Little wet arms wrap around my thigh and I look down to see Maddie smiling up at me. Her brown curls are plastered across her eyes and I reach down to push them back.

"Oh, it's you, Maddie!" I laugh. "You were hiding from me."

She giggles and runs away just as quickly as she came. Cam waves at me from the opposite end of the Slip 'N Slide, then goes back to explaining something to Whitley. From his mimed running and stretched arms, it looks like they're discussing proper sliding form. Knowing Whitley like I do, she's not listening to a word he says. She's going to do it her own way regardless.

She takes off running while he's still mid-sentence, landing on her side instead of her stomach and sliding all the way to the end with one outstretched arm, like a napping Superwoman. "Hey, Mama," she says before she runs to wait for her next turn.

"I've forgotten what Florida Octobers are like." Dawson comes to stand next to me. "I wasn't invited to many fall Slip 'N Slide days in Virginia."

"Like everything else on this island, the seasons never change." I fold my arms across my chest and focus on the kids. Behind us, Cole follows Caroline into the house with the steaks, leaving us alone.

"I've noticed some changes since I've been back," he says. "But all of the little things are definitely the same."

I look over at him. His gaze is on the lower half of my body, and for a second, I think he's looking at my legs. Then I realize he's staring at my shoes. I cross one ankle over the other, trying to shield my Vans from his view.

"Are you making fun of me?" I ask.

"No!" He lifts his head up to meet my eyes. "They're the first thing I noticed when we got in our accident last weekend. If you had looked completely different, I still would have known it was you thanks to the checkered shoes."

Curiosity grabs me. "Are you saying I still look the same?"

"Down to the ponytail." He grins. "Or should I say, *up* to the ponytail?"

I elbow him, a spark of unexpected joy heating my face. "You always were kind of a nerd. Speaking of, where are your glasses?"

"Ohhhh, so you're noting things about me too, then?" His voice takes on a different tone.

"It was simply an observation."

"Do you like them?" he asks.

"Like what?" I play dumb.

"The glasses, G.G."

The nickname again.

129

"I think they're...mature." I raise an eyebrow at him. "They work for you. Like everything always has."

Oh, fuck. Are we flirting?

Cam runs past, sprinkling drops of water on us in his wake. I shiver despite the heat.

"There's another thing that will always be 'you' to me," Dawson says, quieter now.

"What's that?"

He looks down again, pointing at my ankle this time. The tiniest ghost tattoo marks my skin, faded from time. It's one of the memories I've pushed into the deepest ravine of my brain —out of sight, buried in mind. I take a quarter turn toward him so he can no longer see it.

"I forget about that, to be honest," I say. "Do you still have yours? Or did you laser it off of your precious shoulder?"

"Of course I still have it." He sounds offended.

"I won't believe it until I see it."

"Are you asking me to take my shirt off right now?" He squints into the sun, and god the eye crinkles are even better thanks to the barely there fine lines on his face. My stomach does a flip.

Shit.

"That's—that's not what I meant!"

"Sure it's not." His eyes don't leave me.

This interaction has taken a wrong turn.

"I'm going to see if Caroline needs any help." I spin on my heel and stomp toward the back door.

"*Stupid, stupid, stupid,*" I mutter under my breath.

"Everything okay?" Cole opens the door as I'm reaching for it.

"Yep," I say. "Go babysit your friend. I'll help Care."

"Can't even leave you two alone for two minutes..." he grumbles as he walks away.

Caroline and I set up the table outside, then carry all of the

130

food out and arrange it on the tablecloth. I grab a few beers for the adults, and Sunny Ds for the kids. While I'm placing the plates and silverware at each spot, I keep looking over at Dawson. Cole is showing him something on his phone, and his back is turned to me. His T-shirt tightens around his shoulders when he crosses hisarms, and I can't help but imagine the little ghost tattoothat sits on top of his right shoulder blade.

If I'm being honest with myself, having him here for lunch doesn't make me hesitant because of the awkwardness of our past, or the current ice cream parlor debacle. What I'm really afraid of is things becoming comfortable between us too quickly. Like they did in his car yesterday. Like they already have today. Like they always have.

"Let's eat!" Caroline yells.

The kids come running to the table in a flurry of dripping water. I wrap Whitley in a towel and set her up with a hot dog next to Cam and Maddie. "You should sit next to him," she whispers to me, pointing at Dawson. "Maybe you can be friends again."

Even my own daughter is out to get me.

"Eat," I say, tapping her on the nose.

As fate would have it, I do have to sit next to Dawson. I grab the bottle opener from the middle of the table, popping the top off my beer and gulping half of it down. A bubble forms in my chest from drinking it too quickly, and I'm reminded yet again that I'm in my 30s now.

"Cheers!" Cole holds his bottle up. The four of us toast and dig into our food.

"Thanks for lunch," I say, cutting my steak into pieces.

"Yes, it's amazing," Dawson mumbles around his first bite.

We eat, making small talk about the upcoming Halloween festival and our work lives. Dawson and I tell Cole and Caroline about our accident, and getting the cars fixed. The kids finish their lunch quickly, excited to get back to the Slip 'N

Slide. Cole goes inside to grab us a second round of beers, then eventually, a third. When we start the fourth round, all of the jitters caused by the man sitting next to me have magically disappeared.

"This is nice," Caroline says, looking at each of us individually and smiling. "It makes me feel young again."

"Hey, we are young," Cole chastises.

"I get what you mean, Care," Dawson agrees. "Younger."

"Exactly!" She points at him with the neck of her beer bottle.

"How's the new place?" Cole asks Dawson.

I peek over my shoulder to check on the kids, pretending not to be as interested in the new subject as I am.

"It's good," Dawson says. "Small, but I don't need anything crazy right now."

"Where are you staying?" I ask.

"I'm renting a house on the north shore. Temporarily, until I find a place I want to buy."

"It's one of the vacation rentals near Primera Beach," Caroline adds. "I was able to get him a six-month lease."

"That's great," I say, smiling at Dawson.

He opens his mouth like he wants to say something, then snaps it shut again. He repeats the same motion two more times before he spits it out.

"Speaking of buying..." he says to me. "I was hoping I could talk to you about the ice cream parlor?"

Annoyance flares through my beer fog, then is swiftly joined by Dad's voice. Our conversation from earlier plays in my head. *I think we should still make an offer*, he'd said.

On the drive here, I'd been fully prepared to discuss the next steps with Caroline. Now, in Dawson's presence, my stubbornness is rearing its ugly head, and not for the good of me and Dad and Sunny Spirits. It wants to take the easy way out and let Dawson have the building so I can avoid situations like this. So I can go back to my normal, mundane life.

Cole and Caroline stare daggers through my face. I stay silent for a few more seconds. Just because I'm about to give up doesn't mean I can't make him sweat a little.

"It's yours if you want it," I tell him. "Really."

Now it's his turn to be quiet. "That's not what I was going to say," he finally says.

"So you don't want it then?" I ask eagerly, hopefully.

"No, I do. I have—"

"You should listen to him, Sage," Caroline interrupts. "Dawson and I have talked about this. At length."

I fight the urge to poke my lower lip out. Isn't Caroline supposed to be on my side here?

Stop being stupid! I yell internally.

"Okay." Scolded, I slump down in my chair a little, cradling my drink for emotional support. "I'm listening."

"Cool." Dawson smiles at me and his shoulders visibly relax. "Obviously the space is pretty small?"

He makes it sound like a question, so I nod in agreement.

"But, since it's on the end of the strip, there are options. And the thought in my head has always been, what if I add onto it? I could expand it—out, or even up since it's the only single-story building on the street."

I think about the little parlor, trying to imagine his vision. "Right," I say so he knows I'm listening. Although, I'm still not sure what this has to do with me.

"If I get the building, and if I'm approved for a construction permit, I was thinking...maybe we could split the space?"

No, is my first thought. Working in the same vicinity as Dawson every single day? Absolutely not.

Yet I find myself asking, "Like...joint ownership? That seems complicated."

He shakes his head. "Not necessarily. At least not right

away. I would buy the property and do the expansion, then you could rent half of it to start and see where it goes from there. We could find a way to renovate things so it feels like we have our own spaces."

"So I would still be renting?" It's not exactly the step forward Dad and I have been wanting to take.

Caroline butts in again. "Yes. But you would have room for Sunny Spirits. You could still have all of the things you told me you want. A lobby. A small museum. A sign out front. More than a desk in the corner of a bookstore."

At the mention of all the possibilities, the wheels in my head start turning. They're all things I'm desperate for—all things that could finally lead to more for our little family business. For Dad and me. For Whitley and her future. We could have our first true home for Sunny Spirits. It could be the start of expanding to other historical cities. It could be the start of things I've only considered out-of-reach daydreams.

But it would also mean Dawson Aiken is my landlord and my next-door business neighbor. Considering our history, is that even a good idea?

"I know we have a...past," Dawson says lowly, as if he's reading my mind. "But I still think we could figure all of this out so it's mutually beneficial."

Unable to verbalize my thoughts, I scan the yard, searching as if I'll find a reply falling out of the blue sky above. Instead, I find Whitley, and the smile plastered across her freckled face as she plays with her friends is the best source of encouragement I could ever ask for.

"Can I think about it?" I ask.

"Of course," Dawson and Caroline say at the same time. Cole's been quiet throughout the conversation, but when I catch his eye he gives me a motivating thumbs-up.

"Is there anyone else interested in buying right now?" I ask Caroline.

"Not yet," she says. "Take a couple of days to consider everything. If the situation becomes more urgent, I'll let you two know."

"Okay then," I say, releasing a nervous breath. "I'll talk to Dad and see what he thinks."

"Thanks, Sage." Dawson briefly lays a hand on my forearm. "Caroline and I can answer any questions you might have."

I turn to look at him, and our eyes connect for a second too long. Then I finish the last of my beer slowly, quietly lost in my own thoughts as the conversation around me changes direction.

CHAPTER 14

DECEMBER 16, 2009

On my birthday, a cold front sweeps through Larkspur.
Normally, when I lead a group back to Ghost to Coast at the end of a tour, everyone is soaked with sweat, desperate for air-conditioning. Tonight, we're all bundled up, blowing into our hands to keep them warm and licking lips that have been chapped by the blustery island wind. My Sunny Spirits crewneck is doing nothing to block the cold, and my frozen fingers fumble the key three times before I'm able to successfully let us all back into the warm, inviting bookstore.

"Unfortunately I don't have any actual tea to offer you," I say after we've gathered near the used book section. "But learning about Madame Roberta and her tea parties is sure to warm you up."

"You should start offering tea during this part of the tour then," Demanding Dude says grumpily from his spot right next to me. He's been difficult to please from the first minute of the tour, so picking out his nickname was easy. I'll tell Dawson about him later. We'll laugh about it and it will make the fact that I had to work on my birthday a little better.

"Thanks for the suggestion. We'll definitely consider it." I smile sweetly at him.

"In fact, I think I'd like to speak to your manager about that and a few other things, at some point," he responds, sticking his stupid pointy nose in the air.

"Okay." I hold on to my smile, hoping it's concealing the building rage. "That would be me. I'd be happy to chat with you after the tour."

"*You're* the manager?" He doesn't give up. "You're a teenager."

"I'm 20. As of today, actually."

My statement leads to the result I was hoping for—everyone else in the group wishing me a happy birthday and drowning out the man's unwarranted complaints. Once they've all quieted down again, I'm able to finish the tour unscathed. Demanding Dude doesn't bother to stick around and talk to me at the end, but I'm sure his grievance-filled email or voicemail will come eventually.

By the time I've finished all of the closing tasks, it's 12:15 A.M. and my birthday is officially over. I'm not one for grandeur, but it's still always a little sad when a day that has special meaning comes to an end. This is the first time I've ever had to work on my birthday. Mom or Dad have always covered in the past if one of the part-timers couldn't. But Dad is "busy" and Mom has been officially gone since the beginning of November, so there's a first time for everything.

A text from Dawson comes in, picking my mood up off of the floor.

DAWSON

How was it tonight?

A second one quickly follows.

DAWSON

I'm sorry you had to work on your birthday.

My heart quickens to an alarming rate, just as it has every time his name has popped up on my phone's screen over the past four months. Then my stomach begins to ache, because I don't know if I've ever missed someone as much as I've missed him this fall. The good news is, I'll only have to miss him for three more days.

After our kiss on the sandbar at the end of the summer, there was one more when I said goodbye to him later that night. It was brief and full of an awkward newness, but still so sweet I haven't been able to stop thinking about it since. Our constant texts and phone calls have consumed me and made my bad days good, and my good days even better. When I finally see him in person again, I'm afraid I might actually explode from a combination of excitement and building anticipation.

It was ok, minus one Demanding Dude on the last tour.

DAWSON

Are you almost off?

Leaving now! I'll call you when I get home.

I lock up and walk down the street toward my moped, shivering and dreading the frigid ride home. The closer I get, the more obvious it becomes that someone is standing next to it. I hesitate, growing stiff with defense. Whoever it is stands just outside the streetlight, making it impossible to see their features. I'm about to play it safe and call Dad when the person moves closer and steps into the light.

Adrenaline like I've never felt before takes over my body.

"Ghost Girl!" Dawson yells.

My feet begin to move again, quickening to a jog and then a full-out run. He meets me halfway, beneath the Christmas lights hanging from the toy shop's awning, and we stop just short of each other, grinning like fools but hesitant to touch because we've spent way more time thinking about it than actually doing it. It feels like an elevated version of our "who will speak first?" game.

We jump toward each other at the same time, his arms going around my waist while mine wrap around his neck. "What are you doing here?" I mumble into the warm curve of his neck. He smells even better than I remember—like sandalwood and spice and *him*.

"My exams finished early," he replies, his breath hot on my ear. "I wanted to surprise you."

He pulls away slightly and I angle my face to look up at him. His cheeks are pink from the cold. His hair is longer than it was in August and gelled haphazardly into place. He threads his fingers into my hair and presses his lips to mine, kissing me until every bit of chill has seeped out of my body.

"Fuck, I feel like I've been waiting forever to do that again," he says, hugging me so tightly my feet lift off the ground.

"It was much less salty this time." I laugh.

He releases me and grabs a piece of my ponytail-free hair between his fingers, then rubs his thumb over the apple of my cheek. "I realized on my drive home that I've never told you in person how beautiful I think you are."

"Thanks. I call it 'ghost tour guide chic.'" I put my hand on my hip and do a spin beneath the twinkling lights.

Grinning, he slings an arm around me and guides me toward the moped. "I have something for you."

"Yeah?"

He grabs a plastic container from the moped's seat and

opens it, revealing two sprinkled cupcakes. One has a candle stuck in it and he pulls a lighter from his pocket to ignite it. The flame dances in his eyes for a brief second and I can't look away.

"Happy birthday," he says, holding the box toward me.

"Technically, it's not my birthday anymore."

"In my opinion, it is. Now make a wish!"

Grabbing his free hand, I squeeze my eyes closed for a couple of seconds, then open them to blow out the candle.

"I didn't actually make a wish," I whisper.

"What? Why?"

"Because my birthday wish was for you to be here," I say. "And you're already next to me."

"You should have made another wish, then." He sticks our connected hands in the pocket of his sweatshirt and I lean into him.

"I should have wished to teleport home with the moped because it's way too cold to drive it," I say with a pout.

He closes the box of cupcakes and tucks it beneath his arm. "We could load it in my truck and I'll take you home. I have tie downs we can use."

"Would that work?"

"For sure." He passes the cupcakes to me and knocks the moped off the kickstand before pushing it across the street to where he's parked. I follow behind, shivering.

"Now I feel bad because I didn't get to do anything for your birthday," I say to his back.

"There will be other Septembers to make up for it." He winks over his shoulder.

By the time we've finished securing the moped my fingers are numb. Dawson opens the passenger door for me and I nearly leap inside, ready to be away from the ocean wind that makes it feel ten times colder than it actually is. He closes me in and I sink into the seat, exhausted from work, but also from the rush of being with him days earlier than expected. His door opens and he pulls himself into his seat, grinning at me.

"I've never been in your truck before," I tell him, breathing deeply. "It smells good, like you."

"Thanks." He laughs. "Make yourself comfortable."

He starts the engine and drives us away from Main Street and all of its holiday decorations. I look around the truck's interior, searching for something that screams the vehicle is his other than the smell and coming up empty-handed. All I can find is a pair of sunglasses and a CD case. Otherwise it looks like he just drove it away from the dealership.

I pick up the CD case. "May I?"

"Sure." He clicks on the overhead light above me so I can see.

"My mom used to tell me and Sawyer that would make her get into an accident," I say, pointing at the light.

"So did my dad. Don't worry, I'll keep us safe," he jokes, moving a hand to the top of my thigh. My lower body tenses up and I'm so distracted by the weight of his palm that I flip through three sheets of disks without actually looking at any of them.

On my fourth flip, a My Chemical Romance album catches my eye and I slide it out of its spot. "Okay, this is a little surprising. I assumed you would be more of a country music boy."

He moves his hand from my leg and presses it against his chest like he's in pain. "I'm a man of excellent taste," he says dramatically. "I like everything. Keep looking and you'll see."

"I still have so much to learn about you."

Keeping the CD perched on the end of my finger, I flip through the rest of the book, past several more punk and alternative bands, moving into pop, and then, just as I suspected, country. "Shania Twain?" I laugh, sliding out a second disk.

"YES," he scoffs. "She's a legend. Plus, I've always thought she was hot."

"She definitely is." I put the Shania disk back in its spot, then My Chemical Romance in the empty spot beneath it before flipping the book closed and putting it back on the floor.

Dawson looks at it like something is bothering him, then forces his eyes back to the road.

"You take a right at the fork by your house," I tell him.

"I know."

"You've never been to my house though," I say.

"Doesn't mean I don't know where you live." He reaches over and pinches my earlobe. "As you know, it's a small island."

"Stalker." I laugh, swatting his hand away. He grabs mine in his and threads our fingers together on the center console.

When we park in front of the cottage, all of the lights inside are still on. The single strand of Christmas lights on our front porch blinks in a pattern of rainbow colors, and our small tree glows inside the front window. "You can come in, if you want," I say shyly. "Dad and Sawyer are making super early breakfast for my birthday dinner."

"They're still awake?" he asks, looking at the time on the dash.

"One thing you have to know about the Murrays..." I explain. "Thanks to Sunny Spirits, none of us have much respect for sleep."

"Even your brother? Doesn't he have school?"

I shrug. "Christmas break starts tomorrow."

"Okay, I'll come in. Your dad won't mind?"

"Nope!"

I collect the box of cupcakes and slide out of the truck, looking back at Dawson. He grabs the CD case from the floor and flips it open, then quickly moves the My Chemical

Romance disk back to its original spot in the front of the book. I frown, confused.

"Sorry, did I mess something up?"

"No!" Looking embarrassed, he pulls his sweatshirt away from his neck. "I was just putting it back in its spot."

Mr. Perfectionist. I almost say it out loud, but change my mind at the last second, thinking back to the time I caught him organizing the desk at Ghost to Coast.

Hand in hand, we talk up the steps. He pauses before I open the door. "Does your dad...know about us?" he asks.

"Yes." I rise to my toes, pecking him on the lips.

"Did your mom? Before she left?"

"Also yes." I push the door open and lead us inside, smiling at him over my shoulder.

It's only when we're in the tiny, cluttered entryway that I panic a little. Without Mom around, our messiness has multiplied by at least three. There are shoes all over the floor, and a three-inch stack of mail on the credenza in the hallway. Dad's books and newspapers have migrated out of the sunroom and onto every available surface in the rest of the cottage. The one saving grace is, currently, the smell of brewing coffee and freshly fried bacon. It floats through the air, making my stomach growl.

What must Dawson think? Knowing how particular he is, this place must feel like a tiny little pigsty compared to his. I sneak a nervous glance at his face.

He's looking around, taking everything in with a smile. We walk into the living room and he goes over to the three-foot Christmas tree, carefully fingering a couple of the ornaments. "It's so cozy in here," he says.

"Sorry for the mess." I pick a couple of throw pillows up off the floor and arrange them on the couch.

"Wedgie? That you?" Dad's voice calls from the kitchen.

Great. We had to go right in with the nickname.

143

"It's me!" I grab Dawson's hand and pull him back into the hall. "Dawson is with me, too."

"Wedgie?" Dawson whispers into my ear. I can feel his grin against my earlobe.

"Apparently I'm a nickname magnet," I explain. "Wedgie, Ghost Girl...that's me."

"Happy birthday!" Dad says when we turn the corner. He's elbow deep in mixing a bowl of pancake batter. The small kitchen is smoky thanks to the bacon, and the small table is set with our only tablecloth and a single lit candle. "Hope you're hungry," he adds.

"I'm starving," I say.

"Good to see you, Mr. Murray," Dawson tells him.

"Please, call me Gerald." Dad sets the bowl on the counter and uses a napkin to wipe a splatter of batter from his glasses.

"Where's Saw?" I ask. "Did he fall asleep?"

"No, he's doing something in his room," Dad says, offering no further information.

I sit the cupcakes on the bar, propping up on my elbows and staring greedily at the bacon. "Can I help with anything?"

"Absolutely not. It's your birthday." He sits a pan on the stove and drops a large dollop of butter into it. "Dawson, if you want you can grab some coffee cups from the cabinet above the sink."

"Dad, he's a gues—"

"I would love to," Dawson interrupts, sticking his tongue out at me behind Dad's back.

"I thought you weren't going to be back until the weekend?" Dad asks him.

"I finished my exams early." Dawson carefully places the cups on the counter.

"He surprised me," I gush. I imagine little heart-shaped bubbles rotating in circles around my head. "He brought me cupcakes, too."

Footsteps thunder down the hall and Sawyer explodes into the room. "Did somebody say cupcakes?"

I open the box to show him. "The four of us can share them for dessert."

"Deal!" Sawyer says, noticing Dawson for the first time. Becoming shy, he shrinks into himself.

"Whaddup, Sawyer?" Dawson holds his fist out and Sawyer bumps it skeptically.

"Are you my sister's boyfriend?" he asks.

Dawson and I look at each other over his head. In all of the months of texting and talking, this is something we've never discussed. I hold my breath, anxious to see what he says.

"Yeah," he finally confirms, grinning at me. "I think I am."

A chill rushes up my spine. Dawson Aiken is my...*boyfriend?*

Six months ago, I would have jumped off a bridge before I believed this would happen.

"Gross," Sawyer says, ruining the mood. "No kissing in the house."

"Yes, sir." I gently kick him in the butt.

"I have a present for you. Wait here!" He runs back to his room, returning a few seconds later with a box wrapped chaotically in snowman-printed paper.

"What is it?" I ask, taking the box from him and shaking it.

"Just open it, Wedgie," he says. "It's from me, and Dad too."

Dawson comes to stand behind me, watching over my shoulder. I rip the paper off and toss it to the floor. A red shoebox sits in my hands, and I grin because I already know what it is.

Impatient, Sawyer walks over and flips the lid off the top. A brand-new pair of slip-on, checkered Vans rest on top of a mound of white tissue paper. "Ta-da!" he says, wiggling jazz fingers around the shoes. Dawson laughs behind me.

"My favorite!" I put the box on the counter and pull him into a hug. "How did you know I would like them?"

He doesn't get the joke, and looks at me like I'm crazy.

"Thanks, dude," I say, then turn to look at Dad. "And Dad, too."

"I talked to your mom today," he says. "She mailed your gift yesterday, so it'll be here soon. She said for you to call her tomorrow."

My mood sours slightly at the mention of Mom. She called before my shift earlier, but I ignored it. Although everything was smoothed over by the time she left, I've still had a difficult time bringing myself to talk to her regularly since she's been gone. I'm hurt. For a lot of reasons, but for her leaving Sawyer behind more than anything. He's creeping toward his teenage years, but that doesn't mean he's ready to be without a full-time mom.

Dawson rubs his hand up and down my back. "You okay?" he asks quietly.

"Yeah." Shaking my head, I smile at him. "I'm great."

And as I look around our tiny, topsy-turvy kitchen, at my dad and my little brother and my *boyfriend*, I'm more hopeful than ever that it's all going to be okay.

CHAPTER 15

PRESENT DAY, OCTOBER 2022

Three days after Dawson's rental proposal, my head is still spinning in circles.

Yesterday, I brought the proposition to Dad. He'd been cynical at first, which I was secretly hoping for. After all, it will be much easier to tell Caroline and Dawson "no thanks" if I can blame it on Dad.

To my chagrin, when I went into more detail about everything we could do with a larger space, he moved from the dark side to the light side rather quickly, ending our conversation with, "If the price is fair and the rental contract is solid, it's a yes from me."

With that, I'd forced a smile and spent the rest of the day drowning in pros and cons.

Now, with Dad and Caroline crossed off my list of possible advice givers, I find myself sitting at The Phantom Eatery's bar, waiting for the one person I know will give me their honest, unbiased opinion: my brother.

"Whatcha drinking?" Sawyer asks as he slides onto the stool next to me, eyes twinkling above his giant grin.

"My feelings." I take a giant gulp of my Vodka Cran-BOOey, one of Phantom's signatures.

"I'll have what she's having," he tells Fran the bartender, then asks me, "Where's Whit?"

"She went to Penelope's after school. I'm off tonight so I'll pick her up later."

He takes a sip of his drink and puts in an order for fried cornbread. My mood brightens slightly at that.

"You're obviously sulking about something." He calls me out. "What's going on?"

"How long do you have?" I joke.

"Well, I leave for work again in three days, so try to wrap it up before then."

I dive into the sordid tale, starting from the day Caroline took me to see the ice cream parlor and told me that Dawson was coming back to town. Sawyer is always my favorite person to talk to, because he has immaculate facial expressions, and throws in little gasps and *What? You're joking* comments at perfect times. He never makes me feel silly or dramatic, or like my feelings aren't valid, and his green eyes stay locked on my matching ones the whole time.

"Why are you just now telling me that Dawson is back?" he asks when I finish. "That's...major."

I shrug, chewing on my bottom lip. "I've been trying not to make it a big deal."

"But it is a big deal, Sage." He pushes his hair out of his eyes. "I was a kid when everything blew up between you two, but that doesn't mean I don't remember how bad it hurt you."

Fran places our cornbread in front of us and I bite into a piece, trying to think of a response, burning my tongue in the process.

"I know," I say, dropping the cornbread. "But that was then. This is now. It's been a long time and we're both adults."

"So you're saying you're completely over everything that happened?" he asks.

"Yep." I avoid his eyes, focusing on the appetizer. He slides it away from me, forcing me to look at him.

"I'm not a dummy," he says with a straight face. "You've barely even dated since then. Besides, well, you know."

"I would hardly call *that* dating," I argue, then my forehead relaxes when Whitley's face pops into my mind. "Though it did give me the best thing that's ever happened to me."

"The best thing that's ever happened to our family, period," Sawyer adds.

For a couple of minutes, we eat and drink in silence, watching Larkspur-ers filter in and out of the restaurant. Sawyer orders us another round of drinks, then sits up taller, ready to get back to business.

"Here's what I think," he says.

"I'm listening."

"It's not the business side of things I'm worried about for you." He twists a straw wrapper in his hands. "Sunny Spirits needs a space. From what I know, Dawson has always been a good, honest guy. I'm sure he will honor everything he's offering."

"Right." He has my full attention. "So what part of it *does* worry you?"

"I know you." His boyish face turns even softer. "Would putting yourself in a position where you're around Dawson that much be good for you? What if old feelings resurface and you get your hopes up and it all goes south again?"

"Whoa, whoa, whoa." I hold a hand up. "Those are things that haven't come close to crossing my mind."

Liar, said mind sneers, somewhat pissed that I'm contradicting it.

I think about Dawson's and my flirty banter session at

Cole and Caroline's on Sunday. About the tiny flare of hope that selfishly lit me up from the inside when I learned that he's divorced. About the combination of familiarity and newness that keeps threatening to pull me in and force me to want someone I swore I would never want again.

"Liar," Sawyer quips.

"Stop it." I kick at him. "I'm not 21 anymore."

"Age has little to do with matters of the heart."

"Who are you, Socrates?"

He rolls his eyes. "Just a guy who spends a lot of time working in the middle of the ocean and has nothing to do but think about human existence."

"You're such a weirdo." I finish my second drink. "But I love you and I know your concerns come from the right place."

"Whatever decision you make will be the right one, Wedge. Just don't forget to take care of yourself in the process."

"I'll try my best."

"Promise?" he asks.

"I promise."

∼

The next morning, I start a group chat with Dawson and Caroline.

> Can we meet up today?

> I've had my time to think.

Waiting for a response, I lie in bed a few more minutes. When nothing comes, I get up and head for the shower. Today is the day

I'm going to make my decision known, and for once, I'm going to look the part of a growing business owner. Well...co-owner. I wash my hair and scrub and shave every inch of my body, then pull a casual black shift dress out from behind the dozens of Sunny Spirits shirts in my closet. My curling iron is almost finished heating up when Whitley's alarm goes off down the hallway.

I listen, waiting for the alarm to stop and for the familiar sound of her feet hitting the floor. She doesn't usually have issues getting out of bed on her own, so after thirty seconds of the blaring alarm I know it's time to go check on her. "Whitley?" I call as I leave the bathroom.

In her bedroom, I step over the clutter on the floor and switch the alarm off. She's curled on her side facing the wall, still breathing deeply. "Whit?" I sit on the edge of her blue bedspread and shake her gently. "Time to get ready for school."

She rolls onto her back, and I know something's off the second she opens her eyes. "I don't feel good, Mama," she says, her throat hoarse.

"Yeah?" I place a hand on her forehead and she flinches.

"Your hands are freezing," she says.

"They're not, but it probably feels that way because you definitely have a fever." I sigh. "Stay here, I'll get the thermometer."

When I return, she's sitting up in bed, kicking the blankets off and pulling her floral pajamas away from her skin. "I can't be sick. I have a math test today," she whines.

"Don't worry about that." I place the thermometer against her forehead and hold the button down.

"What does it say?" she asks. "Am I dying?"

"No." I smile and show her the flashing 101.3 on the screen. "But you're not going anywhere besides this bed today. And maybe the doctor if Motrin doesn't help."

"What if I just get ready anyway and see if I feel better after?"

I raise an eyebrow at her and shake my head, then stand to help her to her feet so I can strip the sweat-dampened sheets from her bed. "Let's get you some fresh blankets and pajamas, and some medicine."

"This is stupid," she says, staring up at me with watery eyes.

"I'm sorry." I push a strand of sweat-soaked hair from her forehead. "Would it help if I made you a special cup of tea?"

"Maybe..."

After Whitley is medicated and situated back in bed with a cup of honey-sweetened hot tea and a Disney movie playing on my laptop, I retrace my steps, searching for my cell phone. I find it on the bathroom counter next to the scalding curling iron, which I unplug because it doesn't look like I'll be needing it anymore.

There are replies from Dawson and Caroline at the top of my notifications.

DAWSON
I'm flexible today. Coffee meeting?

CAROLINE
Works for me. 11:00 good?

I slump against the bathroom door and release a pent-up breath.

Change of plans.

Whitley is sick. I need to figure my day out.

Caroline replies immediately.

CAROLINE

Oh no!

CAROLINE

What's wrong?

A cold, I think. Fever and sore throat.

DAWSON

Sorry to hear that.

I stare at his name for a few seconds, then move on to calling Whitley's school and texting Dad to see if he can come watch her at our house when it's time to go give my tours later.

Another message from Caroline comes in a few minutes later.

CAROLINE

What if we come to you? We won't disturb Whit. We could sit in the sunroom.

I consider it, then decide I don't want to put anyone out.

Y'all don't have to do that.

DAWSON

I don't mind.

CAROLINE

Me neither! 11:00, then?

I push away from the door and walk out of the bathroom, surveying the mess in the rest of the house. *Sounds good*, I respond against my better judgment.

Whitley is sound asleep when I peek into her room, so I gently close the door to block out the sounds of the maniacal cleaning spree I'm about to go on. Before I start though, I plug the curling iron back in and finish applying my makeup. Operation "Sage the Ghost Boss" is back in session.

At 10:55, Caroline walks through the front door without knocking. "It's me," she whispers loudly.

"In here," I say from the sunroom.

"Holy shit!" Caroline passes the Spine Chiller in her hand to me before taking a seat. "You look hot."

"Bless you, child." I bow my head at her jokingly to thank her for the coffee. "And hot is a stretch. Maybe...passable?"

"Nope. Hot is the right word."

"Thanks." I push my loosely curled hair behind my shoulders and pick a piece of lint off the black shift dress, which is actually way more comfortable than my shorts would have been. "I had some extra time on my hands for once."

"How's Whit?" Caroline asks.

"She's good. Sleeping again right now. The fever is down already."

There's a soft knock at the door and I put my drink on the coffee table before going to answer it. Dawson stands on my front porch in a gray tee and light wash jeans. He's wearing a black ball cap and his glasses, a bouquet of flowers in one hand and a plastic takeout bag in the other. He says something that sounds like "wow" under his breath and when he grins, an unexpected heat builds in my lower abdomen and my cheeks grow so hot I fear I may be catching Whitley's fever.

"S-sorry. Did you say something?" I ask.

"No. Uhh, yes. I mean...you look really nice today. Not that you don't always look nice. You just look different today. In a good way, obviously."

I let him trip over his words, a grin spreading across my face as he digs the hole deeper and deeper. "Breathe, Ghost Boy."

"These are for Whitley." He holds the flowers out to me

when I let him into the hallway. "And I brought y'all some lunch. Soup for Whitley, and beans and cornbread for you. I know that used to be your favorite meal from Phantom, so I thought it might still be?"

"Good guess." I take the bag of food from him and begin walking toward the kitchen. "This is so nice. You didn't have to."

"I wanted to." He follows me, peering around the freshly cleaned cottage. The slightest smell of bleach still lingers in the air. "It looks the same in here."

"Every year I say I'm going to make some updates, and every year I never do." I sit the food on the counter and fill a vase with water for the flowers.

"Is Buster still hanging around?" he asks, propping his hip against the counter and folding his arms over his chest.

"Of course." I laugh. "He particularly likes the sunroom, so don't be surprised if you feel something jump onto the couch to sit beside you."

"So you admit he exists now?" He peeks at me over the top of his glasses.

"It's more of a joke than anything," I say, leading him back to the sunroom.

It's a perfect day outside, so clear and blue that the water and the sky outside the bay windows seem to merge into one entity. I take a seat next to Caroline on the couch and Dawson wanders over to admire the view. He sticks his hands in his pockets and I allow my eyes to roam over his body, from his wavy hair, to the spot where his T-shirt bunches on his lower back, to the outline of his calves in his jeans.

"Nice view," Caroline says, pulling my attention to her. She raises her eyebrows at me, a playful smile on her face.

"It is," Dawson agrees.

"Don't you think so too, Sage?" Caroline asks.

Knowing the ocean isn't the view she's referring to, I flatten my mouth into a line and ignore her.

Dawson removes a hand from his pocket and traces a fingertip over a small crack in the corner of one of the window panes. "Has this been here long?" he asks.

"Since the last hurricane," I say. "One of the many things I need to fix."

"I can help." He takes a seat in the armchair across from Caroline and I.

I can't accept any more help from you, is what I want to say. Instead, I take a big sip of my coffee. Caroline and Dawson exchange a glance with each other, then with me. Remembering why we're here, I suddenly feel nervous.

"I hate to jump right in, but you know patience isn't my strongest trait," Caroline says.

"So I can't make you beg for an answer?" I joke. "That's no fun."

"I won't lie, you've made a decision much faster than I thought you would," Dawson says.

Sitting up taller, I clear my throat and cross one knee over the other. Dawson's eyes follow the movement. I pull the dress tighter over my thighs, feeling self-conscious. "Dad and I are desperate for change with Sunny Spirits. Especially me," I say honestly. "With a rental agreement and everything else we discussed, I know it'll work for us."

"Great!" Caroline says in her realtor voice. She reaches for her phone and immediately opens her calendar.

Dawson's lips lift into a hesitant smile. "This sounds like a yes, but you also seem unsure."

Caroline falters, looking between the two of us.

"It is a yes," I confirm. "And I'm not unsure. Not about the agreement. With the purchase and the remodel and all of the permits, there will be more than enough time to smooth out the details."

"Awesome!" Caroline's optimism is renewed and she goes back to her task.

Dawson scoots to the edge of his chair and rests his elbows on his knees. "What are you unsure about? Because if there's anything, I want to talk about it now."

Once again, Caroline pauses. "He's right," she says, studying my face. "You're not sold on something."

"It's nothing to do with...anything important." I wave my hand through the air, hoping to brush away whatever skepticism Dawson is catching a whiff of.

"Are you sure?" he asks.

About the 'you' part of this? No, I think.

"Yes!" I say with my most confident grin.

As I told myself last night when I made this decision, having to be in close proximity to the ex-love of my life is a small price to pay for a giant Sunny Spirits leap. I just have to get over a few lingering feelings...cross off a few items of unfinished personal business. Then Dawson will be nothing more than my landlord and life will be sweet. It'll be easy.

You're delusional, my brain crossfires.

Dawson settles back in his chair and Caroline gives me a look that says *We'll chat about the rest of this later*.

"Okay, Care," Dawson says. "I'm ready to buy an old ice cream parlor."

"Can you come to my office tomorrow morning around 9:30?" she asks him. "We can start on your offer then."

"I'll be there."

"How long will everything take?" I ask.

"It's hard to say." Caroline smooths her hair. "At least 30 days for the sale to go through."

"Then a few more months to obtain permits and do all of the work," Dawson adds. "We could have the doors of both businesses open by spring. Early summer, maybe."

"That seems like forever and tomorrow at the same time,"

I say, my doubts already smothered by the visions of everything Dad and I want to do.

"Exciting stuff!" Caroline claps her hands together. "I'm proud of you two."

"Thanks," Dawson and I say in unison, exchanging shy smiles with each other.

"Mama?" Whitley's voice comes from the doorway and I jump to my feet, rushing over to her.

"Are you okay?" I ask, kneeling to her level. "Did we wake you? I'm sorry."

"No." She looks over my shoulder at Dawson and Caroline. "I'm hungry."

"That's a good sign you're getting better," I say, standing. "And guess what? Dawson brought you some soup."

"What kind?" she asks.

"Chicken noodle!" Dawson says, climbing to his feet and walking toward us. "I can warm it up for you if your mom doesn't mind."

"Okay. Bowls are—"

"In the cabinet to the right of the stove?" he asks. "That's where they used to be."

I laugh. "And that's where they are still. Good memory."

"Come on. It's really good soup. You'll love it." He places a gentle hand on Whitley's shoulder and guides her down the hall toward the kitchen. I lean against the sunroom doorway, watching them go. It feels like a scene from a different universe —a universe where all of the alternate realities I've missed out on reside.

"No offense, but you reek of uncertainty," Caroline whispers as she comes to stand next to me.

"Shhhh," I silence her, not wanting Dawson to hear.

"I know him being back here has to be confusing for you," she continues quietly. "But you're doing a good job."

"I'm trying. And I'll keep trying until the weirdness is gone and everything feels strictly platonic."

"What if..." Caroline inhales shakily. "Well, never mind."

"What?"

"Well, it's just that some people aren't meant to have a platonic relationship. And I've always felt that you and Dawson are two of those people."

"Don't tell me things like that, Care. Please."

"Sorry," she apologizes immediately. "That's the first time I've ever felt like I could voice it. It's hard to look at y'all together again and not secretly hope for it. But that probably comes from a place of selfishness."

I lean my head against the wall and listen to Dawson and Whitley's voices flowing down the hallway from the kitchen. "I understand selfishness," I say lowly. "It's the reason I'm still messed up over the past. Over him."

She rubs a hand up and down my arm. "What's meant to be, will always be."

"So everyone says." I laugh. The sentiment is eerily similar to something Dad said to me a few days ago.

"I have to go show a house. Want me to shoo Dawson out first?"

"Nah, I can do it."

"Love you!" She slips out the front door.

In the kitchen, I find Whitley yawning over a bowl of half-eaten soup and Dawson drinking a glass of water. "Hey." He places another bowl at the spot next to Whitley. "I went ahead and warmed your lunch up, too."

"Oh, thanks." I take a seat, salivating over the steaming bowl of lima beans and rice.

"Do you want some?"

"I'm okay. I have a lunch meeting with a potential assistant." He scratches the side of his head. "That feels weird to say."

"It's all part of being a big-time business owner like me," I joke.

He finishes his water and leans against the refrigerator. "Speaking of business, do you have to work later?"

"Unfortunately." I sneak a peek at my uncharacteristically quiet daughter. Her chin is rested in one palm and her eyelids are fighting to stay open. "Dad or Sawyer will come watch this one. I'm just waiting for one of them to confirm."

"There's no one else who can give the tours?"

I take a bite of cornbread and shake my head. "Not today."

"I could do them." He walks closer. "You should stay home with Whitley."

My spoon clatters into the bowl and I wipe my mouth. "I can't ask you to do that."

"You didn't ask, I offered. I know it's been a while since my guiding days, but it can't be that different, right?" He downs the last of the water and begins washing the empty glass.

"You've already fed us lunch and offered to fix the crack in the sunroom window." I laugh. "I can't let you go to work for me, too."

"Don't forget the flowers, Mama," Whitley says, running a finger over a vibrant yellow rose petal.

"See? And you brought Whitley flowers, too. We've met our favor quota for the next year, Daws."

Shit, now I'm the one throwing nicknames around.

"Let me help." He folds his arms on top of the counter and for a second, I think he's going to reach for my hand. I pull it out of his reach.

"I'm sure you have better things to do."

"Mama, don't be stubborn. I want you to stay with me." She leans her head on my shoulder.

"Did you two plan this or something?" I raise my eyebrows at Dawson. He shrugs, then winks at Whitley.

"You don't even have to pay me," Dawson says.

"If you do this, I will absolutely be paying you."

"So I can cover for you then?"

I take another bite of beans, chewing slowly and allow myself time to think. "I guess I could pay you as a freelancer. You'll have to sign a waiver, too."

"A waiver?" He laughs. "That says what? You're not responsible for any potential harm caused by the undead?"

"Hilarious," I mumble around another bite. "And, I'm paying you time and a half for the inconvenience."

"I won't deposit the check." His eyes twinkle.

"Then I'll shove cash into your back pocket when you least expect it."

"Are you looking for an excuse to touch my bu—" He stops mid-sentence, pressing his fingers to his lips when he remembers we're in the company of a child. Said child would normally pick up on a joke like that in no time, but at the moment she's so doped up on cold medicine she's barely listening to the conversation.

I can't resist the lamest comeback on the planet. "You wish."

FUCK! How does every conversation go in this direction?

We're in our 30s, for Pete's sake.

"I'll text you any details you might need," I tell him. "I'll also let Ms. Knox and Dad know you're filling in, so there are no surprises."

"Sounds like a plan." He pats his pockets, searching for his keys. "I'll get outta here so y'all can get settled."

"Thanks again. For all of your help." I stand from the stool and help Whitley up from hers.

"Yes, thank you," she says beside me.

"Any time, ladies. Get some rest." Dawson backs out of

the room. A couple of seconds later, I hear the front door open then close again. His smell lingers around us in the kitchen.

"Can we watch another movie?" Whitley asks.

"Of course. I have an idea. What if we set up a chill zone in the living room and watch movies all day?"

"Yes!" She smiles through her Motrin fog.

We're settling on the couch with every blanket and pillow in the house when my phone pings with a text.

> **DAWSON**
>
> We'll talk about your window later. Don't think I'm going to forget about it.

Smiling, I roll my eyes and toss the phone aside. Another message comes in as it hits the couch cushion so I snatch it back up.

> **DAWSON**
>
> And instead of paying me for tonight, maybe you can buy me dinner sometime instead?

My heart rate quadruples, threatening to crash through my rib cage.

> I'll think about it.

I put my phone on silent and pretend to focus on the opening credits of The Parent Trap.

It's happened. The line I've been trying so hard to avoid has officially been crossed—and at a much faster rate than I've been anticipating.

CHAPTER 16

SUMMER 2010

The second week of May, Dawson returns to Larkspur for the summer and all feels right in the world again.

Three months stretch ahead of us, and after only a few days spent together in person over the past year, I feel desperate to make every second of those three months count. When he walks into Ghost to Coast for his first tour shift, wearing one of our new Sunny Spirits T-shirts and his classic knee-weakening smile, it takes all of my self-control not to bombard him and drag him off to somewhere more private.

Him, my heart sings.

Who even are you, Sage? my suppressed inner grump scoffs.

"Hi," I breathe out as he meets me behind the desk.

"Hi." He grabs one of my hands and squeezes, making up for the fact that we can't kiss on the clock.

There'll be time for that later. I hope tonight's tours go by fast.

"I thought I was going to be late." He wipes a bead of sweat from his forehead. "I had to park two streets over. I've never seen things so busy this early in the season."

"Tonight's tours are also packed."

"Good." He grins. "I love big groups."

"There's something I need to show you, though..." I say, opening the booking system and pulling up the list of participants on the first tour. "You might already know, but if not, this is your head's up."

"Ugh, is it a group full of kids?" He wrinkles his nose and squints at the screen.

"No..." I watch him read through the list of names, waiting for his reaction to the last two: Edward and Cynthia Aiken.

"What the hell?" Dawson's mouth drops into a flat line and his eyes go dark.

"So you didn't know?"

"No," he snaps.

"Sorry," I say, shrinking a little at his tone.

"No, no, I'm sorry." He lifts my hand to his mouth and kisses it. "You're the last person I want to take this out on."

"Maybe they want to see what the tour is all about?" I ask hopefully.

"I doubt it. His ego just wants to know why I want to spend another summer working here instead of with him."

He grabs the duster from beneath the desk and starts going to town, wiping everything so forcefully that the computer monitor topples backward. I catch it just before it crashes to the floor, then gently take the duster from him. His face turns a deep shade of maroon. "I have to go to the bathroom," he mutters before rushing away. I stare helplessly after him.

Five minutes later, he returns with his shirt tucked in. His hair is neat and wet with water from the sink. He gives me an embarrassed smile then opens the tour list again, like he's double checking to make sure he didn't imagine the names.

"Do...you want me to give this tour?" I ask tentatively. "Will your parents make you too nervous?"

Knowing what I already know about his tumultuous relationship with his parents, I feel like I should ask a deeper question; like I should try to get to the root of what's bothering him. This feels like a safer option at the moment, though.

"It's okay." He checks the time. "I have ten minutes before people start showing up. Ten minutes to get my shit together and stop acting like an ass."

"You're not acting like an ass," I say, stepping closer so our hips touch.

"You should know something," he says, looking deep into my eyes.

"I'm listening."

"I haven't told my parents about us yet," he admits. "Please don't think it's anything to do with you. It's them. Well, Dad really. He's never encouraged me to date. He's always said there will be time for that after school; that dating is a distraction from what's important."

"But you're 20 years old," I say bluntly.

"Duh." Smirking, he pinches one of my hips. "It's just always been easier to let him think he's right to avoid arguments. And it was easy until last summer. Until you."

"I am pretty irresistible," I joke, moving even closer to him, knowing we're being unprofessional but also not caring.

Dawson looks around the bookstore, which is empty except for one customer who's chatting with Ms. Knox at the cash register. He lowers his face until his mouth is right next to my ear. "I can't wait until we can be alone later."

Goosebumps spread quickly over my arms and legs and my breath gets caught in my chest. His hands feel at home on my hips, but I already know they'll feel just as right on every other spot they haven't been yet. He feels warm and solid and safe—all things that I rarely feel separately, let alone all at once.

The bell on the front door rattles and we leap apart and look to see who's entered, anticipating his parents. It's only the bookstore patron leaving though.

"I am going to tell them, by the way," Dawson says, waking the sleeping computer monitor. "About you. About us."

"I believe you. Take your time."

I can't say I'm all too eager to build a relationship with Dawson's parents. His dad has always rubbed me the wrong way, and that feeling only doubles every time Dawson opens up to me a little more. It doesn't help that Ed and Cynthia are the last to arrive for check-in, completely late with barely one minute before the tour is supposed to begin.

Edward Aiken promenades through Ghost to Coast with the air of someone who has never operated on anyone's time-line but his own. Dawson's mom follows closely behind, looking slightly anxious. Over their shoulders, I can see Ms. Knox staring at them with her mouth hanging slightly open. I wouldn't be surprised if this is the first time the two of them have ever set foot in here. They don't seem like the type to support their locally owned bookstore.

"Surprise," Ed says when he reaches the desk. Like Dawson's, his grin reaches his eyes, but it reads more like a sneer. His gaze roams over me, lingering just a second too long. I don't bother smiling back at him.

"I would ask why you didn't bother to tell me you were coming tonight," Dawson says, "but you're late, so any chit-chat will have to wait."

"I told you we needed to be here earlier," his mom says, staring at the floor. Her diamond earrings sparkle in the over-head light.

"Don't be ridiculous," Ed says. "It's 5:00 on the dot. We're right on time, as far as I'm concerned."

"Your confirmation email does say to arrive at least ten minutes early," I point out, unable to help myself.

Ed ignores me, but Cynthia surprises me by smiling apologetically.

"I'll gather the rest of the group while you check them in," I tell Dawson, touching his elbow lightly without thinking. His dad's eyes follow the movement then stay glued to me as I walk away.

"Is that Gerald Murray's daughter?" I hear him ask.

"Yep." Dawson slaps two participant waivers on the desk in front of his parents. "Sign these and we'll get started."

When Dawson joins the group another minute later, I immediately start thinking of nicknames for his parents. We're at the bed and breakfast before I settle on Tweedledee and Tweedledum, but then I decide that's too mean and I would feel guilty for calling them that behind Dawson's back.

Damn. I'm so soft now.

"I guess you could say," Dawson says, smiling cheekily at the group, "even in the afterlife, Mayor McBride still likes to have his cake and eat it too."

Everyone except his dad chuckles. Ed's arms are crossed tightly against his chest and his nose is wrinkled like something smells bad. We're currently swathed in a mixture of flowery scents from the B&B's gardens, so I know that's not actually the case.

"I don't think there's any truth to this story," Ed says loudly, drawing the attention of the group members. It's the first time he's spoken since we left Ghost to Coast.

"What do you mean?" Dawson asks, fighting to keep the smile on his face.

"Well…" Moving his hands to his pockets and puffing his chest out, Ed looks around to make sure he has everyone's attention. "I've lived in Larkspur my entire life, and I've never heard of Mayor McBride or any silly cake baking contests."

Some of the other guests whisper amongst themselves.

"My dad, everyone." Dawson's attempt at staying light-hearted is dwindling.

"I guess whoever started these tours has a really good imagination." Ed chuckles, and rage flares in my chest.

I stare at him until he locks eyes with me. They're the same color as Dawson's, but completely devoid of any warmth. "Have you ever actually studied the island's history? You might not know, but Larkspur does have a library, and it's full of newspapers and other resources that help us keep history at the forefront of our tours," I say.

If looks could kill, I'd be a smoldering pile of bones on the bed and breakfast's front lawn. At least it wouldn't be the worst place to die. On the off chance that the ghost part of Mayor McBride's story is true, I could join him in haunting the old house and eating cake every night. I could even claim my own bedroom and terrorize all of the tourists who sleep there.

Ed's glare rattles me out of the daydream, and the conversation I had with Dad when we hired Dawson last summer pops into my head. A trickle of regret snakes through my anger.

We don't want to piss off Ed Aiken...

The problem with that is, now that I'm falling in love with his son, I want nothing more than to piss him off.

Love? The word echoes through my brain.

Dawson looks at me, and everything about him only confirms the sentiment. Too bad it's the worst possible time to work through this.

"I highly doubt any old newspaper will confirm the existence of a cake-eating ghost." Ed doesn't let his point go.

"You have a few minutes to take a look around the property," Dawson tells the group, changing the subject. "Take some pictures and enjoy the gardens. We'll move to our next stop soon!"

Everyone but Ed and Cynthia disperse.

"Dad, what are you doing?" Dawson hisses.

"Trying to strike up a conversation! There's nothing wrong with a healthy debate," Ed says.

"Sunny Spirits isn't here for 'debates.'" Dawson makes air quotes. "The tours are for education and entertainment. Of course the existence of ghosts can't be proven, but the people and places we discuss are rooted in research."

"It's true," Cynthia says, smoothing her blonde hair. "The women's board considered reviving the cake contest at one point. For charity."

Feeling like I should leave, I start to walk away but Dawson grabs my backpack strap and holds me next to him. "Sage's dad worked hard to create Sunny Spirits," he says. "I'm sure he'd be happy to answer any questions you have."

"Sage, is it?" Ed drawls. "That's a...nice name. Appropriate."

"I've never heard that one before." I force a laugh.

"I think it's lovely," Cynthia says.

Maybe I underestimated her. I'm glad I decided not to refer to her as Tweedledee. Besides, Dawson's dad is obnoxious enough to hold both nicknames.

"It is." Dawson grabs my hand. "And everything else about her is lovely too."

Ed's eyes truly miss nothing. He stares at our intertwined fingers and I squirm. If I'd known we were going to do this now, I would have been a little less of a smart-ass toward him. I look at Dawson with wide eyes.

"Aha," Ed says. "I wanted to see for myself what could possibly make this job so great that you're leaving me hanging for the second summer in a row, but now it's apparent that it has nothing to do with the actual job."

"You have two assistants and hundreds of employees working the charters on Larkspur and across the state. I don't think that's leaving you hanging," Dawson replies.

"Sage, you'll have to come over for dinner soon." Cynthia changes the subject. Unlike her husband, she's beaming at Dawson and me. I want to rescue her from beneath her husband's arm of steel.

"Yeah..." Ed pulls her even closer, the fake smile plastered back on his face. "I thought Dawson might meet someone at school, but apparently he's more attracted to the locals."

He's a master of passive aggressiveness, and I'm pinned between a rock and a hard place—wanting to stand up for myself, but also wanting to make things as easy as possible for Dawson. I decide staying quiet is the best option. If this is how Ed Aiken speaks to people in public, I can't imagine what he's spent years saying to his son behind closed doors.

No wonder Dawson is terrified to be anything less than perfect.

"It's time to continue the tour," Dawson says.

"I don't think we'll be joining for the rest. I have things to do," Ed says.

Cynthia opens her mouth like she wants to protest, then promptly snaps it shut when her husband looks down at her.

"Are you sure?" I find my voice. "You'll miss the part where we talk about your great-great grandfather and his poisoned-tea love triangle."

"I *hate* to miss it," he says in a tone absent of disappointment. "Sarah, we'll plan dinner soon."

"It's *Sage*," Dawson and I say at the same time.

Ed walks away and Cynthia rushes over to hug her son. "You're doing a great job," she tells him, then touches my arm. "Sage, we'll talk soon."

By the time they're out of sight, Dawson's breathing so hard I'm afraid he's going to pass out. Tears brim his eyes and his face is the color of the scarlet roses in the garden behind us. I pull a bottle of water out of my backpack and open it for him. "Drink this and breathe," I say quietly, not wanting the nearby tour guests to overhear. "I'll finish this tour. You're okay."

He nods silently and takes the water from me.

"Gather round!" I revive my guide voice. "Our next stop is extra exciting, because it's a brand-new addition to Sunny Spirits tours. You'll be one of the first groups to experience the creepy atmosphere of the toy store's haunted loft, which is said to be guarded by one of the island's most well-known spirits— Dr. Leech."

"Thank you," Dawson whispers in my ear, falling into step beside me.

"Any time," I whisper back before continuing my monologue over my shoulder. "Tricky Treats Toys used to be home to Dr. Leech's practice. He's never been quite willing to give up the space, and that often makes things difficult for the toy shop's employees."

By the time the first tour is finally finished, Dawson is feeling more like himself. He leads the next two tours without a hitch, even though, as he feared earlier, the second group is actually full of nervous children. To round off his shift, the final group has not one, not two, but three guests who are just as skeptical and argumentative as Ed Aiken.

At the end of the night, Dawson locks Ghost to Coast's door behind the last guest and slides to the floor. "That was a hell of a first day back," he says, looking up at me dramatically.

"Are you sure you can handle it, Ghost Boy? I'm sure I could easily find a replacement for you." I hold a hand out to him and he grabs it. I try to pull him up but he's stronger than me, and before I know it, I'm in his lap.

"That's a rude thing to say, *Wedgie*."

My mouth falls open and I try to wiggle away. "Hey, that's a family only nickname!"

He wraps an arm around me, pinning me to his chest. Laughing, I peek nervously out of the glass behind him, waiting for someone to walk by on the sidewalk and catch a confusing glimpse of the two of us on the floor.

"I'm sorry about your parents," I say, running a thumb over his cheek. "Hopefully I didn't make things worse by being rude to your dad."

"Don't worry about that." He presses his forehead to mine. "It was kinda hot."

He kisses me, and I get lost in it for a moment before I remember that we could be spotted at any second. Ms. Knox is cool, but I don't think she'd appreciate hearing about two twenty-year-olds putting on a show in her store.

"Come on." I push off of his lap and back to my feet. "Let's finish up so we can get out of here." "Orrrr..." He stands next to me. "We could stay for a while."

"Why? It's late, and we want to be alone, remember?" I rise to my toes to peck him on the lips then turn to head for the Sunny Spirits desk.

I've barely made it five steps before his arms wrap around my waist from behind. "In case you haven't noticed, we're already alone," he says between kisses on my neck.

"Technically." I spin to face him, motioning to the giant front windows. "The problem is the lack of privacy."

"That's an easy fix. Follow me." He grabs my hand and pulls me toward the used book section, flipping the switch to the single remaining light off as we pass by it. In complete darkness, we stumble past the first five rows of books. At the sixth, Dawson turns sharply and leads me to the very end before pressing me against one of the shelves.

"What are we doing?" I giggle nervously, trying my hardest to focus and find his face through the blackness. I can't see him, but I can feel him. His breath against my cheek. His hard chest against mine. His hips pressed urgently against my stomach.

"We're doing this."

His mouth finds mine and I inhale sharply, parting my lips to taste as much of him as possible. His tongue intertwines with mine and his shoulders pin me tighter against the shelf. Tiny splinters dig into the back of my neck. As if sensing my discomfort, Dawson places a hand behind me, protecting my skin from the scratchy shelf.

"Do you think about this when we're not together?" he asks, pulling away and trailing kisses across my jaw and down my neck.

"Every day," I whisper breathlessly. With each kiss, my body arches against him. Unlike the few other times we've made out, I don't try to control it.

His lips brush mine again and his free hand finds its way up my shirt. He pauses just above the waistband of my shorts, briefly splaying his fingers across my stomach before wandering his palm around my side and up my back. His fingertips dance across my bra strap. "Can I?" he murmurs into my mouth.

"Yes." My nipples press against the soft fabric of my bra, despite the nerves that are building.

Releasing my neck, he undoes the clasp, then slides both hands over my rib cage and around my breasts. For a moment, I forget how to breathe. My hips once again tilt toward his, and through the fabric of his shorts I can feel him hard against my lower stomach. Needing to feel more of him, I loop a couple of fingers into his waistband, then confidently slide my hands into the back of his boxers to squeeze his butt.

"Just as I thought." I smile against his mouth. "It feels as perfect as it looks."

Laughing, he slowly pushes my shirt and bra up until my

breasts are fully exposed between us. He lowers his mouth to each one, drawing one nipple into his mouth, then moving on to the other. A jolt of electricity zips through my pelvis.

"Just as I thought," he repeats. "They feel and taste as perfect as *they* look."

"Oh my god," I pant into his hair, mesmerized by the fact that anything can feel this good.

We kiss for a few more minutes, allowing our hands to roam and explore. All too soon, Dawson stands up straight and begins pulling my bra and shirt back into place, kissing my forehead as he does so.

"Can't we stay here all night?" I joke.

"We could," he says. "But anything more than this feels sacred, and I want that to happen somewhere more special than a musty old bookstore."

"Hey, I love this musty old bookstore."

"Me too." He takes my hand and leads me away from my new favorite spot in said bookstore. "Mainly because I get to spend so much time here with you."

"Do you think Madame Roberta was watching?" I joke.

"Nah," Dawson says, flipping one of the lights back on. "I gave her the night off."

CHAPTER 17

PRESENT DAY, OCTOBER 2022

"Ta-DA!" Whitley sashays out of her bedroom in a pickle costume that is so alarmingly green it hurts my eyes.

I squint, laughing at the way her auburn ponytail sticks out of the hole we cut in the back. "You're the cutest pickle I ever did see!"

"Mama, it's not supposed to be cute. It's supposed to be funny."

"It can be both," I say, using my thumb to smooth out the green paint in her eyebrows. "I'm laughing, aren't I?"

"Yeah..."

"I never asked." I kneel to double knot her sneakers. "Why a pickle?"

She shrugs. "Me and Grampa were talking about costumes and he was eating a pickle."

"It was that easy, huh?"

"Yep!"

I grab my purse off the counter and slip my Vans on. For the first time this season I'm wearing jeans. It's the beginning of Larkspur's weekend-long Halloween festival, and the weather couldn't have picked a more perfect time to give us a small break from the heat.

"I have a surprise for you," I tell Whitley, rummaging around my bag for what I'm looking for. I'm about to blame Buster when my hand lands on it. "Do you want to see?

"Please!" She shuffles over in a blur of lime green.

Bit by bit, I produce a can of spray glitter. Whitley takes it from me to see what it is, then squeals.

"I know pickles aren't glittery, but I used my imagination. Do you want to use it?" I ask.

"Yes, yes!"

"Let's go outside and I'll spray you down."

A few minutes later, she's drying in a spot of direct sunlight. She holds her arms out and spins, admiring the sparkly green costume. "Call me Princess Pickle!" she yells.

"Your chariot awaits, princess." I fold her into the car and help her buckle the seat belt around the outrageous costume.

"I hope the judges have a sense of humor," she says as we search for a place to park. "Hey, who's judging this year anyway?"

"Ms. Knox," I say. "And...Dawson. I'm not sure who else."

"Dawson?" Whitley repeats. "Good. He brought me flowers so I think he'll be on my side. Ms. Knox, too."

The parking on Main Street is blocked off for foot traffic, and the square is packed with people—some I recognize, and many I don't. Tourists and locals from nearby towns flock to Larkspur for the Halloween festival every year, and for good reason.

In addition to the existing downtown businesses, food trucks and tent vendors are set up in the square and all along Main. The fall decorations and canopy of fairy lights above the street give everything an ethereal feel during the day, and a fun, spooky vibe as it gets dark. There are costume contests for all ages, hay rides around the island, bobbing for apples, and enough other activities to last for the entire weekend.

On our walk from the car, Whitley and I point out different costumes and snacks we want to try. "Why don't you ever dress up, Mama?" she asks, admiring a woman dressed like Elsa from *Frozen*.

"It's just not my thing," I say. "It's more fun to help you dress up."

Whitley has always loved the Halloween festival. I'm sure it's for the same reasons other kids do—costumes and candy and the feeling of magic. But I like to let myself think that she actually loves it for deeper reasons. Like she somehow knows that the festival is a major part of how she came to be; that she wouldn't be here if I hadn't been in this specific place at an earlier time.

The stage for the costume contest is set up in the very center of the square, with several rows of chairs for spectators and a small table for the judges at the front. There are four judges at the table. I spot Ms. Knox's silver hair on one end. Dawson sits next to her, his broad shoulders making her small frame look even smaller. From a distance, I can't tell who makes up the rest of the judging panel.

I lead Whitley to the left side of the stage to line up with the other elementary-aged kids. "Penelope!" she yells, spotting a shimmery blue butterfly. Penelope runs to her and I giggle at the sight of a butterfly and a pickle hugging in a puff of glitter. It travels through the air and coats my cardigan and the costumes of other nearby kids.

This is why I usually say no glitter.

"You two look perfect!" I tell them, pulling out my cell phone. "Let me take your picture. I'll send it to your mom too, Penelope."

"Okay!" Penelope puts her arm around Whitley and they grin at me with smiles that are missing at least one tooth each.

"Good luck," I say. "I'm going to find a seat."

When I turn around, Ms. Knox is standing so closely behind me I nearly plow her to the ground. She wobbles and I grab her by the shoulders. "Easy there." I laugh.

"You're covered in glitter!" she says, swiping at the front of my tank top.

"You can thank my pickle for that."

We look at Whitley and she waves at Ms. Knox. "Am I missing a joke?" Ms. Knox whispers. "I don't get it."

"Nope, she's just a sparkly pickle." I laugh.

"You've gotta stop letting your dad plan her costumes," she says. "Next year, I'll help."

"Next year she might think she's too old and cool to dress up, so I enjoy the chaos while it's here."

"Good point." Ms. Knox glances over her shoulder at the judge's table. "Hey, I was hoping you could do me a favor."

"Sure, what's up?"

"I'm supposed to be judging today, but I'm not feeling well."

"Okay?" She seems fine, so I look her over, searching for signs of illness.

"I was hoping you could fill in for me?" She looks at the judges again. The one next to Dawson waves at her and I realize it's Larkspur's current mayor, Mayor Grady.

Dawson locks eyes with me and grins. I look back at Ms. Knox, smelling something fishy.

"Are you sure you're sick?" I ask.

She slumps her shoulders and forces a cough into her palm. "Yes. Very."

"Whitley is in the contest. It wouldn't be fair for me to judge." I'm searching for any excuse not to take that seat next to Dawson.

"Don't worry about that." She pats my forearm with the

hand she just fake-coughed into. "I've already okayed it with Mayor Grady."

"I don't know..." I look at Dawson again.

"Please?" Ms. Knox widens her eyes at me, pleading. "You know they like to have local business owners on the panel. You check that box."

"So would Dad." I look around and find him in the third row of the audience, next to Eve.

"Oh, he won't do it. You know that."

I point two fingers at my eyes, then at Ms. Knox. "Don't think I don't know what you're doing here, lady," I joke.

"I have no idea what you mean." She rolls her shoulders back and coughs into her hand again. "I'm a sick old woman."

"Mmmmhmmmm."

"Come on, I'll take you to your seat." She grabs me by the elbow and leads me to the other judges.

Dawson and Mayor Grady wave at us as we approach. It's only when we're at the table that I realize the fourth judge at the other end of the table is Edward Aiken.

"Everyone, you know Sage, co-owner of Sunny Spirits," Ms. Knox says. "I'm under the weather so she's going to take my spot today."

"Good to have you, Sage!" Mayor Grady says enthusiastically. His veneers are blindingly white in the afternoon sun.

Ed slants his eyes in my direction, but doesn't say anything. Just as I have for the past decade, I feel the urge to stick my tongue out at him. Ms. Knox pulls her vacated chair out and all but shoves me into it. "Y'all have fun!" she says as she runs away. I watch her take the empty seat next to Eve and Dad instead of going home to get some rest.

Judas, I think, avoiding Dawson's face as I turn back around.

"Fancy meeting you here," he says.

"At least you knew you were going to be here..." I reply. "How does this even work?"

"It's easy." He reaches across me to pick up the stack of papers at my spot. "Each age category has a scoresheet of numbers that correspond with the contestant numbers. You rate each costume one through ten, then the numbers are tallied at the end and the highest scores win first, second, and third."

His arm brushes mine when he reaches to put the ballots back. I discreetly attempt to scoot my chair further away from his. In retaliation, he not-so-discreetly moves his chair closer to me again. The old classic Dawson smirk is on his face, and it elevates my blood pressure.

"I shouldn't be surprised that you still have an annoying streak," I say.

"I shouldn't be surprised that you're still super easy to annoy." He folds his hands on the table in front of him.

"You didn't wanna sit by daddy dearest?" I whisper, peeking around him to look at Ed. He and Mayor Grady are deep in conversation, but talking quietly enough that I can't figure out what they're discussing.

"We're not on speaking terms," Dawson says, uncomfortably scratching his neck. "Haven't been for a while."

"Oh. I'm sorry," I say. "Has that made it harder to come back to Larkspur?"

"Not really. I love Larkspur. Plus, I have Mom. Cole and Caroline. Y—I mean, other...people." His mouth twitches.

Was he about to say me?

Don't go there, Sage.

"Here come the first contestants," Mayor Grady says, pointing our attention to the stage.

Each kid who files onto the stage has a number pinned to their costume. The volunteers line them up horizontally and make sure their numbers are visible. Whitley stands between

Penelope the Butterfly and a little boy dressed like Dwight from *The Office*, the number "12" hanging off the bottom of her pickle. She searches the crowd, a look of surprise filling her face when she sees me at the judge's table.

"What are you doing?!" she mouths at me.

"I'll tell you later," I mouth back.

"Wait." Dawson grabs my forearm. "Is Whitley a cucumber?"

"A pickle," I correct. "With glitter."

He bursts into laughter, his shoulders shaking so hard he almost knocks me out of my chair. "That's hilarious," he says, rubbing a hand across his face. "Immediate ten out of ten for me."

It looks like Whitley's mission to be "just funny" has been accomplished.

Mayor Grady stands from the table and walks to a microphone stand at the base of the stage. "Welcome, everyone, to Larkspur Island's annual Halloween Festival!"

People all around the square stop to clap, some of them juggling candy apples and bags of popcorn. The kids on stage hop nervously from one foot to the other, suddenly aware that all eyes are on them.

"We're going to kick things off with a Larkspur tradition, the costume contest! Our first group of participants is already on stage. Please give a round of applause for our five-to-eleven-year-old contestants! Everyone will have the opportunity to say their name, and what they're dressed as. Make sure you keep clapping to show these kids how awesome their costumes are." Mayor Grady passes the mic to one of the volunteers and returns to his seat.

The volunteer makes her way down the line. Some of the children scream their names and costumes into the microphone, and some speak so quietly you can barely hear them. There are a few mermaids, a construction worker, and even a mini–Michael Myers. Caroline's kids are numbers four and five—Maddie is one of the mermaids and Cam is a football player. I write my scores down as each costume is introduced.

"And what's your name?" the volunteer asks Whitley when it's her turn.

"I'm Whitley, and I'm a pickle!" she says excitedly. "It was my Grampa's idea. Hi, Grampa!" She waves and I turn to grin at Dad, rolling my eyes.

After Dwight, a Barbie, and an ice cream sundae are introduced, the kids' contest comes to an end and they file off stage to watch the adult contest before winners are announced.

"What are you doing?" Whitley looks panicked as she bumps her way off the stage and through the crowd to me. "Why didn't you tell me you were a judge?"

"It happened last-minute," I say. "Go sit with Grampa."

"Fine," she huffs, then calls, "Hi Dawson, bye Dawson!" as she dodders away.

"She was excited when I told her you were a judge," I say.

"So she likes me then?" he asks.

"For some reason," I joke. "The flowers and soup also had something to do with it."

"If only you were as easy to win over," he mumbles.

"What did you say?" There's no way I heard him correctly.

"Nothing." His leg bumps mine under the table. "Look, the next group is coming out."

The adult contestants line up on stage. When I spot number 14, my mouth falls open and all thoughts of the man next to me are swiftly moved to the back burner. Cole is on stage wearing the tightest-fitting firefighter costume I've ever seen in my life. The buttons on his stomach are straining and the shorts are so small I fear he may have to be cut out of them. A shrill cat-call whistle sounds from the audience and I look for the source, laughing when I discover it's Caroline.

"No fuckin' way." Dawson falls into another fit of laughter. Cole catches his eye and blows a kiss at him.

"I could have gone the rest of my life without seeing this," I joke.

"You and me both," Dawson says. "I thought this was a family-friendly event?"

I watch as he writes a "10" beside Cole's number with a grin on his face.

After the adults are finished, there's a brief intermission while Mayor Grady collects our score sheets and takes them to the volunteers to be tallied. Ed stands and walks into the crowd, too cowardly to sit next to his son without a buffer. I try to wave Caroline and Cole over to serve as my own buffer between Dawson and I, but they're too busy being social butterflies to notice. Cole's costume seems to be a crowd favorite.

"You never responded to my text," Dawson says suddenly, turning his body toward me.

"What text?" I play dumb.

"About buying me dinner. You responded to everything else when I gave the tours for you that night."

"I don't think I saw that one," I say.

"You're so mean." Dawson laughs.

"Does it sound nicer if I say I forgot to respond?" I shift to face him and my knees angle against his.

"Not really." He studies my face, a twinkle in his eyes.

I always loved the twinkle.

"It's just...do you really think it's a good idea for us to have dinner?" I ask.

"Why wouldn't it be?" he asks.

I stare at him like he's stupid.

He steeples his fingertips together. "Maybe I should try to approach this like you would," he says. "Bluntly."

I raise my eyebrows.

"I would like to...spend time with you, Ghost Girl. Because I like you. I liked you ten-plus years ago and it turns out, I still like you now."

My first thought is to run away and disappear into the costumes and other distractions in the square. My second is to scream, because this is scary—the scariest thing that's happened to me since finding out I was pregnant with Whitley. My body doesn't fully respond to either of these cues, so instead I kind of jump in my chair unexpectedly and let out a yelp that sounds more like a hiccup.

"This seems easier for you than it is for me." My voice shakes.

"I don't know if it's easier," he says. "Maybe we're just both still more like our younger selves than we think."

"How so?" He piques my interest.

"Well, I've always been the one to gravitate toward our connection. And you've always been the one to fight it kicking and screaming."

A high-pitched ringing noise fills my ears. For a second, I think it's the all-too-familiar, anxiety-induced tinnitus, then I realize it's the microphone. Mayor Grady is back on the stage, ready to announce the costume contest winners.

Saved by the bell, I think, turning away from Dawson.

"Who's ready for our top three children's contest winners?" Mayor Grady asks enthusiastically. The crowd cheers.

"Your second runner-up is everyone's favorite pickle, Miss Whitley! Come on up here, Whitley!"

Clapping, I let out a whoop as Whitley and her pickle waddle their way to the stage. One of the volunteers gives her a third-place ribbon and a bag of candy. She's joined by the first runner-up, the construction worker, and the winner, Penelope the butterfly. I use my phone to take a few photos of them and Whitley beams at me through her painted face.

"She was robbed," Dawson whispers in my ear. He's close enough for me to smell the aftershave on his neck and the Winterfresh gum he's been chewing.

"I'll have to file a complaint," I joke.

"Please have dinner with me." Still an inch from my face, he changes the subject. "If nothing else, we can start talking about plans for the parlor. We don't have to discuss anything you're not ready to."

Whitley comes up as Mayor Grady is announcing the first runner-up for the adults. "Look at my ribbon!" she says excitedly.

"It's beautiful. We'll hang it on your wall when we get home." I squeeze her to my side.

"Congratulations, Whitley. I love your costume," Dawson says.

"Thank you." She passes him a piece of candy from her prize bag. He opens the Kit-Kat and offers me half, which I accept.

"Since you shared your candy, I'll respond to your dinner text," I say.

"I was hoping that would work."

"Keep an eye on your phone later, because I will expect a reply back." I arch an eyebrow at him.

In the background, Mayor Grady announces Cole as the winner of the adult costume contest. I watch him do a stupid little run to the stage to collect his prize, wishing the entire time that Dawson were the one in the sexy firefighter costume.

CHAPTER 18

SUMMER 2010

"How's the book coming?" I ask Dad as I set a plate of grilled cheese sandwiches on the table between him and Sawyer. "Sorry I haven't asked much about it lately."

He brushes me off. "It's okay, you're a busy working girl with a boyfriend now. The book is going okay...I've been stuck on the same chapter for weeks, writing and rewriting over and over."

"Do you think you'll ever be happy with it?" I ask.

"It's not that I'm not happy with it." He ladles some tomato soup into Sawyer's bowl. "I just want it to be...perfect."

"But there's no such thing as perfect, Dad," Sawyer says. "Your best is perfect. That's what my teacher, Mrs. Everly, told us all the time last year."

Dad and I smile at each other. "That's great advice," I tell Sawyer.

"It is," Dad agrees, reaching over to ruffle Sawyer's hair. "Maybe you could write me a note that says that. I'll stick it to the top of my computer so I can see it while I'm writing."

"Okay!" Sawyer says around a spoonful of soup.

"Could you write two notes?" I ask, thinking of Dawson. "I know someone else who could use that reminder."

"Sure."

Dawson is working tonight's tour shift, but I decided not to join like I normally would so I could spend some time with Dad and Sawyer. We're off to a great start with Sawyer's favorite dinner of grilled cheese and tomato soup, and we have the start of a *Star Wars* movie marathon lined up next.

"Is Dawson coming over later?" Sawyer asks. He's becoming quite infatuated with having someone he views as a cool older friend around.

"No, he's working and it will be too late when he's finished," I say.

"Why don't you ever go to his house?" he asks.

I exchange glances with Dad. It's been a couple of weeks since Ed and Cynthia infiltrated Dawson's tour. Out of guilt I told Dad about everything that happened, worried that Ed would do something stupid like write a bad review or start openly gossiping about Sunny Spirits around town. There's been nothing so far, but the tension between him and Dawson is thicker than ever.

"Because our house is more fun." I grin at Sawyer, then pop the last of my grilled cheese into my mouth.

"It's because of me," Sawyer says. Dad and I laugh.

A while later, we're halfway through *The Phantom Menace*. Never able to make it through an entire movie, Dad is already passed out in his corner of the couch. Sawyer is working his way through a popsicle, and I'm texting Dawson off and on.

DAWSON

This couple will not stop making out! His hand hasn't left her ass and people look uncomfortable. Do I say something?

> Go ahead and book them a room at the B&B when you make it there.

DAWSON

> Maybe I'm just jealous. I'd rather book us a room.

I bury my face in the pillow on my lap, grinning like a fool.

> I think people would talk.

DAWSON

> I don't care if you don't.

I'm halfway through my next response when my phone starts ringing. Mom's name shows on top of the screen and I sigh. "It's Mom," I tell Sawyer. "Keep watching, I'm going to take this."

"I want to talk to her after you!" he says.

Nodding, I roll off the couch and answer on the scurry to my room. "Hey, Mom."

"I'm surprised you answered," she says. "I didn't know if you were working tonight. Not that you usually take my calls when you aren't working..."

I ignore the remark, not wanting to start the conversation with an argument. "Well, you have me now. How are you?"

"I'm really good," she says. And she does sound good. Her voice is bright and less tired than it used to be.

Most days, it's hard to believe Mom has been gone as long as she has—in a few months, it will be a year. I think we'd all known how unhappy she'd become here. In fact, I'm pretty sure the slowly unfolding series of unfortunate events began for her the second she moved to Larkspur to be with Dad years and years ago.

Sure, things were mostly good through my birth, and Sawyer's too. Then Dad started the book, which turned into a much longer ordeal than any of us could have expected. Mom was keeping the business afloat, operating the household, and doing most of the parenting, which now that I'm older, I realize never came naturally to her.

When the spark between her and Dad died, that was the final straw.

"I'm the type of person who will do anything for love," she'd told me the day we had lunch at Phantom after her and Dad's big fight, *"but now the love is no longer there to keep me going."*

What about me? What about Sawyer? Is our love not enough?

Those are the questions I never brought myself to ask. But when she decided to leave and move to Atlanta without a second look behind her, that was a good enough answer for me.

"How's the new job?" I ask. "Well, I guess it's not so new anymore."

"It's great! I have my six-month review soon, and I'll be up for a raise," she says. "Office management feels like a breeze after years of trying to learn how to run a business."

"I bet." I fall onto my bed and pick at a loose thread on my comforter.

"You probably understand that better than anyone now. How is everything with Sunny Spirits? You doing okay?"

"It's good. Dad let me make some changes to the logo. We started the summer with new T-shirts and merch."

"That sounds exciting," she says.

"It was fun." I roll onto my back and stare up at the old cottage ceiling. "Made up for the other stuff that sucks...like bookkeeping."

A door opens and closes on Mom's end of the call, and I try to imagine her apartment. It feels like she's a world away. The hardest part about her being gone is having no concept of what her daily life looks like. I can still only imagine her here with us.

"That will get better the more you do it." Mom laughs.

Easy for you to say, I think. She's moved on and she's happy now. I'm even more stuck on this island than I was before she left. Dawson makes it better when he's here, but when he's at school I grow more and more desperate to experience something different. Something that I *want* to do for myself.

"How's Dawson?" Mom asks in an attempt to keep me from going quiet.

"He's...perfect." I smile up at the ceiling.

"Good."

I can tell by her tone that she's already running out of things to chat about, so I pivot before things become too awkward. "Sawyer wants to talk to you. I'll pass you to him."

"Oh, okay. I love you."

"Love you too." I walk to the living room and pause the movie before handing Sawyer the phone.

While he's talking to her, I clean the kitchen. With the sound of my brother's laughter and easy conversation in the background, I scrub the empty plates and glasses with enough force to crack them all into pieces. I can't pinpoint exactly what shifted my mood—all I know is I'm feeling frustrated at no one thing in particular.

When Sawyer is off the phone, we start *Attack of the Clones*. I doze off somewhere in the middle, and when I wake up the credits are rolling and Sawyer is snoring with his head in Dad's lap. I switch the TV off and cover them with a blanket before checking the time on my phone. It's 11:15, but now I feel wide awake, and my earlier frustration has settled into my bones and made me antsy. The house is too quiet and unsettling.

I need to go somewhere. Anywhere.

In my room, I find the moped key and shove the iPod Shuffle Dawson got me for Christmas into my pocket next to my phone. Then I tiptoe out of the house and steer toward Main Street.

Through the windows of Ghost to Coast, I can see Dawson giving his final tour monologue. Instead of going in, I wait outside until the last guest is gone. A few minutes later, Dawson turns off the lights and locks up.

He spots me the second he exits the building, his face lighting up. "What are you doing here? I didn't think I would see you tonight."

"Dad and Sawyer have already passed out and I was feeling restless." I walk to him and wrap my arms around his waist. He kisses me slowly.

"I'm glad you're here," he says against my lips.

"We should do something...something crazy," I say, my mood lifted by the rush of adrenaline his kisses always give me.

"Crazy?" He scratches his head. "This is Larkspur. Everything closes by midnight, even the bars. And even then, everyone around here knows we're not 21."

"So let's do something else. Let's *go* somewhere else."

"Okay?" A mischievous smile tugs at his lips. "I'm down to do anything as long as it's with you."

He pulls his keys from his pocket and starts walking toward his truck. I grab his arm.

"Let's take the moped," I tell him. "It's a nice night. It has a full tank. We can drive and see where we end up."

"Can we both fit on that thing?" He laughs.

"Yep." I step closer to him until every part of our bodies touch. "You just have to sit very close and hold on tight."

"Yes, ma'am," he says breathlessly.

I release him and walk to the moped. "I only have one helmet, though."

"You wear it." He takes the helmet from me and fastens it

to my head, then kisses the tip of my nose. "It looks cuter on you."

Dawson settles behind me and I start the tiny engine, then wheel us shakily onto the road, driving slowly to get used to the weight of two people. By the time we're coming up on the turn to the bridge that leads to Hayworth, I feel confident with Dawson behind me, comforted by the feeling of his arms around my waist.

"Should we keep going straight or take the bridge?" I yell over my shoulder.

"The bridge!" he says excitedly.

I make the turn, drawing a breath as water slowly surrounds us on all sides. It's still and purple beneath the light of the moon, and the salty smell whips around us, tying together a moment that I already know will become one of my most cherished memories. A strong gust of wind sends us closer to the shoulder at the peak of the bridge, and Dawson puts his hands on top of mine to help me regain control.

"Thanks!" I yell.

"I've always got your back, G.G." He laughs into my ear.

The small town of Hayworth is almost as devoid of nightlife as Larkspur. We continue to drive around, taking random turns and detours based off Dawson's commands of "right" and "left" and "straight." Eventually we come across a 24-hour diner, and I turn into the parking lot and kill the engine.

"Good call. I'm starving," Dawson says.

Inside, we order burgers and chocolate shakes to go. We're the only customers other than a group of tipsy twenty-some-things, and the gray-haired waitress couldn't look less enthused to be there as she passes us our greasy bag of food. We take it outside and sit on the curb next to the moped, beneath the glitchy flashing diner sign.

I take a bite of my burger before pulling my iPod out of

my pocket. I put one earbud in and pass Dawson the other, then scroll through the library, trying to decide what to listen to.

"Can I pick?" Dawson asks, biting his straw.

"Please." I pass him the iPod. A minute later, Yellowcard pumps into my ear.

The burgers are greasy and the shakes are watery, but even on the dirty concrete of a crumbling parking lot, his company makes the meal feel gourmet. Dawson finishes his food and lays a hand on my leg. The neon diner lights paint his face a shade of blue as he leans to kiss my shoulder. When he sits up, his face is serious.

"No one has ever made me feel the way you do, Sage." As he says it, the song changes from "Lights and Sounds" to "Only One," and the timing feels too perfect.

"I know how you feel," I tell him. I move the shakes from between us so I can scoot closer.

"I've been thinking more and more about something over the past few days," he says. "It would be a big decision."

"What kind of decision?" I ask, laying my head on his shoulder.

He rests his cheek on top of my head. "I don't think I want to go back to school in the fall," he says quietly, slowly. "I like it fine, but I don't know if it's where I'm supposed to be."

I can't determine if the feeling that flows through me is happiness over the thought of Dawson being in Larkspur full-time, or guilt over the thought of holding him back from something someone as smart as him is meant to do.

"That *would* be a big decision," I murmur, thinking about my conversation with Mom. About my own feelings of being forced into a life I'm not sure I want. "Do any of us really know where we're supposed to be, though?"

"I do." He lifts his head and puts his finger under my chin, forcing me to look at him.

"Where?" I ask.

"I'm supposed to be wherever you are."

Tears prick the corners of my eyes. I place my hands on his cheeks and pull his face to mine. A smelly, dingy diner parking lot is the last place I would ever expect to lose track of time, but it happens. I don't know if we kiss for minutes, hours, or days beneath the busted flashing sign, until I open my eyes and everything looks the same. The earphones lay in a tangle on the concrete between us. I didn't even notice that they fell out.

I love you, I think.

But I don't want to be the first to say it. Rather, I don't want to say it here.

"Your dad would be furious, you know," I say instead.

"I don't care." His face hardens. "I'm done doing things exactly the way he wants me to do them." "I'm so honored to be the initiator of your rebellious phase," I joke. "You should be." He tugs on my ponytail. "What's something you've always wanted to do, but have never done because you know your dad would hate it?" I ask.

"It's cliché." He smirks. "But getting a tattoo."

"Oh really?" I ask. An idea begins to formulate.

"Yeah, I know it's kind of stupid..."

"It's not!" I jump to my feet and hold my hand out to help him up, then pull him toward the front door of the diner.

"What are you doing?" he asks.

"Excuse me," I say, waking the waitress from her nap behind the counter. "Are there any tattoo parlors around here?"

"Two streets over," she says wearily. "It'll be the only thing open so you can't miss it."

"Thank you!" I tell her, then lead Dawson back to the moped.

"Are you serious right now?" he asks, laughing.

"As a heart attack." I buckle my helmet and pat the empty space of seat behind me. "Hop on, Clyde."

"Anything for you, Bonnie."

He takes his place and we disappear back into the dark streets of Hayworth, eventually stopping in front of another crumbling building with bars on the windows and a neon flashing sign that simply says "TATTOOS." I hesitate before turning off the engine.

"I'm suddenly not so sure about this," I say over my shoulder.

Dawson reaches around me and turns the key before removing it and putting it in his pocket. "Too late. We're doing this."

"We?" I squeak.

"Yes." He pulls me off the moped and removes the helmet, kissing the top of my mussed hair. "You said you wanted to do something crazy, remember?"

I stumble along behind him as he pulls me toward the sketchy storefront. "I was really just thinking I would watch you get one."

"Where's the fun in that?" He opens the door and ushers me inside. I let him because the sudden excitement is burning like a fire in his eyes, making his handsome face even more hypnotizing.

The parlor is empty with the exception of one guy behind the front desk. This is the first time I've ever set foot in a tattoo shop, but he looks exactly like what I would imagine a stereotypical tattoo artist to look like—black mohawk, leather pants, and so many tattoos on his own skin that I don't know where to look first. He smiles enthusiastically, and it seems out of place, but also makes me relax. From the looks of it, he's probably excited to finally have some potential clients.

"Sick shirts!" he tells us, noting our matching Sunny Spirits apparel. "I love ghosts."

"Thanks," Dawson says, matching his eagerness. "We were hoping you could squeeze us in for a couple of tattoos?"

"Squeeze *him* in." I step forward, smiling at the artist.

"No, *us*," Dawson argues, grabbing my hand.

His touch immediately wears me down another notch.

"I'm guessing you're new to this?" the artist asks, standing from his seat. He towers over both of us.

"How could you tell?" I joke.

"We're open to advice," Dawson adds.

Mohawk Man walks around the desk. "My best advice would be to start with something small."

"Okay..." Dawson turns to me. "G.G., we're doing something small. What should we do?"

I peer up into his hazel eyes, secretly already knowing the answer to the question I'm about to ask. I lower my voice. "Are we really about to get matching tattoos?"

"They don't necessarily have to match." He laughs. "And of course I'm not going to force you. It's your decision. Although, imagine reminiscing on this in ten or twenty years." The corner of his mouth lifts sweetly.

Resting my forehead against his chest, I breathe in his smell and try to wrap my head around a decision I've already made. If Dawson believes we're going to be together to talk about this in our thirties or forties, then I believe it. If Dawson wants us to get tattoos together, who am I to argue?

Besides, what makes me happier lately than being connected to him in some way—whether that's literally or figuratively?

I lift my head to find the tattoo artist staring at us with a slight smile on his face. "You two remind me of me and my wife when we first started dating," he says. "I know I look tough, but I still believe there's no better feeling than young love."

Love.

There's the word again. Dawson and I exchange a shy glance and I take a step back, suddenly feeling embarrassed.

"Okay, Ghost Boy," I say. "What should we get?"

Dawson shrugs and looks over my shoulder at the sample sketches covering the parlor's wall. His gaze then falls back over my face and rests on the top corner of my T-shirt. I look down, prepared to brush a stray bit of burger or some other scrap off my chest.

All that's there is the Sunny Spirits ghost.

We lock eyes and Dawson grins. "It only makes sense," he says.

I want to argue, but he's not wrong.

"Can you do this?" I ask, turning to Mohawk Man and pointing to the cute little spirit on my shirt.

"Easily," he answers. "Great choice. Like I said earlier, ghosts are cool."

CHAPTER 19

SUMMER 2010

"I suppose you're wondering why I've gathered you here today." Cole plops two Spine Chillers on the table in front of Dawson and I, then takes his seat.

"I was wondering that." Dawson blows his straw paper at Cole. "But now I'm wondering why you're acting like you're about to ask us to join you in selling some scammy product."

"Funny." Cole makes a face at Dawson. "But this is serious. The most serious thing I've ever done in my life."

My Spidey Senses begin to tingle and I watch in slow motion as Cole reaches into his pocket and produces a small, black velvet box. He opens it and sets it on the table between our coffees. At the sight of the classic oval-shaped diamond ring, tears begin rolling down my face.

I jump out of my chair and run around the table to squish Cole into a hug. Laughing, Dawson joins us, creating a group hug that draws the attention of everyone in Beans N' Boos. When we finally go back to our seats, Cole is dabbing at the corners of his eyes.

"That's even better than the reaction I was hoping for," he says, his tan skin glowing.

"When?" I ask, bouncing up and down in my seat.

"Sunday. And I was hoping you two could help me? I've planned a little scavenger hunt..."

Cole fills us in on his plan and we perfect the details. I'm good at keeping secrets, but I'm so excited it's probably still best to avoid Caroline for the next few days. Me being giddy for no reason (in her mind) will seem suspicious.

Per Cole's instructions, I initiate the plan the night before.

> Let's hang out tomorrow. Coffee and beach day?

CAROLINE

> Yes!!!

> Pick you up at 10? We'll take the moped. It will be fun!

CAROLINE

> See you then!

The next morning, the sun is shining brightly and the sky couldn't be a brighter shade of blue. Caroline waits for me on her front porch and I beep my goofy little horn as I slide to a stop in front of her house. She runs out to meet me, wearing a floral spaghetti strap sundress over her bathing suit. Her hair is in a bun and she looks beautiful and natural, just like she always does.

"Hey hey," I say.

"I'm excited to spend the day with you," she says, climbing onto the seat behind me and squeezing my shoulders. "I need to talk to you about Cole at some point. He's been weird lately."

"Boys!" I yell over my shoulder with faux disgust as we drive away.

We're halfway to our first destination when Caroline becomes suspicious. "I thought we were going to Beans?" she yells.

"I have to make one quick stop!"

"What are we doing at the marina?" she asks when I park and shut off the engine.

"Don't ask questions," I say. "Follow me."

"O-kayyyy..."

We walk down the dock until we reach Cole's dad's boat. Caroline looks even more skeptical when I turn to face her. "I think there's something for you next to the steering wheel."

She doesn't look convinced and makes no move to get into the boat. I make a show of tapping my foot and checking a fake watch. "We don't have all day, Care."

"Fine," she sighs out. "I'm so confused."

I watch as she jumps into the boat and wobbles to the wheel. Just as Cole promised, there's a rolled-up sheet of paper tucked next to it. She unrolls it slowly and reads it, her face a question mark. "Sage...what is happening?" she asks as she crawls back onto the dock and passes me the paper. I already know what it says but I pretend to read it anyway.

Caroline,

This is where we shared our first kiss. Remember that night? It's hard to believe that was only a little over a year ago. This is your first clue. For what, I'm not telling you. ;) To find your second clue, you should go to the place we spent four years flirting more than learning. I love you.

"This looks fun!" I say, pretending to be clueless.

"I guess we should go to the high school?" she thinks out loud.

"You got it." I usher her back to the moped.

When we get close to the school, I notice Dawson's truck in the parking lot. Knowing I'm about to see him, my stomach starts fluttering. My boyfriend and I are helping our best friends get engaged. Has there ever been a better day?

Dawson waits in front of the school, next to the cute Larkspur High otter statue, holding a bouquet of daisies. I park a few feet away and wave at him, but leave the motor running. Today isn't about me, and if I get anywhere near him right now, there's no way I'll be able to resist kissing and hugging him and generally delaying our task.

"Dawson has something for you," I tell Caroline.

She swings her leg over the seat and runs to him. He gives her a hug and the daisies, then pulls an envelope out of his pocket. She rips it open and devours the next note. "Thanks, Daws!" she calls as she runs back to me.

"Clue two." She passes it to me and tries to find a comfortable way to hold the flowers. "Sage, is what I think is going to happen about to happen?"

"I have no idea," I lie, reading the note slowly to avoid making eye contact with her.

Caroline,

Remember all of those times we used to pass each other in the courtyard? Dawson could never resist stopping to flirt with Sage, but I never minded because that meant I got to see you, too. I hope you like the flowers. You only have one final stop...I'm too excited to draw this out.

Meet me at the place we like to go for our evening walks and watch the sun set. See you there.

I smile at the memory Cole mentioned. Would any of us be where we are now without the events of our high school courtyard? I pass the note back to her and pull away from the school, blowing Dawson a kiss as we go.

"Where to, my lady?" I yell over my shoulder.

"Primera Beach!" she says.

It's our longest drive of the morning. The breeze picks up as we near the coast, blowing stray petals from the daisies in Caroline's cradled arm. I haven't been able to stop grinning like a fool.

My best friend is going to get married. My best friend has found the love of her life.

What makes it even better is, I think I've found mine, too. And I never even knew it was something I wanted until it happened.

In the beach parking lot, I wrap Caroline in a hug when we climb off the moped for the final time. "I love you," I tell her. "Go find your man."

"Are you coming?" she asks.

"Nope, you're flying solo."

"I'm nervous," she says, taking one of my hands.

"For what?" I wink. "Godspeed, my friend."

She backs away from me, turning when she reaches the edge of the parking lot, and disappears into the Larkspur-spotted sand dunes with her daisies. A minute later, Dawson's truck pulls into the parking lot next to me. He hops out and tackles me, spinning me around in circles.

"We did it!" he says.

"Without a single hiccup." I kiss him when he sets me down.

"One day," he says between kisses. "That will be us."

I lean into him, hiding my blush in his chest. "You think so?" I murmur happily.

"I have no doubt." He presses his lips to my hair.

"I wish I didn't have to work later," I whine.

"Me too. I would do the tours with you but I promised Mom and Dad I'd spend some time with them tonight."

"I'll survive," I joke.

"Meet me when you get off, though?" he asks. "At Skeleton Beach?"

"I'll be there."

My phone buzzes in my pocket and I pull it out. Caroline has sent me a picture of her, Cole, and a lovely, shiny diamond ring.

With the exception of Dawson, Skeleton Beach is quiet and empty per usual. And that's just the way I like it.

"I'm dead," I say as I collapse next to him on top of the blanket he brought for us. "Leave me here. Make me part of the tour and do my spirit justice, please."

"That bad?" Dawson laughs, scooting closer to me.

"Every guest in the last group was a Screaming Lady," I say. "Every. Single. One."

"That's brutal. Would a kiss make it better?

"There's nothing your kisses couldn't make better," I say, leaning in for one. "How was your night?"

He answers with a scoff.

"That bad?" I repeat his earlier question.

He sighs and kicks his shoes off. "I wanted to talk to my

parents about not going back to school in the fall, but I chickened out."

"Oh," I say. We haven't talked about this since the night we went to Hayworth. Instinctively, I reach down to trace the ghost on my ankle. It's almost fully healed, only slightly bumpy in a couple of places. "Maybe you should think about it a little longer?"

"As far as I'm concerned, there's nothing to think about," he says, lying back and pulling me down with him. "I want to be here with you. I can still finish my degree online. I can keep working for Sunny Spirits. Maybe we can even find a place to live. Together."

The thought of sharing a space with Dawson gives me goosebumps. How lucky would I be to go to sleep next to him every night? To wake up next to him every morning? To share food and a living space and a shower. To share a home.

Maybe he *is* supposed to be here. Maybe his dad wouldn't take it so bad.

"You're quiet," he says, running his hand down my ponytail.

"Sorry," I say. "Just thinking."

"About what?"

"It's just, what if you quit school and regret it later?" I swallow. "What if you regret...me?"

He rolls me so I'm on top of him and wraps his arms around me. "You take that back right now," he says, kissing my forehead. "That's the last thing you need to worry about."

"You swear on your alphabetized CD case?" I joke.

He purses his lips. "Sorry, that's asking a little too much."

I laugh and he rolls us again so he's on top of me. He bends his head to kiss me, softly at first, then with more need. I part my legs so he's lying between them and stick my hands under his shirt to feel his strong back, running my fingers over his tattoo. We keep kissing until we're moving greedily against each other, sparking every part of our bodies to life.

"Dawson," I whisper as he's kissing my neck.

"Hm?"

"I want to...you know."

He sits up on his knees and looks down at me.

"Now? Here?" he asks.

"Why not? It's just us." I sit up and begin pushing his shirt over his shoulders.

When it's off, I grab the hem of my shirt and pull it over my head, then remove my bra and cast it aside before lying back down on the blanket. We stare at each other, pale in the moonlight. Dawson's chest heaves and I lean up to kiss it. Behind him, the waves drown out the sound of my heart in my ears.

"You are magic," he says, running his hands up my sides. They settle on my breasts and I hold them there for a second before reaching for his belt buckle. His breathing intensifies as I slide his jeans down on his hips and slip my hand into his boxers. We both gasp when my hand closes around him. I stroke him slowly while he unbuttons my shorts, then he stands to take his jeans off and slide my shorts and panties down my legs and off my ankles.

For a few moments, all we do is gawk at each other. On an open beach, surrounded by nothing but curling wooden statues, I should feel self-conscious. Nervous. Unsure.

But it couldn't feel more right.

I drag him on top of me, skin to skin, kissing him until every part of me feels liquid. "Have you done this before?" I whisper.

He shakes his head. "Have you?"

"No," I say. "Do you have a..."

"Yes." He trails kisses from my lips to my lower stomach,

then sits back on his heels to find the condom in the pocket of his jeans. I watch him roll it on, then he's back on top of me.

He slides a hand between my legs and my hips jolt when he inserts a finger in me, never breaking eye contact. He's hard against my thigh and I want to touch him, but being a rookie, I'm nervous about something happening to the condom.

The stars in the sky circle his head. The pressure between my legs builds as he slowly moves his finger in and out, and I'm pretty sure I have stars circling around my head too.

I slide my hands down his back, letting them settle on his upper thighs. He removes his finger and I wrap my legs around his waist, anticipating what comes next.

"We're gonna have sand in places there really shouldn't be sand," he says randomly.

I bust out laughing.

"Are you trying to ruin the mood?" I ask, moving my hands to his butt.

"Not possible, when you're beneath me looking like this."

"So make love to me, Dawson."

He reaches between us to readjust, then grabs on to my hips, pushing himself into me inch by inch. A moan escapes his lips and I kiss them, lifting my hips and causing him to make another sound into my mouth.

"I do love you, Sage," he says, quickening his pace. "I'll never love anyone like I love you."

I hold on to him tighter, and we move together until we both fall apart. "I love you too," I say into his hair. "So much it scares me."

CHAPTER 20

PRESENT DAY, OCTOBER 2022

The pasta boils over while I'm in the bathroom finishing my makeup, and I can't help but feel like it's an omen for the way the rest of the evening is going to go.

"Fuck me, am I right?" I grumble to no one as I mop up the slimy pasta water on the stove and floor.

I should have picked up a pizza. Or met Dawson at one of the restaurants in town. Unfortunately, being seen in public with him too much makes me nervous. Time changes a lot of things, but people don't forget about the past when it comes to romantic relationships. Who knows what kind of speculation about us would make its way around town.

She hit his car and made him pay for the damage to hers.

She's sleeping with him because she wants a piece of the building he's buying.

She's the reason he left his wife.

I'm not ready to be the target of a rumor. And Dawson doesn't deserve that either.

My phone chimes with a text from Caroline.

CAROLINE

Is he there yet?

Not yet.

CAROLINE

Are you nervous?

What's there to be nervous about? I'm viewing this as a business meeting.

CAROLINE

Do people usually make out at business meetings?

She ends her question with the emoji of a monkey covering both of his eyes.

Not. Gonna. Happen.

CAROLINE

I'll ask you again later.

I'm ending this conversation. Bye!

CAROLINE

Fine. I'm holding your daughter hostage until I get the details.

I'm in the process of sending her three middle-finger emojis when there's a knock at the door.

"Coming!" I make a quick dash to the bathroom to check my hair and smooth my dress, then run to let Dawson in.

He's holding a giant pumpkin in his arms. "I brought this for you." He grins over the top of it.

"Do you ever come empty-handed?" I laugh.

"It's a perfect pumpkin!" he says. "I saw it at the grocery store and thought, 'Whitley might like to carve that.'"

Must he be so kind and thoughtful?

"That was really nice." I take the pumpkin from him and haul it to the kitchen. "I hate pumpkin guts, so I hope you also plan to come help her carve it."

"Is that another invitation to come to your house in the near future?" he asks hopefully.

I plop the pumpkin onto the counter and turn to look at him, twisting my mouth to the side. "Yeah, I guess it is."

"Invitation accepted. I also brought a tape measure." He produces it from his pocket.

Confused, I stare at him.

"For the window I'm going to fix. I need to know how big it is."

"I was hoping you'd forgotten about that," I say honestly.

"Why?"

"Because I'm already deep in Dawson favor debt."

"By letting me fix it, you'd actually be doing me a favor," he says.

"How?" I raise a single eyebrow.

"Well, if you trust me enough to give me creative liberty, I can replace it with stained glass that will look great in your sunroom. Then I can also add it to my portfolio." He grins hopefully.

Every time I've seen him since he's returned to Larkspur, he's been wearing some type of neutral color. Today he's wearing a red T-shirt that makes the silver flecks in his hair stand out and his eyes look dark and mysterious. His glasses didn't make the cut and I'm kind of bummed about it.

"That does sound pretty..." I say.

"Awesome." He pulls a few inches of the tape measure out and flourishes it around. "I'll be right back, then."

He disappears around the corner, toward the sunroom. Grabbing the garlic bread from the oven, I place a few pieces on a plate and set it on the table next to the pasta. It's warm in the kitchen, so I quickly pull my hair up into a ponytail, unable to stand it on my neck any longer.

"Mmm, spaghetti?" Dawson says, coming up behind me. He tosses the tape measure onto the kitchen counter along with his keys.

"It's one of the few things I know how to make well." I scrutinize the spread on the table.

"Luckily it's my favorite food," he says, pulling my chair out for me.

"No, it's not," I scoff.

"You're right." He grins. "But I do really like it."

We dig in, making small talk for the first few minutes. I get the notion that he's feeling me out—trying to decide how personal we should take the conversation. It's the first time we've been truly alone since that day in his car, and being alone in the cottage is much more intimate. Especially surrounded by memories of all the places our past selves tried to find moments of privacy in this little cottage.

The corner of my old tiny bedroom, which is now a den again. The alcove by the front door. The kitchen pantry. Like so many other places on this island, they're all tainted with past debaucheries.

I can't help but wonder if he's thinking about them, too.

"Can I be nosey about something?" I ask when my first glass of wine is half-empty.

"Sure." He dabs his mouth with a napkin.

"What's going on with your dad?"

"I had a feeling you might ask me that tonight," he says.

"You don't have to talk about it if you don't want to."

"I don't mind, but I'm going to need some more of that first." He points to the bottle of red wine.

I refill his glass. "My pleasure."

"After...you and me," he starts slowly, "I decided to stay in Richmond instead of coming back home. Doing my own thing instead of rushing back to take my place at Aiken Inc. is something he wasn't thrilled about, obviously."

"I can only imagine," I say, settling into my chair.

"He ignored me for a while. Then I met Eliza, and we eventually got engaged." He looks away from me at the mention of his ex. "When we started planning the wedding, Dad came crawling back with an apology. Things were strained for a while, but at least we were on speaking terms."

I break a piece of garlic bread in half and dunk it in my leftover sauce, listening attentively.

"Several years later, Eliza and I separated. He pretended to be upset...said a few things about me ruining his only hope for grandchildren. From there came another apology, which I now know only happened because he wanted to take advantage of the situation and try to get me to succumb to coming back and 'doing my part' for the business. He got pissed when I said no, and when Mom told him I was moving back but starting my own business, he completely lost it. He told me I was a lost cause, and his biggest regret in life was not having more children to make up for the disappointment he feels in me."

His voice is gravelly and shaky by the time he finishes.

"Oh my god," I say. I reach across the table and grab his hand. "Dawson...you're far from disappointing. He was wrong about you in the past, and he's wrong about you now."

"Maybe." He flips his hand over and threads his fingers through mine. "I've accepted that I'll spend the rest of my life trying to undo all of the damage he's done to me. Maybe one day I'll be free of it. Or maybe I won't. Either way, I can rest in the satisfaction that I've never fully surrendered to him."

"You *will* be free of it one day," I say. "He's the one who will have to live with the guilt when he comes to his senses."

"I'm not sure the man is capable of feeling guilt, but maybe."

We sip our wine. I realize I'm still holding his hand, and gently pull mine away. He leaves his there for a moment, like he hopes I might give mine back. Then he slowly curls his fingers and moves his hand to his lap.

"Your dad seems good," he says. "Did he ever try to publish his book?"

"You're never going to believe this." I cross my arms on the table. "He's still writing it."

Dawson snorts into his glass. My expression doesn't change.

"Oh, you're not shittin' me, are you?" he asks.

"I wish I were."

"Well, I still believe in him," he says sweetly.

I wish I could more than I do, I think.

"How about your mom?" he asks, getting a bit more spaghetti and offering me some. I shake my head.

"She's good. She remarried last year." I smile slightly. "We see them about once a month or so."

"I don't know whether or not to say congratulations," Dawson says around a bite of noodles.

"Is that your way of asking me if I like the guy?" I ask.

"Pretty much." He smirks and pushes his plate away.

"He's a good guy," I say. "He's also Whitley and Sawyer approved."

"Oh my gosh, Sawyer! How the heck is he doing?"

We spend at least thirty more minutes catching up on the topics of work and family. We drain the first bottle of wine, and I offer to open another. Dawson declines since he'll eventually have to drive home.

"I would take some coffee though, if you have it," he says.

"That sounds really good actually." I stand up and push my chair in. "It'll go great with the cake."

"You made cake?" he asks excitedly.

"I *purchased* cake," I correct. "From Beans. The lemon pound cake."

"Fuck yeah." He pumps his fist in the air and begins cleaning off the table.

"Leave that. I'll take care of it later." I grab his arm and force the bowl of leftover pasta out of his hand.

"No way." He grabs it back from me.

I roll my eyes. "You're insufferable."

"I always liked it when you talked dirty to me." He grins and takes a step closer.

"I should have known name-calling was one of your turn-ons," I joke.

"Are you kink-shaming me?" He moves even closer.

I look up at him, rendered speechless by his body heat and the intensity of his stare. My heart thumps in my chest. If he reached for me right now, I think I would let him hold me. If he tried to kiss me, I wouldn't fight him.

He licks his lips and I feel defenseless. Because fuck, his mouth is still beautiful. My body begins to tingle as I'm swept away in a tide of memories—memories of every place his mouth has touched my skin. Like my ghost tattoo, they're permanent and impossible to brush off. I can't see them, but they're there. On my neck. On my stomach. On my inner thighs.

Everywhere.

No, my brain says as he takes another step closer.

I skirt around him and trip into the kitchen. My hands are shaking so hard that I spill two spoonfuls of coffee grounds on the counter before successfully starting the machine. I squeeze my eyes shut and wish for him to somehow be gone when I turn around. Not because I *don't* want him here. More so because convincing myself that I don't want him is becoming exhausting.

Dishes rattle as he places them in the sink and I spin to

face him, breathing heavily for no other reason than my body can't keep up with my emotions. "I hate this," I say before I can stop it.

"What?" He looks taken aback.

"This." I motion between us. "I needed things to feel different with you—friendly, platonic...whatever you want to call it. For my sanity. For *our* sanity. But it's not different. When I'm around you I still feel like I felt more than ten years ago, and it's not fair. I. Hate. It."

As I speak, his face goes from puzzled, to sad, to defeated. It redirects my hate from the situation at hand to myself. I want to pluck all of my words from the air and shove them back down my throat.

He sticks his hands in his pockets and stares at the floor. Coffee filters into the pot next to me, breaking through the deafening silence. He chews on his bottom lip, and when his eyes return to mine, they're misty and wounded.

"Wanna know something funny?" he asks.

"What?" I snap, confused.

"While you've been desperate for there to be nothing between us," he says, "I've been desperate for the exact opposite. And I knew that spark was still there the second you stepped out into the night after running me over."

"I didn't run *you* over," I argue. "Just your car. My aim was off."

This coerces a small smile from both of us.

"The logistics don't matter," he says. "What does matter is we're at an impasse."

I slump against the counter, feeling drained. He comes to lean next to me. Our reflection bounces off of the kitchen window, against the night outside. We look otherworldly—ghostly. It's like peeking into a portal from the past.

"I don't know what to do," I finally say. "One side of me knows there's no good reason I shouldn't explore this. The other side is terrified of somehow being the one to screw it all up again."

He moves to stand in front of me, erasing our image from the dark window. "You can't keep yourself imprisoned over something that happened a third of your life ago, Sage."

"I can and I will." I lift my chin defiantly. "Plus, you'll be my landlord soon and I'm a seasoned professional."

"Okay, then." He moves a hand to the counter, caging me in on one side. "Tell me honestly, right now, that you don't want anything to happen between us again, and I'll walk out the door with no questions asked."

"Dawson, that's not fa—"

"Say it," he interrupts, "and we'll be nothing but *platonic* from here on out."

I try to say it. I really do. But I physically can't form the words.

"I...can't," I admit, defeated.

He places his other hand on the counter, completely closing me in. The alarm bells in my head are deafening, but they're no match for the way he's looking at me. He's so familiar. So beautiful. So...Dawson.

My Ghost Boy.

He moves closer and our bodies mold together. His breath is on my cheek and I feel a rusty old door creak open deep within me, letting him in. He's the only person I've ever given a key. The only person I've ever wanted to have one.

End this. My fear makes one final attempt at shutting this down.

"Kiss me," Dawson whispers.

With those two words, the last of my defiance evaporates. Tentatively I reach up and push his hair off his forehead. Then I thread my fingers through it and pull his face to mine.

A sob forms in my throat the second our lips touch. Because how many times have I secretly wished for this? How many nights have I lain awake, restless and destroyed over the fact that I would never have the opportunity to kiss Dawson Aiken again?

How long have I been haunted by desire for one person and one person only?

Dawson moans into my mouth and a single tear escapes my right eye. He relaxes into me, pressing my back harder against the counter. I rise to my toes and wrap my arms around his neck, refusing to let the slightest bit of distance sneak between us.

His hands explore my neck and shoulders before moving down my back, then to my hips. He grabs the backs of my thighs and swiftly lifts me onto the counter. I wrap my legs around his waist.

The coffee sits forgotten. The box of lemon pound cake lies somewhere behind me on the counter, potentially squashed. The man between my thighs kisses me senseless. My tears continue to flow silently, dampening our cheeks and filling our tongues with the familiar saltiness of our very first kiss so long ago.

It's only when he pulls away that I notice there are tears swimming in his eyes, too.

I use my thumbs to wipe his cheeks, then wrap my arms around his shoulders and pull his head back into my chest, afraid to let go.

"I've missed you, Ghost Girl," he says against my collar-bone. "I've missed you so much."

We stay like this for the next hour, kissing and holding each other silently in the kitchen. "Is it weird now to ask if there's any update on the building?" I joke, eventually breaking the silence.

Dawson laughs and helps me back down to the floor.

"Not at all." He keeps his arms wrapped around my waist.

"We're still in due diligence. Maybe you can come with me to do a walk through soon."

"I already know what it looks like," I say.

"But it will give us a head start on what we want to change." He sways us back and forth.

"What *you* want to change," I correct.

"I want your ideas, too," he says.

"Was all of this just a ploy to spend more time with me?" I ask, narrowing my eyes.

"Nope. But it's my favorite perk."

On the table, my phone pings. I force myself away from the comfort of Dawson's chest and walk to retrieve it. "I didn't realize what time it was," I say. "Caroline is on her way with Whitley."

"I should leave before she gets here. She'll be able to smell us on each other. She's relentless."

"You have no idea," I joke, thinking about her earlier texts.

He grabs his keys from the counter then pauses, furrowing his brows. "That's...strange. I thought I put my tape measure right here too."

"You definitely did. I saw you." I scan the surface, but there's no sign of the tape measure.

We exchange a glance and he voices what I'm thinking with a grin. "Buster?"

"Come on." I tap him on the chest with the back of my hand. "You know that's just a joke."

"But is it?" he asks, his smile as wide as his eyes.

For the first time ever, the mention of Buster raises the hair on the back of my neck. I watched Dawson put that tape measure next to his keys. We're the only people here and we haven't left the room all evening. I shiver, hating the feeling of my lifelong beliefs being challenged.

"It's around here somewhere. I'll bring it to you when it pops up," I say.

At the front door, Dawson presses me against it and kisses me again. "Where do we go from here?" he asks when he pulls away.

"I think we just...float. Take things naturally."

Smiling, he spins me away from the door and opens it. "I'll float with you forever if that's what I have to do."

I stand on the porch and watch him walk to his car and back out of the driveway. Then I go back inside and stand in the hallway with my fingers pressed to my kiss-chapped lips, wondering how I've gone from being sad and miserable to feeling like the last ten years never happened within a matter of weeks.

On my walk back to the kitchen, I pause outside of the sunroom and look in at the cracked window. Something on the windowsill catches my eye. I walk closer, switching a lamp on along the way. My breath hitches in my throat.

It's Dawson's tape measure. I poke it, convinced it has to be a mirage, but it's solid beneath my finger. Snatching it up, I immediately take it and put it in my purse.

Apparently Dawson isn't the only doubt it's time for me to contemplate.

CHAPTER 21

SUMMER 2010

You can do this, I think as I put the moped in park in front of Dawson's house.

They're just parents. They're just people.

Plus, they created Dawson. So how bad can they really be?

I'm wearing the nicest dress I own—the only dress I own. It's blue with capped sleeves and a flowy skirt. It's also a size too small because I haven't worn it since the homecoming dance Caroline dragged me to our junior year. All of these factors made the drive over very uncomfortable. Mopeds and dresses don't mix.

My knees quake when I walk up the steps to the front door. Or, what I assume is the front door. The house is so massive it's hard to tell. Swallowing, I pull my dress down for the tenth time in 30 seconds and press the doorbell with a shaking hand. A dramatic chime rings through the house. Through the frosted glass of the door, I see someone approach.

"Whoa," Dawson says when he steps onto the porch. "You're the prettiest thing I've ever seen."

I squirm in my uncomfortable dress. "Is it okay?"

"It's more than okay." He leans in to kiss me, running a hand down the length of my hair when he pulls away. "And your hair...I love when you wear it down."

His compliments make me feel a bit more comfortable and I attempt a smile. He's wearing a gray button-down over a white T-shirt and jeans. He looks perfect—but in my opinion he never looks anything less than.

"It's gonna be okay," he says quietly. "I've been trying to stay on Dad's good side all week, so he should behave."

I grab his hand and he squeezes.

"Come on. Let's go inside." He smiles at me.

The foyer is almost as big as our cottage. A shimmering chandelier hangs over a round entryway table, and the marble floor is spotless and shiny. Our footsteps echo through the downstairs hallways and up into the unfathomably high ceilings. I look around, already feeling out of place.

"We have some time before dinner," he tells me. "Do you want to see my room?"

I grin, feeling my first hint of excitement. "More than anything!"

He leads me up the grand, curving staircase. It's even quieter upstairs in the hallway, which has at least four doors on either side. I follow him to the third door on the right and he pushes it open. The smell of him washes over me, and I'm thankful there's at least one room in this house that I could feel at home in.

"Holy shit." I step inside, greedily attempting to take in everything at once. "It's like *Hey Arnold*'s room."

He laughs. "Not nearly as cool. No skylights."

"You're right." I look from the perfectly made bed to the floor-to-ceiling shelves on the far wall. "It's cooler."

The shelves are filled with countless model cars, each one dust-free and shined to perfection. I walk over to get a closer look, mesmerized by the sheer amount of them. "Did you make all of these?" I ask.

"With my grandpa," he says, smiling softly. "It was our thing, before he passed."

"That's sweet." I walk along the length of the shelves. "What was he like?"

"Mom always used to say he and I were the same person, just generations apart." He reaches out and straightens a deep blue Mustang by half an inch, a faraway look on his face. "Were you close to any of your grandparents?"

Unable to stay in one place for too long, I walk over to his bed and run my hand across the crisp white duvet. "I never knew any of them," I say.

"I'm sorry."

"It's okay," I say. "You can't miss what you never had. And Ms. Knox has always been kind of like a grandmother to me, so that's pretty cool."

He comes to stand next to me, then pulls me down to sit on the edge of the bed with him. "You have no idea how much I've imagined having you here," he says, kissing my neck. "I wish we had longer to enjoy it."

"One of us really needs *our* own place," I joke.

"We will have our own place," he says. "One day. Soon."

"You might hate living with me. I'm not neat like you. I'm the complete opposite."

"I don't care about that." He pushes my hair behind my shoulder and trails the tip of his finger along my collarbone. "Being organized has kind of been forced onto me. Mom and Dad are both neat freaks. I've learned to depend on cleanliness the older I get though—my environment is one thing I feel like I can control. It makes me feel...secure. Safe, somehow."

"That makes sense. Don't you ever just want to let go a little though?"

"All the time. I'm trying to figure out how, but I think it'll take a while."

"Let me know if I can help," I say.

"Trust me." He presses his lips to the tip of my nose. "You've already helped me overcome more than you know."

"I love you, Dawson."

"I love you more." He kisses me slowly, but it still ends too soon. "Let's go downstairs."

The dining room table seats twelve, and I wonder if Dawson eats dinner here every night he's home—him, his parents, and nine empty chairs. Tall white candles in silver candlesticks line the center of the table, and each place is set with more plates and silverware than I know what to do with. I'm out of my element...I know I am. But if the cutlery is still the most intimidating thing at the end of this evening, I will happily count my lucky stars.

"Sage, hi." Dawson's mom enters the room, dressed in all white. She's attractive. The kind of woman who's hard to imagine ever being less than flawless from head to toe.

"Hi, Mrs. Aiken." I stand to shake her hand, but she surprises me by hugging me.

"You can call me Cynthia." She smiles. "What an adorable dress!"

"Thank you," I say, shyly. "And thanks for having me over."

"I'm sorry it took so long. Ed's schedule can be a bit unpredictable."

"Speaking of..." Dawson mutters.

Ed thunders into the room, immediately commanding everyone's attention. Each time I see him, I like him less. It's hard not to, knowing what I know—knowing all of the things Dawson has told me. Maybe tonight will be the night I'm able to find something redeemable about him, though. He looks like he just stepped straight out of the pages of a Tommy

Bahama catalog, but not even the cheery Hawaiian print on his shirt can soften the "I'm better than you" expression on his face.

"Nice to see you, Sage." He holds his hand out and I take it. His grip is almost too tight and he stares deep into my eyes when he shakes, like he's trying to put me in my place for the rest of the evening. Dawson protectively places his hand on my lower back.

Dawson and his mom don't sit until Ed does. I follow their lead and spread my napkin in my lap, staring at the empty table and wondering where dinner is going to come from. Right on cue, three people walk into the room carrying trays of food. They arrange it on the table with warm smiles, then remove the lids from the dishes, filling the room with mouthwatering smells.

Of course the Aikens have house staff. I should have known.

Could Dawson and I be any different?

"Thank you," Ed says curtly as they leave the room. "Sage, do you like Beef Wellington?"

"I've never had it," I say honestly. "But I'm sure I will."

We make our plates and I wait for Dawson to start eating, watching him out of the corner of my eye to see what fork and knife he uses. He smiles encouragingly at me and squeezes my leg under the table before digging into his plate.

"This is delicious," I say after swallowing my first bite.

"It's one of Dawson's favorites," Ed says.

"So," Cynthia says after a minute or so of silence. "I know you two went to school together. Were you friends?"

Dawson and I smile at each other. "Kind of," he says at the same time I say, "Not really."

"We basically annoyed each other," Dawson clarifies. "But in a good way, I think."

"I agree," I say.

"That doesn't make sense," Ed chimes in. "You either liked each other or you didn't."

"Everything isn't always black and white, honey," Cynthia says quietly. He shoots her a look and she returns her attention to her French green beans.

"She was too cool for me and she knew it," Dawson jokes.

"I don't recall ever seeing you at any of the football games," Ed tells me.

"Oh, sports aren't really my thing. My best friend Caroline did make me go to a couple, though."

"Hm," Ed grunts.

I've never been so revolted by a human being. I've watched him schmooze his way around Larkspur, so I know he's capable of at least pretending to be friendly. I guess he only brings that personality out for people he believes worthy of it. Dawson's jaw is tense as he aggressively cuts into his food.

"Are you in school now, Sage?" Cynthia asks.

"No, ma'am. Maybe one day though."

"So you just work telling ghost stories?" Ed asks.

"She manages Sunny Spirits, Dad. She's 20 years old and she basically runs a business," Dawson says. "And she's great at it."

"Thank you," I tell him.

"Is it really a sustainable business though?" Ed doesn't give up.

"I think it's fun and creative," Cynthia says. I can see how hard she's trying to keep the conversation light.

"We have plans to expand to other historic Florida cities, one day." I sit my fork down and stare in Ed's direction. "You have fishing charters all over, right? Same concept."

"The difference is"—Ed motions between him and Dawson—"our business is viable."

"*Your* business, Dad," Dawson corrects. "Sunny Spirits is also viable."

"*Our* business," Ed argues. "*Your* future."

Dawson's face turns red and he lets his fork clatter onto his plate. "You know, since we're on the subject, there's something I've been wanting to talk to you and Mom about."

Oh no.

"Sure, what is it?" Cynthia asks.

Please no, Dawson. Not while I'm here.

Dawson takes a deep breath and grabs my hand under the table. "I don't want to go back to school this fall. I can find an online program to finish my degree."

The dining room goes so silent I can hear a clock ticking in the next room over. Cynthia freezes, eyes locked on her husband. Ed finishes chewing and swallows his bite, then slowly wipes his mouth with his napkin. His eyes are cold and unblinking, and I wish I were literally anywhere else.

"I'm already two years in," Dawson continues, his voice confident. "I want to be here, with Sage."

I would be proud of him if I wasn't overly scared right now. Our hands are clasped together so tightly we may come out of this with a few broken phalanges.

"Out of the question," Ed growls. "We'll talk about this later."

"I'm an adult and I can make my own deci—" Dawson starts.

"I *said*, we'll talk about it later," Ed snarls.

I let go of Dawson's hand. I need a second to breathe.

"Where's your bathroom?" I ask Cynthia quietly.

Her eyes are full of apology. "Take a right in the hall and it's the last door on the left."

"Thank you." I turn to Dawson. "I'll be right back."

"I need to make a quick call," I hear Ed say as I exit the room. His chair legs squeak on the floor and I rush down the hallway to disappear before he emerges behind me.

The bathroom is bigger than my bedroom, but I don't

know why I'm surprised. I run my hands under the cold water and press them to my cheeks. My face feels like it's on fire. I'm proud of Dawson for standing up for himself, but I'm also terrified—for both of us. For him because he's going to have to face his dad's wrath. For me because I can't shake the feeling that this is all my fault.

Of course I want him here with me. But is it worth the risk of having him ruin his relationship with his parents? Is it worth him throwing his education away?

I take a couple of minutes to calm down and prepare myself for what I'm about to walk back into, then I slip out of the bathroom. Ed is standing in the hallway, and I'm so startled I nearly slam the door back closed in his face. "Excuse me," I say, trying to skirt around him. He blocks my path.

"Are you happy?" he whispers.

Stepping back, I put as much distance between us as possible. "I'm going to find Dawson."

"I don't know what you've been saying to him, but I will not let my son ruin his future."

"This isn't something I've talked him into." My voice waivers. "Have you ever stopped to think that his so-called future is one you've let him have no say in? Maybe you should let him make his own decisions."

I'm feeling more and more uncomfortable. Angry tears are building behind my eyes.

"You've been a real wild card." He rubs his chin. "I always thought he would meet someone in college. Someone driven. Educated. Someone who could come back here and be his true equal. Instead, he's fallen for Larkspur riffraff."

Riffraff?

A lump forms in my throat and it's getting harder to breathe.

"So glad I can be here to shake things up." I raise my chin, hoping it makes me look somewhat defiant.

Ed moves to one side and I take the opportunity to run around him.

"Sarah?" he calls after me.

"It's Sage," I hiss, whirling around.

"I think you know I have a lot of pull on this island." He studies his fingernails. "And from what I understand, your little ghost story business is the only thing keeping a roof over your family's head."

My stomach plummets to the floor. Beef Wellington crawls its way up my esophagus. My ears begin to ring, and I feel myself losing control.

"Are you...threatening me?" I manage to squeak.

He shrugs. "If you're as smart as Dawson thinks you are, you'll figure it out."

Breathe. Breathe. Breathe, I tell myself.

But I have no composure left. I turn and run down the hallway, straight past the dining room. "Sage?" I hear Dawson's voice.

I don't stop. I find my way back to the front door and run outside, letting it slam behind me. I desperately pat my pockets, searching for the moped key.

"Sage!" Dawson runs outside, heading straight for me.

Still fighting to breathe, I lean over and rest my head against the seat of the moped.

"What's wrong?" Dawson grabs me around the waist and lifts me to standing, holding me against him. My breath comes in short, desperate bursts.

"Breathe, baby," he whispers into my ear. His palm rubs circles on my back. "I've got you."

He holds me until I can stand on my own two feet. The whole time, my dad's voice plays on repeat in my head: *You don't want to piss off Ed Aiken.*

CHAPTER 22

SUMMER 2010

July is a month full of fireworks.

And not just because of the holiday. Since the dinner at his parents' house, everything between Dawson and me has felt tumultuous—fragile. After I panicked, I told him that I thought he should go back to school. That it wasn't worth the fight with his dad, and we've survived one year already so we can easily survive two more. That I only panicked because of the worry over the situation.

From the look on his face, you would have thought I'd slapped him and told him I hated him. Even when we discuss it now, he looks at me with such sad eyes I can barely live with myself. So that's why on the days we're not fighting and crying, we're in makeup mode, using every spare moment to touch, kiss, and fuck away the feelings of uncertainty that neither of us can bring ourselves to fully face.

Of course I'd rather have him here, but we're no longer the only two people with cards in this game. I can't tell him that, though. If he knew what his dad said to me outside the bathroom that night, everything would become an even bigger mess.

I don't know if I'll ever be able to tell him. I'm between a rock and a hard place, and all the while I'm worrying myself to death about what Ed expects from me. Will he be happy if Dawson simply decides to finish school? Does he expect me to step out of Dawson's life completely?

There's no way I can do that. There's no way Dawson would *let* me. I used to think people were dramatic when they would make statements about not being able to live without another person. Now I know exactly how it feels. Dawson is my anchor. My sun and my moon and all of those other silly metaphors that are used to describe how important someone is to you. I need him like I need water, or oxygen.

The selfish side of me has racked my brain to the point of asking whether or not my family really needs Sunny Spirits, if it came to that. I could get another job. Maybe two. However many I would need to make sure Dad, Sawyer, and I are taken care of.

As long as it meant I got to keep Dawson.

Maybe Ed is right and I am just Larkspur riffraff. What if Dawson would be better off without me? He makes me the best version of myself, but do I really do the same for him?

As August nears, things only become less clear, and there's no one I can talk to about it. So I just let everything sit and stew and bubble over in my brain while time flies by.

"You're quiet," Caroline says as we unpack a box of her clothes. After being on the waitlist for months, she and Cole finally got approved for one of the apartments in the island's only complex. Dawson and I are helping them move in today.

"I haven't had any caffeine," I say.

"That was a dumb decision," she jokes, folding another T-shirt and placing it in the middle drawer of their new dresser. "But I'm also not buying it."

I look out the window, down into the parking lot where the boys are unloading a couch from the back of Dawson's truck. A few weeks ago, the sight of Dawson sweaty and golden in the late afternoon sun would have filled me with a primal desire. Now, it still does, but that desire is also joined by apprehension and the sinking feeling that I'm doing something wrong.

"Buying what?" I ask.

"That nothing is wrong," she says. "Cole said Dawson has been off lately too. You can talk to me and I won't say anything to Cole, you know."

"I know," I sigh out. And I want to believe her, but I can't. "I'm just thinking about work stuff."

"Something you should know about yourself is you're not a good liar when there's something actually wrong." She tosses one of her shirts at me.

"Can we talk about something else?" I ask. "Like the fact that you're getting married in less than six months?"

"We've talked enough about that," she says. "But speaking of, are you free to go to Hayworth next week to try on maid of honor dresses?"

"Wouldn't miss it. Let me know the day and I'll be there."

The apartment door bangs open and the boys' raised voices interrupt us.

"Watch your step!"

"Angle it to your right."

"Perfect! Sit it right here."

Caroline walks out of the bedroom to supervise and I follow. Dawson and Cole are both shirtless and drenched and they drop onto the couch at the same time, breathing heavily. "Couldn't you have gotten a first-floor unit?" Dawson asks.

"Do you know how long we've been waiting to get a unit at all?" Cole says. "I would have moved into a tenth-floor apartment if they existed."

"Get your sweaty asses off my couch!" Caroline says, trying to pull Cole up by his forearms.

"It's a used couch, babe. Trust me, there have been plenty of other sweaty asses on it already."

Dawson laughs, and I take a seat on the arm next to him. He wraps his arms around my waist and pulls me into his lap. Not caring that he's sweaty, I snuggle against him and kiss the top of his head, breathing in his smell.

"I told you we needed a new couch," Caroline says, flopping down between us and Cole.

"You need to sell a few more houses first," Cole argues.

She whips her head to look at Cole. "Maybe you need to build more houses so I can do that."

"Cool. I'll tell my boss that my fiancée needs us to work faster."

Dawson and I silently watch the two of them and he smirks, tightening his hold on me. I look around the apartment, feeling jealous of Cole and Caroline for the first time, wishing that it were me and Dawson getting ready to spend our first night in our new place. Dawson kisses my cheek and runs his finger along the inside of my waistband. That's all it takes for me to know it's time for us to be alone.

"Can we help with anything else before we go?" I ask, lifting myself off the couch. Dawson follows.

"No, you've done more than enough. Thank you so much." Caroline stands and gives us a hug.

"For real," Cole says, fist bumping us. "We'll have you over for dinner before Dawson leaves.

I wait to see how Dawson replies, but all he says is, "Sounds good."

He grabs his shirt off the kitchen counter and pulls it over his head on our way out the door.

"I was hoping you'd leave that off," I joke.

His eyes darken. "I will if you will."

In his truck, we drive toward Skeleton Beach and park as close to the treeline as possible. Dawson cracks the windows and cuts the engine before moving his seat back and pulling me over to straddle him. We remove our clothes in a flurry of contorted arms and legs, and then he's inside me, his mouth on my shoulder and his hands guiding my hips.

When we're finished, we hold each other in silence, breathing heavily and letting our hearts return to their normal rhythms.

"I'm gonna go back," he says quietly.

Surprised, I sit up to look at him. "What?"

"Only because you think I should." He runs his thumb across my lower lip. "I'll try one more semester. But if I'm miserable, that's it." I stare at him, trying to decide what I'm feeling. Sadness over the fact that I'm going to have to go another three to four months without seeing my soulmate? Relief that Ed will feel like he's won? Happiness that he's doing what's best for his potential? "When did you decide?" I ask, moving back to my seat and pulling my T-shirt on.

"Yesterday."

"Have...have you told your dad yet?"

"Yep." He finds his boxers and shimmies into them. "As you can imagine, he's thrilled."

Good, I think. Even though Ed Aiken is the last person I want to see get his way.

I lean my head against the seat and reach for his hand. "Why aren't you a senior already?" I joke.

He laughs and cocoons my hand in both of his. "I wish you could come with me."

"Me too," I say.

More than anything.

"Maybe you could come visit me some time? For my birthday or something?" he says, his face brightening. "I can show you around Richmond. Give you a tour of campus. We can get a hotel because, well, roommates."

Excitement flares through me at the idea. "Do you think that would work?"

"Why not?" He starts the truck. "You work on getting the time off, and I'll figure out the rest."

"Deal." I settle into my seat.

We roll the windows down and Dawson drives me home with his hand on my thigh. With each mile, the events of the past few weeks seem to get sucked out the window, into the salty island air and out to sea.

CHAPTER 23
PRESENT DAY, NOVEMBER 2022

"Can anyone tell me who this is?" I ask my early afternoon tour group.

Leo, our other full-time guide, has been back from paternity leave for a few weeks, and I've been enjoying the adjustment back to working semi-normal hours.

A young guy with frizzy hair steps forward and squints at the plaque situated at the base of the statue in question. "Henry Howell?" he reads, but it sounds like a question.

"Right." I smile. "And who was he?"

His girlfriend joins him. "This says he was Larkspur's first mayor," she says.

"That he was!" I place a hand on Henry's bronze shoulder. "Mayor Howell is the reason this square is here. In fact, it was his first order of business when he took his position in 1860. He believed that a central square would be the key to bringing the people of Larkspur together. Every day, he would walk over to visit with whoever was around, sometimes sitting on his favorite bench for hours at a time. That's why, to this day, he's still considered the island's fav—"

A movement at the edge of the square catches my eye, and

I glance over. Dawson is standing a short distance away, watching me with a smile on his face. He has one hand in his pocket and the slightly cool fall breeze ruffles his hair. When we make eye contact his smile doubles, and he nods at me, like he's apologizing for distracting me.

"Sorry…" I say, my cheeks growing warm. "Where was I?"

"He's still considered the island's favorite mayor?" Really Tall Man says.

"Oh, yes. He was! The benches in the square have since been replaced, but the new ones are in the exact spots as the original ones. Any guesses as to which was Mayor Howell's favorite?"

Everyone points in different directions. I join the woman in front of me in pointing to the bench in the back right corner. "Yep! That was his spot. Would you believe me if I told you he still likes to hang out there?"

I sneak another look at Dawson. He's still watching silently, appreciatively.

"Have you seen him?" Frizzy-Haired Man asks.

"Not personally," I admit. "But there have been many reports from locals and visitors alike of running into a friendly man dressed in 1800s clothing late at night, and he's always sitting in the mayor's favorite spot."

"He sounds like a ghost I wouldn't mind meeting," an elderly woman in the back of the group jokes.

"Most of Larkspur's ghosts are friendly," I say. "And you'll see even more when we get to McBride Mansion, we have a history of quirky mayors. Speaking of, let's head that way."

I lead the group away from the statue, motioning for Dawson to join me as I walk ahead of the group.

"What are you doing here?" I ask, feeling like a middle schooler who just ran into her crush outside of class.

"Just confirming something." He squints down at me.

I bite the inside of my lip. "Confirming *what?*"

"That you're still the hottest tour guide around," he whispers, peeking at the group over his shoulder.

"Maybe that can be Cole's Halloween costume next year. Hot ghost tour guide," I joke.

He laughs and reaches for my hand, swiftly dropping it when he remembers I'm working.

"Hey, what are you doing when you get off?" he asks.

"I have to get Whit from Dad's at some point, but nothing other than that," I say. "Why?"

"Come to my place. I want to show you something."

"That's your worst pick-up line to date." I wrinkle my nose.

"Hardy har." He rolls his eyes at me. "It's not that. I want to show you the work I've done for your window so far."

We stop at the end of Main, and I check to make sure I have everyone before continuing. "Text me your address," I say. "And I'll think about it."

"It's a date." He winks at me before turning back in the opposite direction.

"I never said that!" I yell after him, then address the group. "Sorry, folks. He used to guide with us and I think he misses it sometimes."

An hour later, I turn things over to Leo for the evening and call Dad to let him know I'll pick Whitley up by six. Then I hop in my car and put Dawson's address in the GPS, heading for the north shore. I drive with the windows down and my old favorite playlist turned up, Anberlin's "Breaking" making me feel like I could be driving to see the Dawson of 12 years ago.

His rental is one of the small modern new-builds facing the water. The house is crisp and white, its only personality coming from the bright yellow front door. The garage begins to open as I park behind him in the driveway, and he walks out to meet me.

"This is nice," I say. "Do you like it?"

"I do." He scoops me into a hug. "The garage is particularly convenient."

We walk up the driveway. "Why aren't you parked in it then?" I ask.

"Because it's not for parking. It's for working."

He leads me into the garage and I find myself surrounded by chaos. Large sheets of glass are stacked against one wall. Several tables are set up around the room, some covered in pots of paint, others in glass cutouts of every shape and size. There's a large sheet of paper spread out in one corner, and something that looks like an oven in the opposite corner.

"What's this?" I ask, walking over to it.

"It's a kiln," he explains, patting the top. "After the glass is painted you have to fire it...kind of like pottery."

"Really?" I ask.

"Yep."

I meander over to a table covered in paper, pencils, and markers. "I guess I've never really thought about how complicated of a process this is."

"I don't know if it's complicated, necessarily." He spins one of the markers. "More like time consuming."

"It's artistry." I pick up one of the papers, realizing it's a sketch. It features a rough drawing of a circular window with a rose pattern.

"Parts of it remind me of when I used to build those model cars with my grandpa," he says. "I guess I never realized how much I like working with my hands until I took that first stained glass class."

He moves closer to me and our shoulders brush. "This is probably nosey," I say. "But how are you going to find the right people to hire? People you can trust with your vision?"

"It'll be easier than you think. I'll do most of the work to start, and slowly train. Those right people will come."

The next table is covered in half-finished sun catchers, like the ones he sells at Ghost to Coast. "Will some of these go to Ms. Knox?" I ask.

"Probably. Her inventory is getting low."

Spinning, I take everything in one more time. "I'm so *proud* of you, Dawson. And is it weird that I'm thrilled to see it's an absolute disaster in here?"

He laughs loudly. "This isn't the hobby to get into if you're afraid of clutter, so it's been strangely therapeutic for my perfectionism."

"Amazing."

"Come." He grabs my hand. "This is what I really wanted to show you."

We walk over to the large sheet of paper on the floor. As we get closer, I can see it's a life-size sketch of my sunroom window. It's colored in pinks, purples, and blues, with what looks like a piece of driftwood across the center. I gasp.

"Is it...?"

"Skeleton Beach," Dawson confirms. "Do you like it?"

The lump that has been residing in my throat way too much lately is back again. "I love it," I choke.

"The pieces are in the kiln," he says. "Over the next few days, I'll put it all together, so maybe we can install it next week."

I swallow, still staring at the sketch because if I turn to look at him, I'll lose my composure. "Thank you. So much."

He moves to stand behind me, and I let him wrap his arms around my waist. He rests his head on my shoulder and presses his cheek against mine. "I would do anything for you, Sage. Do you know that? I would and I will do whatever I have to do to keep you this time."

This time.

I'm not sure I deserve a "this time." But I know I want to keep him, too.

"I would like that," I say through a smile.

"Do you still go there?" Dawson mumbles into my neck. "Skeleton Beach, I mean."

"I went the day Caroline told me you were moving back," I reply honestly. "But that was the first time in years.

"Why that day?" he asks.

"I'd avoided it for so long because I knew it would only make me think of you." I run a hand along one of his forearms. "When I realized my streak of avoiding you was going to come to an end, I knew I *had* to think about you. It seemed like the right place to come to terms with things."

He kisses my shoulder. "It was our spot," he says. "Wanna know a secret?"

"No," I joke.

The kiss on my shoulder turns into a gentle bite and I elbow at him, laughing.

"It's the first place I went the night I got home," he tells me. "After our accident. Seeing you once was all it took for me to realize that I was still a goner for you. Really, it was just confirmation. Deep down I already knew I never stopped being one."

"We'll have to go together again." I settle even deeper against his chest. "I've actually always wanted to take Whitley. I've never shown her and I know she would love it."

"Maybe we can all go soon."

"That would be nice." I turn over my shoulder and kiss the tip of his nose. His mouth finds mine and he parts my lips with his tongue. His kiss is deep and hungry, and awakens my appetite too. My appetite for him. When it comes to kissing Dawson, there's no such thing as satiation—only the want for more.

With a groan, he breaks the kiss and moves me forward, walking us as one unit so he can hit the button to close the garage. I laugh at the gesture, and he kisses the lobe of my ear.

Bit by bit, the sunlight disappears until the only source of light comes from the strip of small windows at the top of the garage door.

"That's better." He spins me to face him, then continues to kiss me like we have all the time in the world.

I liquefy beneath his hands, growing more and more languid until it's almost impossible to stand. He backs me toward the sketch-covered table, pausing to clear off half of it before perching me on the edge, recreating the scene from my kitchen a couple of weeks ago. The difference is, now, it's evident that there's more than making out on our minds.

"If anything feels like too much," he pants against my neck, "say the word and we'll stop."

"Okay," I say, clutching on to the belt at his lower back.

"Do you trust me?"

"I always have."

He moves a hand to the back of my neck. "Lie down for me."

With his help, I slowly lie back onto the table, far past the point of return. Far past the point of questioning whether or not Dawson and I are doing the right thing by being together. Because since he's been back, I can't help but feel like all that matters is we are together. That we're getting this second chance to be everything we're supposed to be.

Pinning my wrists above my head, he bends and kisses me once more, then stands and moves his hands down to push up the hem of my shirt. I tense slightly, self-conscious in a way that I never used to be. "Please remember that I'm not 20 anymore." I poke fun at myself. "And I'm a mom and my body shows that."

His face reappears above mine. "Which by default, has made an already beautiful body even more beautiful." He kisses my forehead. "Be nice to yourself."

He disappears again and I feel the featherlight touch of his lips on my stomach. He unbuttons my shorts and drags them down my legs until I'm left lying in my underwear. I reach for him, but he gently places my hands back above my head and holds them there. His lips return to mine and his other hand slides into my panties, palming me before he slips a finger in and draws a line up my center that makes me convulse beneath him.

"Tell me you've thought about this, Sage," he says.

"More than you know," I whimper, trying to free my hands. "Which is why I want to touch you, too."

"Shhh," he says, rubbing circles that make me see fireworks. "We're floating, remember? There will be time for so much more. For now, it's my turn to show you how much I thought about you."

Satisfied that I'll keep my hands in place, he vanishes back out of my line of vision. My underwear are pulled over my ankles and discarded somewhere I can't see. I feel Dawson's hands on my knees. He spreads my legs and kisses up my thighs, likes he remembers the exact spot of every place his lips touched before. For a brief second, his breath is cool against me, then it's quickly replaced by the warm sensation of his tongue.

I cave and move my hands to his head, threading my fingers through his hair. It's been so long since I've done this with anyone. Too long, which is probably why it feels so good it almost hurts. Out of instinct I try to scoot away, but he wraps his arms behind my knees and pulls me back to him. Stray markers and sheets of paper go flying off the table.

"Dawson," I gasp, "I'm going to—"

He buries his face even deeper, intensifying every little movement of his mouth until I feel myself tip over the edge. I grip the sides of the table, arching my hips toward the sky, until the adrenaline slows and I can float back down to earth. Down to *him.*

It's impossible to open my eyes, but I feel him stand and fold his body over mine bit by bit. He rests his head on my chest and wraps a section of my ponytail around his finger.

"Your heart is beating so fast." I can hear the smirk in his voice.

I take a deep breath, finding my words. "I have no idea why," I joke.

Standing, he runs a hand down my leg and traces the tattoo on my ankle, then takes both of my hands in his and helps me up to a seated position. I'm finally able to crack my eyes open, and the first sight I see is his beautiful face. It makes me want to cry.

"Am I dreaming?" I ask.

He laughs and grabs my panties and shorts from the table behind him. I'm not sure I can trust my legs to stand so I can put them on. As if he knows that, he starts putting them on for me. I slide off the table to pull them up and fumble the button with shaking fingers.

"You've always been so lovely when you lose control," he says, drawing me into his chest.

I'm not sure if it's the dopamine floating around my brain, or his smell, or the feeling of him against me, but the floodgates open and I begin sobbing into his shirt. And not a few silent tears. Shoulder-racking, chest-caving sobs.

"Hey." He lifts my chin, frowning at my tear-covered face with concerned eyes. "What's wrong?"

"That's the thing." The hiccups threaten to come. "I-I don't know. I think I'm just overwhelmed. In a good way."

"You're supposed to be the tough one," he jokes, sympathy tears pooling in his eyes.

Looking at the sheets of glass behind him, I take a few deep breaths and attempt to get it together. "Every time I look at you, I see so many things."

"What do you mean?" He wraps an arm around my shoulders and leads me to the door that takes us into the house.

On the short walk, I collect my thoughts. He sets me on a stool at the sterile white counter and pulls two bottles of water out of the fridge. I take a gulp, feeling my nerves settle.

"I see who you are now, and you're the man I've always imagined you'd be," I say. "But I also see the boy you were over ten years ago, along with every memory we ever made together. From the first day you called me Ghost Girl, to the day we said our final goodbye at Caroline and Cole's wedding. It's a flood every time."

"I know." He sits next to me. "That happens to me too. I see you now, more stunning and amazing than you'll ever realize. But I'd be lying if I said I didn't also see the girl who broke my heart into pieces more than a decade ago."

A few moments of silence pass.

"I remember everything that happened over those last months in perfect detail," I say quietly, looking at him. "It's followed me forever. How are we supposed to get rid of it?"

He pushes my flyaways behind my ear and leans in to kiss me. Once again, the flood in question comes from all sides, submerging me in a pool of memories. This time, Dawson keeps me afloat.

He moves away and stares me deep in the eyes. "We forgive ourselves," he says. "Because we deserve to. And because we're meant to be together regardless of the past."

CHAPTER 24

SEPTEMBER 2010

When Dawson isn't around, every day feels like walking uphill in a windstorm while it's pouring rain.

What makes it even harder is, I've rarely left Larkspur, let alone the state of Florida, so I have no idea how to even fathom the distance between here and Richmond. Miles mean nothing to me. The number of hours seems like a lie—it certainly has to be more. There's no way to describe the way I feel his absence in my bones.

It also gives me way too much time to think.

I should have told Dawson to stay here with me, his dad be damned. But it's too late for that now. Besides, even if he were here, I would still be dealing with the consequences of Ed Aiken and his words. Words that have taken characteristics about myself that I used to only occasionally ponder, and made them the focus of my everyday self-talk.

Uneducated.

Larkspur riffraff.

Not good enough for my son.

Without Dawson here to ground me, I fully believe them. And scrolling through his Facebook every day and seeing photos of him on campus with groups of friends that include other girls does nothing to quiet my inner demons. He's where he should be, and I'm where I should be.

I may dabble in the "paranormal," but I never signed up to deal with demons.

In two days, I'll be leaving to go to Richmond to visit Dawson for his birthday. I wish it were today. I'm not sure I'll make it that long without completely breaking down, and it's becoming harder and harder to hide the way I'm feeling from him. It's getting more difficult to envision a future together. Even after he's finished with college, can anything really change?

You'll never be good enough, the demons say again.

On this particular day of September, a vicious storm forces us to cancel all of the tours. Since I have an unexpected day off, Caroline invites me over to help her address wedding invitations while the rain pours and the lighting flashes outside. Rather, to keep her company while she addresses them, since I have the penmanship of a five-year-old.

"Are you excited for your trip?" she asks.

"I can't wait," I say, sealing the envelope she passes to me.

"I can tell you miss him. You haven't been yourself the past few weeks."

"I haven't?" I ask, playing dumb.

She uses the pen she's holding to tap me on the knuckles. "You're quiet. Withdrawn. When was the last time I saw you before today?"

I look down at the table. "I've been working a lot."

Caroline focuses on scrawling an address onto a new envelope. Her handwriting is loopy and free-flowing. It reminds me of some of the driftwood on Skeleton Beach, with its curled edges and consistent swirls.

I chew on my lip, trying to decide if I really want to ask Caroline what I'm about to ask her. When it comes to matters of the heart, I've always preferred to keep them bottled up inside. It's easier that way. It's easier without the opinions of others—even those you love. Even when you know they're going to give you nothing but support and try their best to make you feel better.

"Can I ask you something?" I say before I can change my mind.

"Of course." She sets her pen down and folds her hands on the table, giving me her full attention.

"Do you think Dawson is too good for me?"

Lightning flashes through the window and her eyebrows fold over her blue eyes. "No!" she emphasizes. "No, no, and absolutely not. Why would you think that?"

I shrug. I don't want to tell her about Ed. But at least I can talk to her about the doubt that's been controlling me since he put fuel on the fire. "It's a thought I had a while ago and I can't shake it. He's so...perfect. He's smart and successful and funny and popular, and kind to top it all off. Always has been and always will be. And I'm...I'm me."

Caroline stands up and moves to the chair next to mine. She turns to face me and takes one of my hands in hers. "Dawson is all of those things," she says. "Tell me, what do you think you are in comparison?"

Looking down at our hands, I rack my brain for words. "I have no goals. I'm grumpy, and sometimes mean. I don't have a future off of this island, at least not one that I can see. I'm stuck."

"I should punch you in the nose right now," Caroline says bluntly. "Maybe that would help you see what I know Dawson sees. What I see. What Cole sees, too."

"Cole can't stand me," I say.

"Oh, Cole loves you now. But don't tell him I told you that. He loves y'all's dynamic too much."

I cross my heart, a smile sneaking its way onto my lips. "So...what do you see?"

She grabs my other hand. "I see someone who is way funnier than she realizes. Someone who is always there for her friends and family, no matter what. Someone who takes shitty situations and turns them a little less shitty. I see my best friend. I see the girl Dawson is madly in love with."

If I look her in the eyes, I'll start crying. I've been doing way too much of that lately, so I keep my head down. "I love you," I say, squeezing her hands.

"I love you too. And I understand how it feels to question your decisions and your future. Larkspur can feel isolating in a lot of ways. But look at me. Look at Cole. We're here with you, and I bet you don't think those mean things about us for making it work, just like you are. I'm sure Dawson would rather be here than at school, too."

"He would," I say honestly. "Did you know he didn't want to go back this semester?"

"So why did he?"

"It's a long story." I sigh. "But it's why I'm having a hard time seeing a future for him and me. He doesn't want to work for his dad, so what happens after he finishes school? Does he find something else to do here? Does he go elsewhere, and we break up when I can't go with him?"

If I were Dawson, I would run far, far away from anywhere his dad is.

"Why couldn't you go with him?" she asks, confused.

"You know why. I have to be here. Mom isn't coming back. Sawyer is still a kid. Dad is so checked out of everything right now that I don't think I could trust him to take Sunny Spirits back over. If we lost the house and the business because of me, I would never be able to live with myself."

She watches me with a sad look in her eyes, like she knows

it's going to be hard to convince me to believe anything other than what I already do. "I know it's not easy to have hope when everything feels overwhelming, but circumstances do change, Sage. By the time you and Dawson have to face that, old doors could be closed and so many new ones could be open."

"I know," I say. "I only wish I could see the future so I could feel better *now*."

"Don't give up on him. Don't give up on the two of you. You're meant to be together. I feel it in my bones."

"You're only saying that because you and Cole love having best friends who are a couple," I joke.

"True." She laughs. "But I've also been watching you guys for years and I've never seen two stronger magnets."

I roll my eyes to the ceiling. "God, you weren't supposed to make me actually feel better," I say.

"You would do the same for me," she says, moving back to her original seat and picking up a new envelope to address.

"I would. Day or night."

∼

The next morning, I'm in the middle of starting my laundry when I get a text from Dawson.

DAWSON

Can you call me?

I smile, already anticipating the sound of his voice. In twenty-four hours, I'll get to hear it straight from his beautiful face. Thanks to Caroline, the rain cloud above my head has dissolved enough that I can see a bit of the sun peeking through.

After starting the washing machine, I take my phone outside and dial his number.

"Hey." He answers on the first ring. I know something is wrong the second I hear his voice.

"Hey. You good?"

"You're never going to believe this," he says, fast and hopeless. I can imagine him pacing, running a hand through his hair.

My stomach drops. "Believe what?"

"My parents are here. In Richmond," he says. "They showed up unexpectedly this morning, to surprise me for my birthday."

Please no.

"Did they know I was coming this weekend?" I ask.

"No," he says shortly. "I never told them because things have been so bad with Dad since, well...you know."

I know more than you do, I think.

I understand why he didn't tell them, but it still feels like a knife to the heart. Is he ashamed of me?

"Okay." It's all I can say.

"I'm so fucking upset!" His voice echoes through whatever room he's in. "I've been looking forward to this weekend since I left Larkspur and now it's ruined. I don't want them here. I want you. Just me and you."

He keeps ranting and I let him, staying silent because I have no idea how to make him feel better. How to make myself feel better. A rug has been ripped out from beneath me, taking all of the good feelings Caroline gave me yesterday along with it.

"I'm sorry," I say.

"As much as I hate to say it, I don't think you should come, Sage."

The knife twists a little deeper.

"We can't do a full weekend with them. I can't watch Dad treat you like a piece of trash beneath his shoe, because you don't deserve that and I might kill him."

My throat is filled with the familiar lump. "Okay," I croak.

"Please don't be upset with me," he says. His voice is combative, and though I know it's not directed at me, I can't stand to hear it.

"I'm not."

"We can re-plan for another weekend." His voice softens.

"Okay," I say again.

"I love you," he says. "I love you and I miss you more than I've ever missed anyone or anything and I have half a mind to sneak away from them and come to you."

"Don't do that. It will only make things worse." I swallow, rage-filled tears lining my eyes.

A door opens and closes on his end of the call.

"I have to go," he says. "I'll call you again as soon as possible. I love you, Sage."

I stare out at the water, feeling nothing. "I love you too."

The call ends, and my arms fall to my sides. For a while, I just stand here in the grass, rooted in place, staring out at the ocean in the distance. A light breeze blows across my face and I blink, expecting tears but there are none. Instead, I feel numb. Defeated. Scared, and hopeless, and hurt.

Things are never going to get better, I think.

Turning, I walk slowly back to the front door. Before I step inside, I turn off my phone.

CHAPTER 25

SEPTEMBER 2010

My phone stays off for the next two days.

Since I don't have work to keep me distracted, I stay buried beneath the covers in my room, leaving only to go to the bathroom and get the occasional glass of water. Dad and Sawyer have no idea what to do with me, and I should feel bad, but I don't. I just want to sleep. If I sleep enough, maybe my brain will reset and I'll wake up feeling better—more positive. Then I can stop feeling sorry for myself and be strong enough to be the person Dawson deserves to have in his life.

Not that he'll still want me after I've ignored him for two days. Two days that include his twenty-first birthday. My phone sits lifeless in my top dresser drawer, and I have no plans to change that any time soon.

I'm a piece of shit.

"Wedgie?" Sawyer says tentatively from the other side of my door.

"Hm?" I grunt.

He peeks around the curtain, his sweet face riddled with concern. "Dad and I are making frozen pizza for dinner. Do you want some?"

"I'm not hungry." I roll so my back is to the door.

I feel him hovering, then his defeated footsteps retreat down the creaky hallway.

A little while later, it's Dad's turn. "I brought you a plate," he says, stepping into my room even though I didn't give him permission.

"I'm not hungry."

"I haven't seen you eat anything in two days." He puts the plate on my nightstand. "You don't have to tell me what's wrong if you don't want to, but you do have to eat."

"Just leave it there," I say to the wall.

Like Sawyer, he lingers, waiting for me to talk to him. When he realizes I'm not going to, he stomps away with a heavy sigh.

The noise of the TV blares through the walls for a while, keeping me company. Then Dad and Sawyer go to bed and the cottage is filled with a lonely silence. In the dark, I roll over and pick a piece of cold pepperoni off of the pizza. When it hits my tongue, I immediately gag and roll it back onto the plate.

A while later, the distant sound of a truck engine cuts through the silence. It rapidly gets louder and closer, but I don't bat an eye, assuming it's one of the neighbors. When I hear the crunch of our gravel driveway, I drag myself from the bed and go to peep out my window. There are lights cutting around the corner of the cottage. They disappear and the engine dies, and a few seconds later someone is beating on our front door so hard I think it may come off its hinges.

I jump, quickly becoming suspicious about who may be on the other side. But there's no way. It couldn't be him.

When I walk into the hall, Sawyer is standing there, staring with wide eyes. Dad flings open his bedroom door, pulling on a shirt as he comes barreling out. "Who the hell?" he says.

"I think I know," I tell them. "Go back to bed."

"Sage, let me—"

"Please go back to bed!" I sound mean and nasty, but if it is Dawson, we're not going to put on a show for my family.

Sawyer and Dad linger while I walk to the door. I unlock it and open it slowly. The light on the front porch filters into the hall, illuminating me and casting the face of the man on our porch in shadows.

"Sage, what the actual hell?" Dawson says, stepping forward and wrapping his arms around me. I'm suddenly very aware of my greasy hair and the pajamas I've been wasting away in for forty-eight hours. I'll add it to the list of reasons he shouldn't want me.

My arms hang limp at my sides. "What are you doing here?" I ask into his shoulder.

"What do you mean?" His voice raises. "Your phone has been going to voicemail for two days! No one else has heard from you either! Caroline said she would come check on you but I told her I was already on my way. I thought something had happened to you!"

I push him back outside and shut the door behind us. "Well, as you can see, I'm alive."

His face changes from angry to pained. He tries to reach for me again but I take a step back.

"What is going on?" he asks, forcing my hands into his. "Something is wrong. You're avoiding me. On my birthday of all days! I've been driving myself crazy. And now you're acting like I'm a stranger who just showed up at your house in the middle of the night."

"You should be at school," I say numbly. "That's where you belong."

I walk down the steps, in the direction of the water. The grass is dewy on my bare feet and there's a chill in the wind that adds to my numbness. Dawson follows, close to my heels. He jumps in front of me and puts his hands on my shoulders, holding me in place. "I belong where you are. First and foremost. Before anywhere else."

My facade finally breaks and I swipe his hands off my shoulders. "No," I growl. "You don't."

The dam breaks and his panic bursts through. "You're not making any fucking sense!" he cries. "Is this because I told you not to come this weekend? You're being cold! And ridiculous."

There they are.

Finally, two words that correctly describe me came out of his mouth.

"Thanks," I sneer, trying to walk around him again.

"What do I have to do to get you to tell me why you're doing this?" Begging, he grabs my arm before I can get out of his reach.

"Stop *touching* me," I say. "I don't want you to touch me."

It hurts too much.

He lifts his hand in surrender and takes a step back.

Even while I'm ripping his heart out, he's so beautiful. His hazel eyes, black in the night, are shiny with tears. He rakes his hands through his hair over and over again, roughly and desperately, turning circles in the grass. I want to hold him. To apologize and explain everything and beg for him to just keep loving me, despite what I've done.

But it's too late. My mind is made up. It has to be.

"I feel like I'm holding you back, Dawson," I say, finally throwing him a bone. "I'm not right for you."

With it said out loud, a weight lifts off my chest.

"You're being crazy, Sage." He twists his hands together, searching my face like he's trying to find the real me inside somewhere. Like I'm an imposter.

I shrug, running my tongue across my teeth. I wish he would stop saying my name.

He doesn't give up. "Can we go somewhere? Please, please, can we just talk? I don't know what to do!"

"You can leave," I say, breathing deeply through my nose. I feel my walls deteriorating, and there's only so long before the tears come.

"I *love* you." He tries once more to grab my hand, but I stand my ground. "And I know you love me. You're not fooling me. You can tear me apart all you want and you still won't be able to convince me that something has suddenly died between us."

I lift my chin, staring him square in the eyes. "Maybe you should start trying a little harder to believe that something has."

Silence surrounds us. His body deflates, and I know I've done it. I've delivered the final punch to his gut.

"Does it mean nothing that I can't live without you?" His voice shakes so violently I can hardly understand him.

My inner walls come tumbling down, and the truth of my feelings rushes in. *I can't live without you, either!* I scream internally. I want to hold him—to tackle him to the ground and kiss him and convince him it has nothing to do with him. To tell him my hopes and fears, and about his dad's shitty threats.

But I won't. Because I know myself well enough to know my insecurities aren't something I'll be able to work through in a way that he's deserving of.

"Please go, Dawson." I reach out and take his hand, squeezing it for what could be the last time. *Needing* to touch him one last time. "Please."

He grasps on to me like he's drowning and I'm his final chance of being saved. How ironic is it that I'm the one who pushed him over the edge of the boat? I pry my hand out of his, watching as he slowly backs away from me, refusing to look anywhere but my face. With every little bit of distance, I have to fight harder not to run after him.

Suddenly, he turns and begins sprinting toward his truck. He climbs in, and the engine sounds angry when it snarls to life. I watch as he turns the truck around, then flies down the driveway. Gravel kicks up behind him, and his tires squeal on the asphalt when he hits the road.

I keep watching until his taillights completely disappear from sight. Then I fall to my knees and sob into the misty grass.

I don't get out of bed for another week.

Dad goes to work for me. Caroline tries to visit but I won't see her. Dawson doesn't come back.

When I finally charge my phone and turn it back on, I have a slew of texts and voicemails from Dawson, Caroline, and even Cole. I delete every single one without reading or listening to them.

Time marches on, and eventually I will too. But this time, I'll do it alone, like I was always meant to.

CHAPTER 26

PRESENT DAY, NOVEMBER 2022

"Knock knock!" Dad calls as we open the door to the old ice cream parlor.

Dawson and Caroline are sitting on two of the sagging red stools, deep in conversation. Smiling, they look over and stand to greet us. My heart somersaults around my chest at the sight of Dawson's grin. My stomach joins the party when I remember it's part of the same mouth that was between my legs a few days ago.

"Hey!" Caroline says.

"Good to see you, Gerald!" Dawson walks over to shake Dad's hand, then turns to me. "Hey, Sage."

"Hi." We stare at each other shyly—sharing a secret that only the two of us are in on.

Caroline being Caroline, she looks back and forth between us, then narrows her eyes and raises an eyebrow at me. I wink at her, hoping to convey that I'll fill her in later. I can see the impatience oozing out of her pores.

"I haven't had a chance to thank you in person for doing this," Dad tells Dawson. "We're so excited. A bigger space is something we've always wanted. Something Sage has worked incredibly hard for." He puts an arm around my shoulders and I preen at the compliment.

"She's always been a hard worker," Dawson says, looking at me appreciatively.

I place a hand on my cheek. "Y'all are making my head big with all of these compliments."

"When the space is finished, Sunny Spirits and Aiken Stained Glass Contractors will be the hottest businesses on Main Street," Caroline says, her voice full of realtor zeal.

"I thought we could do a walk-through?" Dawson says. "To start getting an idea for how to reorganize. I told Sage I want your opinions on this, too. Then we can hit the ground running when the sale goes through."

"We really appreciate it," Dad says. "Now that I'm standing here, it's much smaller than I remember."

"Really?" I ask, looking around the dusty, abandoned parlor. "It's bigger for me."

"Don't worry about the size, either way," Dawson says. "Here's what I'm thinking."

He walks toward the front door and I immediately become distracted by his butt in his jeans. Caroline elbows me and whispers, "Pay attention."

"I was thinking we could have a shared reception space." Dawson spreads his arms to indicate the area around him. "We're two different businesses, and we'll have some kind of separation so we don't distract each other..."

With that phrase he looks directly at me, a twinkle in his eye. I twist my mouth to the side, trying to hide my grin. I'd really like to tell him that being distracted by him is a-okay, when it comes to work and non-work alike.

"Anyway," he continues, shaking his head to find his train of thought. "Shared reception could be handy. Now, here's what I'm thinking for the extension."

He leads us around the parlor, explaining his ideas for

which walls to knock down and where to build new ones. Dad listens intently, holding a hand to his mouth and nodding in agreement. I nod too, but if I'm being honest, I'm only listening to about half of the rebuild discussion. I'm too focused on all of Dawson's excited expressions. Too attracted to the passion he obviously has for this project.

"What about the kitchen?" Dad asks. "Will that stay?"

"Honestly, that's the one thing I haven't thought about super hard yet," Dawson says.

"Maybe I could help?" Dad asks. "Can I take a look?"

"Be my guest." Dawson sweeps his arm toward the kitchen in the back of the room. "I'll come with and we can brainstorm."

"We'll wait here," Caroline tells them, speaking for me. "I want to talk to Sage about something."

Dawson gives me one last smile before they walk away, and Caroline drags me over to the front window. We stare out through the grime, watching people walk up and down the sidewalks and through the square. It's cooler today, and everyone is enjoying the opportunity to be outside in jacket weather.

"Spill," she says quietly.

I pause, listening to Dad and Dawson's booming conversation and laughter. It echoes through the kitchen and out into the main space, reminding me of old times with them shooting the shit in the cottage kitchen.

"I think you already know," I tell her. "What's to spill?"

She moves closer, speaking even quieter. "I want the dirty details. Have you kissed? Have you talked about the past? Have you...*boinked*?"

I snort. "You did not just use the word boinked."

"You're making this harder than it needs to be, pal." She smooths her French twist.

"The answers to your questions are yes, yes, and partially,"

I say.

"Partially? What does that even mean?" Her voice squeaks in exasperation.

Dad and Dawson's voices grow quieter and I look over my shoulder, making sure they're not sneaking up on us.

"Use your imagination," I tell her. "Although, my daughter thinks adults don't have any imagination."

Caroline laughs then turns to lean against the window so she can look at me. "You've talked about things, then?"

"Most things." I shrug, lowering my voice to a whisper. "Turns out we've both been haunted by our past for a long time. It will take some work. Starting with me fully forgiving myself for the way I went about the breakup."

Caroline looks down at the floor. "You know, he came to our apartment that night. The night you ended things."

"You've never told me that." I lean against the window beside her.

"I never felt like I could. You were so adamant about not speaking about him." She glances at me. "He was...destroyed, Sage."

I swallow. "I know. Which is why it's been so hard to forgive myself."

"Do you know what I told him?" Caroline asks.

I shake my head.

"I told him to give you some time. That you would come around," she says. "But you never did."

I think about that night. About my selfishness. About the look on his face. About the wet grass on my feet and the debilitating feeling of my world ending.

"I would have," I whisper. "But then I got pregnant."

Caroline scoots closer so our shoulders are touching. "Forgive yourself, my friend. Forgive yourself, then *give* yourself the chance to become what you two were always meant to be."

Smiling, I pull Caroline into a hug. That's how Dad and

Dawson find us—clutching each other's shoulders in front of the smutty parlor window.

"Did we miss something?" Dawson asks, smirking.

Caroline pats my cheek as she pulls away. "Can't a girl hug her best friend?"

Dad laughs. "You've always been thick as thieves."

Caroline walks over to the stools and grabs her bag from the floor, dusting it off. "I have another appointment to get to, but please let me know if anything comes up. This place should be yours soon, Daws! Can you lock up? I trust you to bring the key back to me tomorrow."

"Sure thing. Thanks, Care." He catches the key when she tosses it to him.

"I've gotta get going, too," Dad says. "Always work to be done."

"I'll walk you out." Caroline jokingly offers him her arm and he takes it with a grin.

"Bye!" I call behind them.

Standing next to Dawson, we watch the two of them walk out the door, then past the parlor's window. When they're out of sight, Dawson grabs me around the waist, lifting me off the floor and smashing his lips to mine. "Having to wait to do that was torturous," he jokes when we separate.

"Update: one of them already knows," I say.

"Caroline?" He wrinkles his nose.

I wrap an arm around his waist. "Obviously."

He holds me to him, leading us over to the stools. We sit across from each other, hands clasped and knees touching.

"So what do you think?" he asks, looking around the space.

"It's going to be great," I say. "I can't wait. You have a knack for envisioning things."

"Thanks." He kisses my hand.

"Did you ever think when you decided not to work for

your dad that you would end up starting your own business?" I ask.

"Not at first. For a while there I thought I was gonna be a finance drone forever. Eliza was, well...never mind. We don't need to talk about that." He looks guilty for saying her name in front of me.

I bump my knee against his. "We can, you know. I would actually like to."

"You sure?"

"Positive."

"Okay..." He sits taller. "I was going to say that she wasn't crazy about the idea of me doing something else. I made good money, and that security was important to her."

"I get that," I say.

"Me too. But sometimes it felt like the money was all she was worried about." He shrugs.

"Is that why things ended?" I ask.

He looks across the room, out the window at the passing islanders. His lip twitches. "That was part of it."

"Can I ask what the other part was?"

His attention comes back to me, and he pulls me to the edge of my stool, pinning one of my knees between both of his. "Sure."

No further explanation comes. His mouth quirks like he's trying to contain a smile.

"So...are you gonna tell me?" I ask.

"You asked if you could ask me a question. You never actually asked me the question itself." He finally grins.

Reaching out, I hit him lightly on the shoulder. "You're so obnoxious."

"As you've told me many times before, Ghost Girl."

"Fine. What happened between you and Eliza?" I use her name to let him know this isn't some weird jealousy thing.

"Like I said, the money was part of it." He rubs his chin.

"But the other reason was she never really felt like I was truly myself around her. She always felt like I was holding something back."

We look at each other. In this dirty old building, surrounded by dilapidated furniture and yellowing walls, he looks out of place and even more perfect. I've always known that he was the reason I never found anyone else—the reason that I've never wanted to. I've never considered that maybe it's been the same for him. I assumed the hurt and hatred he must have eventually felt toward me fueled him and kept him driven to do more with his life and meet someone he would realize actually was better than me.

"I'm sorry," I say. "I'm sure that was hard."

"It was. But it was the best thing for both of us. We're on good terms. She met someone a few months ago, and it seems to be going well."

A muffled clanging sound comes from the kitchen, startling both of us. We jump and look at the darkened doorway, then each other.

"Must be the building settling," I say.

Nodding, he turns to look one more time before relaxing.

"What about you? Did you ever meet anyone?" he asks.

I fold my lips together and shake my head. "Not since Whitley's dad. And you already know that was a one-night occurrence."

"Wow. Really?"

I nod.

"How often does Whitley see him?" he asks.

"Never." I roll my shoulders back. The subject of Whitley's dad always makes me tense up. "He lives in Tennessee. He came to see her a couple of times after she was born, but ultimately decided he didn't want to be a part of her life."

Dawson's jaw tenses. "Forgive me, but that's really shitty."

"No need to apologize," I say. "He *is* shitty. And if I think

263

about it too hard it makes me so angry I can't function. But then I remember that without him, I wouldn't have Whitley. And that always calms me down."

He moves a hand to my thigh and runs a thumb over the bare skin. "Seeing you as a mom is really cool. Whitley is a neat kid. I can't wait to get to know her better."

"She's already a fan of you," I say.

He beams. "Yeah?"

"It might be something to do with the soup and the flowers and the giant ass pumpkin you've given her." I smirk.

Another noise comes from the kitchen, louder this time. Dawson lets go of me and stands up, walking around the bar to stick his head through the kitchen door. He flips the light on and stands there for a moment, trying to figure out where the sound is coming from. I move to join him, surveying the empty, dusty room. After standing and listening for a minute or so, the room is still completely silent and empty. We raise our eyebrows at each other.

"Don't you dare say it," I warn him.

"Too late, I'm going to," he says. "I don't suppose your dad has any insight on the ice cream parlor's history?"

"I would be more surprised if he didn't," I reply, eyes roaming skeptically.

"Our own ghost," Dawson says appreciatively.

"You're one of the only people I know who could be excited about that possibility." I laugh.

He turns the kitchen light off and finds the key Caroline gave him in his pocket. "You should be too. How convenient is it for Sunny Spirits to have its own ghost?"

"Pretty damn convenient," I say, following Dawson to the front door. "I only hope it's not the most unfriendly ghost on Larkspur."

I blame the fact that I'm even entertaining this on Buster.

"Are you and Whit free tonight?" he asks as we step onto

Main Street.

"We can be," I say. "Why?"

"I'll pick y'all up at 5:00." He doesn't give any further context. "Bring jackets."

"Okay. But *again*, why?" I look up at him and roll my eyes.

He puts his arm around me and pulls me beneath his shoulder. "*Again*," he whispers, "just bring jackets and come hungry."

The first thing I notice when I open the back door of Dawson's Audi for Whitley is the picnic basket on the floorboard. The smell of something delicious wafts out of the car and Whitley voices exactly what I'm thinking.

"I don't know what's in there, but it's making me hungry!"

Laughing, Dawson turns to look at her. "I'm sorry Whit, I only brought enough for me and your mom," he jokes.

"Whatever!" She sticks her tongue out at him and buckles her seat belt. "I'm young, not dumb."

His laughter grows louder. "I would never think that."

I slide into the front seat and his hand finds my thigh before I've closed the door behind me. "Hey," I say, growing shy at the sight of him in his dark jeans and hoodie. His lips are red and his dark hair is wavy and windblown from the blustery day. My stomach drops even further when I see his glasses have made a reappearance. I couldn't dream up a better-looking man if I tried.

"Hey." He grins, and I miss his hand when he moves it to the gearshift.

"Where are we going?" Whitley asks almost immediately. Her windbreaker rustles as she leans forward in the seat.

Dawson turns us out of the driveway and glances at her in

the rearview mirror. "Somewhere pretty cool," he says. "Somewhere you've never been."

Feeling my first bit of suspicion, I raise an eyebrow at him.

"It must be off the island, then," Whitley says. "I've been everywhere on Larkspur."

"Not everywhere..." I say before turning to silently mouth "Skeleton Beach?" at Dawson.

He nods, and I reach for his hand. He threads our fingers together on top of the center console and I look out the window, watching as trees turn to sand dunes, then back to lush, green forest. A few minutes later, Dawson parks us in the familiar, overgrown parking lot. Like always, there are no other cars around.

Maybe Dad is right. Maybe Skeleton Beach is haunted. Perhaps there is some unexplained paranormal phenomenon that only makes this part of the beach visible to certain people. Why else would no one else ever be around to appreciate it? Why else has it always seemed like a secret, no matter how much time passes?

Who are you, Sage? I ask, snapping myself out of my daydream.

"You can carry this," Dawson tells Whitley, piling a giant blanket into her arms and mashing it down so she can see over the top.

"Where are we?" she asks, glancing around the parking lot. "This place looks sus."

"Sus?" Dawson and I ask at the same time. Normally I'm the one having to explain words to her.

She rolls her eyes. "*Suspicious,*" she says, like it's common knowledge.

Dawson and I exchange a *Damn, we're old* glance, and he leans into the car to grab the picnic basket and a big red kite I didn't notice earlier. He holds the kite up, blocking us from Whitley's sight long enough to give me a kiss. A gust of wind sweeps through the parking lot, cooling the blush in my cheeks and nearly sweeping the kite away. I pull it against my chest and roll the string up so I won't trip over it.

"We have a short walk," Dawson tells Whitley, placing a hand on her shoulder to guide her toward the trail. I walk behind, smiling at the sight of the two of them walking side by side—Whitley's head barely reaching Dawson's elbow. He moves ahead to brush aside stray branches and monitor tripping hazards.

When the trail dumps us out onto the beach, Whitley gasps and almost drops the blanket from her arms. "Whoa!" she says, walking to the nearest piece of driftwood to run the tip of her finger along it. "What is this place?"

I continue to navigate through the labyrinth, searching for the perfect clearing to set up our picnic. Whitley and Dawson follow. "Grampa calls it Skeleton Beach," I tell her. "He first showed it to me when I was a little girl."

"So you've been here before." She stumbles up behind me and I take the blanket, trading her for the kite. "Why haven't you ever brought me?"

Dawson hovers behind, smiling at me over her head.

"It's a secret place," I say, thinking on my feet. "I wanted to make sure you were old enough to keep the secret."

"Oh, I know how to keep secrets. Ask Penelope!"

Dawson sets the picnic basket on the ground and helps me spread the blanket over the sand. The combination of him and the blanket and the beach only makes me think of one memory—of a night long ago on a different blanket, beneath a deep night sky. The memory doesn't jar me like it would have a few weeks ago. Instead, it fills me with excitement to create a new one. One that still involves me and Dawson, but also my daughter.

The wind lifts one of the corners of the blanket and Whitley jumps on top of it, pinning it back in place. Dawson and I sit on either side of her and he begins unloading the goods from the picnic basket—chicken strips, macaroni and cheese, fried cornbread, and corn on the cob, all from The Phantom Eatery. Last but not least, he produces three slices of the lemon pound cake from Beans.

It's all food I've eaten a million times before, but in this setting with my current company, it looks better than ever. We fix our plates and huddle together in the cold wind, letting the food fill our stomachs and warm our fingers. Dawson and Whitley have a contest to see who can eat all of the corn off their cob first, and he declares her the winner despite the fact she missed at least fifty percent of the kernels.

"How did you know about this place, Dawson?" she asks him as I pass her a paper towel.

"Your mom and I used to come here. When we were younger," he says.

"When you were friends?" she asks.

"Yep," I say. "And now we're friends again so here we are."

Dawson scoots closer to me and Whitley looks back and forth between us.

"You're not friends." She scrunches her nose. "Friends don't kiss and hold hands."

"We don't do that," I try to lie.

Whitley places her hand on my knee. "It's okay if you like someone, Mama. I'm not a *little* kid anymore. You don't have to hide things from me. I like Dawson, too." She smiles at him and I watch him melt into the blanket next to me.

"Thanks, Whit," he says. "That's a very grown-up thing to say."

"I know."

Dawson pushes himself to his knees and reaches over her to grab the forgotten kite. "Are you too old to fly this?"

"I don't know," she says. "I've never tried to fly one before."

"I have to teach you then!" He stands and holds his free hand out to help her up.

"Mama, are you coming?" she asks.

"I'm going to clean all of this up." I motion to the half-eaten food. "Then I'll come."

"Okay!"

I lean back onto my hands and stretch my legs out in front of me on the blanket, watching Dawson and Whitley walk hand in hand through the driftwood and down to the water's edge. He shows her how to lick her finger and hold it up to determine the direction of the wind, then unfurls the string and helps her find a grip before letting the kite soar into the gray sky. Surprised by the force from the kite, Whitley stumbles several steps forward, and the wind carries her laughter through the air and into my ears.

"Whoa!" Dawson says, helping her regain control.

"It's too strong!" Whitley yells through a fit of giggles.

"But you're stronger!" he replies.

Smiling, I sit up and flip the lid of the picnic basket open. It's almost impossible to focus on the task at hand, because I can't keep my eyes off the perfect scene in front of me. It's something I've never witnessed before...the possibility of my daughter having a father. The possibility of having someone in my life who would want to be that for Whitley. The possibility of *Dawson* being that for Whitley.

She's always had Dad and Sawyer, and for that I'm thankful. But I've always wished she could have more. Now, there's a hope there that I've never felt before.

Hope.

It's what has been missing from my life for far too long. Almost like Dawson took mine with him in 2010, and now he's brought it back to me. I've never been fond of the idea of placing all of your hope in someone else, but maybe it's okay.

Perhaps, sometimes, hope comes in the form of a person.

CHAPTER 27
OCTOBER 2010

The annual Halloween festival rolls around, marking over a month since I last saw the face or heard the voice of Dawson Aiken.

Most days show me grace and pass quickly, but every now and then a random Tuesday or Saturday drags so slowly that I have no choice but to get stuck in a kaleidoscope of regret, thinking about every part of our relationship from start to finish over and over and over again in the same pattern. In the past few weeks, I've learned to appreciate the act of throwing myself into work—leading every available tour and spending the time away from tours organizing our finances, upgrading our website, and setting us up on every existing social media platform.

On the first day of the festival, Dad finds me in Ms. Knox's office at Ghost to Coast, eyes glued to the computer. I look away long enough to force a smile at him, then return to the spreadsheet on the screen. He pulls a chair up next to me and takes a seat, groaning in that way people do as they age.

"You should be out enjoying the festivities," he says.

"It's the same every year," I say. "Nothing I haven't done a million times before."

He sighs deeply. "You deserve to have some fun, Sage. I saw Caroline and Cole out there on my way in. Go join them. There's nothing to do until the tours tonight and I'll cover those so you can have a whole day to yourself."

I don't *want* a whole day to myself. I don't want to have *fun*.

"Maybe in a little while," I say without looking at him.

Sighing again, he reaches across me and flips the top of the laptop shut, jarring me out of my trance. Anger flares through me and I spin in my chair to face him. Leaning back, he folds his arms across his chest and stares me down, giving me a taste of my own medicine.

"This is no longer a recommendation, Wedgie. I'm tired of seeing you like this. Never giving yourself a break and being sad and mopey when you have no choice but to take one. The Sage I know was once full of fire. I haven't seen any of that lately and I miss it. Your mom told me you need some tough love, so I'm here to give it to you." He lifts his chin, putting on a rare blunt parent schtick.

With every one of his words my eyes narrow until I'm in a full-blown scowl. "I'm not a kid. You can't make me do anything," I argue. "Plus, Mom lost her right to be involved in my life and feelings when she left."

"Don't say that," Dad says.

"Speaking of parenting, if you're here, where is Sawyer?"

"He's with Adrienne and Eve at the costume contest."

Like every time I hear Ms. Knox called by her first name, I have to figure out who he's talking about.

"I thought he didn't want to dress up?" I ask.

"He didn't, but he wanted to watch. Go join them. I promise you won't be disappointed in Cole's costume this year." He smiles gently, placing a hand on my shoulder.

I look from him to the laptop, thinking about all of the things I could do to keep my mind busy today. Maybe Dad is right, though. I've been listening to the sounds of the festival flowing through the front of the closed shop all morning. Maybe I could have a different distraction today.

"Only because you asked me to," I say.

"Excellent." Dad's green eyes lighten and he claps his hands together.

Outside, the day is overcast and moody. The salty Larkspur breeze blows the smells of popcorn, candy apples, and fried foods along Main. For a minute, the nostalgia of it all makes me forget everything else, and I feel my shoulders relax. I pull up my jeans and adjust my T-shirt, which are both askew from hours of sitting, thenbegin walking toward the square, keeping my eyes peeledfor Caroline.

I find her standing in line for a funnel cake. "Sage! Hey!" She looks relieved to see me and wraps me in a hug. Along with everything other than work, I've been neglecting our friendship since what happened with Dawson. In the case of her and Cole, it goes deeper than just not wanting to see anyone. They're Dawson's friends too, so I'm embarrassed. I haven't wanted to see the look in their eyes...particularly Cole's.

What must they think of me?

"Wanna share one?" I ask, pointing to the funnel cakes. "My treat."

She looks so happy to see me, not a sight of disdain in her sweet face. "You know I do," she says.

We take the funnel cake over to the square and find an empty patch of grass to sit on. My appetite has been minimal recently, so the powdered sugar is particularly sweet and decadent on my tongue. Once again, I feel something in me relax.

"Where's Cole?" I ask, scanning the crowds of costumed people. In my search I notice a young auburn-haired guy on the bench across from us, dressed in jeans in a flannel shirt. He's looking at me and Caroline, and our eyes lock briefly before I look away.

"Taking photos with the other costume contest winners," she says. "Third place."

"He placed again?" I laugh. The sound is foreign to my ears. When was the last time I laughed?

"You know he lives for this every year," she says around a mouthful of fried dough.

"What's his costume?"

Looking up, she points. "See for yourself."

Cole is walking toward us, and my mouth falls open. He's wearing bright pink leggings with a neon orange leotard over the top. His head is covered by a long blonde wig, and over the top of that is a sweatband the same color as the leggings. His broad shoulders have the straps of the leotard stretched to the point of no return. Eyes follow him as he makes his way through the throngs of people, proudly wearing a third-place medal around his neck.

"My god," I whisper. "Is he a..."

"Workout Barbie," she confirms, like it's completely normal for her to see her fiancé dressed like this.

"Where does he come up with this stuff?" I wave at Cole when he sees us and his face softens.

"I don't ask questions, I just help make the costumes," Caroline says.

"Hey." Cole drops to his knees on the grass in front of us. He pecks Caroline on the lips then surprises me by pulling me into a hug. Once again, over Cole's shoulder, I lock eyes with the auburn-haired guy who is still staring at me. I thought the first time was a coincidence, but now I'm not so sure.

"Congratulations," I tell Cole, tapping his medal with the tip of my finger. "I'll have to come take one of your jazzercise classes sometime."

He laughs, brushing the blonde wig out of his eyes. I'm relieved to see no signs of hatred in them. "How are you, Sage?"

My brain battles over whether to be honest or lie. "I'm here," I finally decide to say. "I'm...okay."

Cole settles between us and helps us finish off the funnel cake. We don't talk about Dawson. Instead we people watch and admire costumes. Cole gets us a second funnel cake and we talk about the wedding, and how it's only just over a month away. Before I know it, the sunless sky is turning dark and the lights strewn up and down the street illuminate everything in a yellow glow.

It's nice to lose track of time because I'm enjoying myself and not because I'm diving into work to punish myself. Dad was right. I needed this. But while I am feeling better, there's still the nagging emptiness in the corner of my mind—the face of someone who should be sitting on the grass next to me and our best friends, with his hand on my thigh and his mouth occasionally on my neck.

The weight of him sits on my shoulders. Around me, the festival goes on and laughter floats through the air. I can only think of him. What is he doing right now? *How* is he doing right now? Has he already met someone else and forgotten about me? Does he hate me? A familiar ringing fills my ears, and my chest begins to constrict.

What I wouldn't do to forget for more than two minutes at a time.

"Who wants to bob for apples?"

Cole's voice echoes down the tunnel, pulling me back to the present. The ringing subsides and the scene in front of me becomes clear again. Cole and Caroline are looking at me expectantly.

"I'll, uh...come watch," I say, swallowing. Hoping that they didn't notice me disappear.

"Great. You can hold my wig." Cole grins and stands, offering Caroline and me a hand.

"It would be an honor," I joke.

At the bobbing booth, I do indeed clutch Cole's wig to my chest while I watch him and Caroline go head-to-head to see who can retrieve the most apples. Cole is ahead by at least three, and every time Caroline comes up for air she looks progressively more pissed off. A crowd has developed around the booth to cheer them on, which only gives Cole more gusto to be the winner.

"Hi," someone says next to me.

It's the auburn-haired boy from the bench earlier. He's smiling at me, freckles spattered across his nose. He's incredibly tall and lanky, and I can smell the scent of his cologne. He searches my face, waiting for me to say something.

"Hi?" It comes out like a question.

"Nice wig." He nods at Cole's hair in my hands.

"Thanks," I say. "I like to have options."

Why is this boy talking to me? There's only been one other boy who has ever wanted to talk to me.

"I'm Lucas." He holds a long-fingered hand out.

I take it tentatively. "Sage..."

"That's a nice name. Are you from around here?"

Part of me wants to run. Part of me is desperate for the attention.

"Born and raised," I say. "Which is how I know you're not."

He laughs. It's harsh and short. Nothing like my favorite laugh. "I'm from Tennessee. Here for a long weekend with my family."

"Cool." I clutch the wig tighter to my chest and return my attention to Cole and Caroline.

"I've...noticed you a few times today." He keeps talking. "I think you're really pretty, so I told myself I would say hi if I got the opportunity."

My need for validation takes a little step forward. "Thank you," I say.

Part of me wants him to leave. Part of me wants him to keep talking. All of me wishes he were someone else. But he's looking at me in a way that reminds me what it's like to feel something. And I'm not strong enough right now to realize that this isn't where I should be seeking reassurance.

"Can I buy you a drink?" he asks. "There's a beer booth up the street."

"I'm only 20," I say.

"Well, I'm 25, and like I said, I'll buy so you don't have to worry about it." He grins and takes a step closer. I can feel the heat from his body.

I stare up at him, studying his face. He looks nice. He seems nice. He looks *and* seems like a distraction. A drink and more conversation could help me make it through the rest of this day.

Besides, wasn't I just thinking that I would do anything to forget for an extended period of time?

"Okay," I agree. "Let me return this wig to my friend first."

He grins, looking triumphant. "I'll wait here."

After leaving Cole's wig with the bobbing booth attendant, I return to Lucas and we walk down the street to the beer stand. It's getting darker and chillier, and I cross my arms over my chest, rubbing the tops of them.

"You cold?" Lucas asks.

"I'm fine," I say.

He removes his flannel from the top of his white T-shirt and passes it to me anyway. Feeling obligated, I pull it on. The fabric is itchy and the smell of his cologne on me makes me feel briefly nauseated. It's not the rightcologne. He's not the right guy.

But, he's someone. And that's all that matters right now.

"Thanks," I mumble.

While he gets in line to order our beer, I stand off to the side, looking around the crowds for familiar faces. A chill rushes through me when my eyes land on Ed and Cynthia Aiken sharing a candy apple in front of Ghost to Coast. They notice me before I can look away. Cynthia gives me a sad wave. Ed grimaces, but his face transforms into an evil grin the second Lucas walks up and passes me a beer.

Shit, I think. *Shit, shit, shit.*

Tears fill my eyes and I begin walking, my only goal being to get out of Ed and Cynthia's line of vision. Lucas is easily hot on my heels with his long legs. Beer sloshes out of the cup and over my hand, adding to the icky feeling covering the rest of my skin.

"Let's sit here," he says, grabbing my elbow and pulling me to the edge of the abandoned costume contest stage.

"Okay." I sit next to him and tilt the cup into my mouth, downing half of the beer in one go.

"Whoa." Lucas chuckles. "That was kind of sexy."

Don't call me that, my brain says. Then, *please call me that again.* "Tell me about yourself," he continues. "I've never met anyone named Sage before." "You'll love this then..." I tell him about Sunny Spirits and growing up on Larkspur. In return, he tells me about how he grew up as a military brat and now works as a lineman. We talk about basic things, but he keeps giving me compliments and buying me beer, and it's good enough to numb the pain. I'm not much of a drinker, so by the third beer I'm feeling woozy—like I'm in a different world surrounded by fire instead of fairy lights.

Lucas runs a hand down my back and I shiver.

"We're staying at the motel a couple of streets over," he says, and I nod, knowing the one he's talking about.

"That's cool," I say, subdued.

"I have my own room." His hand settles on my right hip. "Do you want to come hang out for a while?"

His touch is heavy and uncomfortable, but I don't push him away. I stare up at the lights, which are now somewhat blurry. Around us, the street dies down, and the memories wait at the edge of my mind, waiting to make their attack and pull me back down.

I would do anything to forget, I think.

"Sure," I tell him.

Then I let him lead me down Main Street, away from the hustle and bustle of the festival and toward his motel room.

CHAPTER 28

DECEMBER 2010

T hree days before Caroline and Cole's wedding, I have to run to the bathroom to vomit the second my eyes open.

I wipe my mouth and sit back on my heels. The bathroom tile digs into my knees as more heaves work their way up my esophagus. When I'm able to stand and wash my face, blood-shot eyes and pale skin greet me in the mirror.

It's a stomach bug, I think. *Dad's sausage and peppers last night were questionable.*

It's the flu, another part of me says.

It's because you have to see Dawson in a few days. This one makes the most sense, but it still doesn't feel completely right.

On the way to Ghost to Coast, I make a stop at the drugstore. After scoping out the area and making sure no one I know is around, I hurriedly buy a pregnancy test and clutch the brown paper bag tightly to my stomach on the short walk to the bookshop.

"Good morning!" Ms. Knox says brightly when I enter.

"Morning," I say, feeling another gag push into my throat. "I have to use the bathroom. Too much coffee."

"No need to ask for my permission," she jokes.

It's the longest three minutes of my life. I stare at the little window on the test, biting my fingernails as the urine slowly absorbs and reveals one line. I hold my breath, praying the first prayer I've ever prayed for there not to be a second one.

The prayer doesn't work. The second pink line appears, bright and glaring in the fluorescent lighting of the bookstore's bathroom. I fall against the wall and slide down to the floor, pressing a hand to my mouth to try to hold in the building sob. It escapes anyway and loudly reverberates around the concrete walls. I pull my knees to my chest and cry into them, unsure of how I'm ever going to get up again.

One time without a condom. One bad decision. That's apparently all it takes.

"Sage?" There's a knock at the door. I can see Ms. Knox's bare feet beneath the crack.

Startled, I wipe my eyes and find my voice. "I'm fine. Be out in a sec."

"You're not fine. I can hear you crying." She rattles the door knob. "Open the door or I'm using the key."

Weakly, I wobble to my feet to unlock the door and crack it open. "I'm just having a bad day," I tell her through the crack.

She pushes her way into the bathroom with more strength than should be able to exist in her small body, bringing the smell of patchouli with her. It's normally a comforting smell, but in the moment, it makes me heave. I make a grab for the pregnancy test but it's too late. Her mouth falls open and she shuts the door behind her, closing us in together.

"Oh, honey," she says quietly, looking between the test and me.

With the test in my fist, I crumple back to the floor, alternating between crying and gagging. She sinks down next to me and pulls me into her chest. She says nothing, only lets me cry until I can't anymore.

"I hate to ask," she finally says. "But is it...Dawson's? I thought that ended."

"It did," I say. "It was someone else."

"Take deep breaths." She runs a hand down my ponytail and stands up to wet a paper towel, which she presses to the back of my neck. It's cool and shocking, and my body releases one more sob before slowly relaxing.

"I'm so stupid," I say to the bathroom floor. "I was only trying to feel...better."

"You are far from stupid," Ms. Knox scolds. "We're going to figure this out. You and me. Until you're ready to tell someone else."

Her care for me makes new tears come. "Thank you," I say, grabbing her hand.

"I love you." She kisses my forehead. "You know you're like a granddaughter to me. I'm always here—for anything."

I blow my nose into a wad of toilet paper, then look at her. "What if I killed someone?" I joke.

She laughs. "There's my Sage. And yes, even if you kill someone. I'll help you hide the body, too."

"Damn," I snort. "You're so dark."

She stays with me until it's time to open the store, even taking it upon herself to call one of Sunny Spirits's part-time guides and get me coverage for the day tours I'm supposed to lead. I stay locked in the office, trying to find some acceptance of everything that has happened in my life since September. I spread a hand across my stomach, trying to fathom how there could possibly be the beginning of a life within me. Trying to fathom how this is going to fit into my own life.

The worst part is, there's still only one person I wish I could talk to.

~

Caroline is the most beautiful bride.

Classic and graceful and stunning in her traditional silk white dress. Cole isn't so bad himself, looking like a small-town James Bond in his tuxedo.

Thank god they're both so impressive to look at. It helps me keep my gaze from floating to the best man behind Cole while I'm serving as Caroline's maid of honor. What their attractiveness doesn't do is keep him from looking at me. I've felt Dawson's eyes on me since he first arrived at McBride Mansion, where the wedding is taking place in the garden, followed by a reception inside. His hazel gaze follows my every move, but I can't return the favor. Not until the day is mostly over.

That's why I wish for it to pass slowly. When dinner and the cake cutting end and the dancing begins, I know my last moments of peace are running out. For a while I float around the room, talking to anyone and everyone to keep Dawson from finding me alone. It's a small wedding though, so eventually I'm out of people to talk to.

We lock eyes across the dance floor, and he uses it as his sign. He pushes through the crowd on the floor, through flying limbs and spilling drinks, until he's standing a foot away. My breath catches in my throat as I allow myself to take in his tuxedo-clad body. His hair is as perfectly styled as it always used to be. He's thinner, and his face has the look of someone who's being haunted 24-7, but overall, he's still breathtaking. Still my Ghost Boy.

"Hi," I say.

"You look incredible," he replies.

I don't deserve his compliments. I smooth my hands over my blue satin bridesmaid dress. Over my stomach, which will soon no longer fit into said dress. "Thank you," I tell him. "So do you."

He steps forward quickly, intentionally, and wraps me into

a hug. It happens so fast I don't have time to react. I'm just suddenly surrounded by him. By his smell and his solidness and his comfort. Melting, I squeeze him against me and hold him until he pulls away.

"Can we talk?" he asks, taking my hand.

I nod and he leads me outside into the garden. It's dark and the ocean breeze is cold. Dawson removes his tuxedo jacket and places it around my shoulders before leading me to the swing on the B&B's front porch. I'm taken back to Lucas giving me his flannel, and I want to rip Dawson's jacket off and give it back to him.

Like everything else he's ever given me, I don't deserve it.

"How are you?" I ask, trying to ground myself.

"Do you want the honest answer?"

I don't know if I can handle it, I think.

"Yes," I say, swallowing around the lump that now lives permanently in my throat.

"I'm not good," he admits. "How are you?"

"Also not good," I say quietly, barking a sad laugh.

We sit next to each other on the swing, rocking back and forth and staring out at the B&B's front lawn. Our hands sit in our laps and our thighs are a few inches apart. He doesn't need to be touching me for me to feel him all over, though. It's how Dawson has always made me feel—like I'm surrounded by all of the best things on earth. Even when life is hard.

"I owe you an apology," I say. "I was...terrible. And on your birthday, of all days."

"It's a birthday I'll never forget." He smiles mournfully. "But I've already forgiven you, Sage."

"Please don't say that," I say. "It's easier to think that you're going to hate me forever."

He angles his body toward me and reaches for one of my hands. "That's impossible. Because I already know I'm going to *love* you forever."

Tears escape around my false eyelashes and he pulls me against him.

"Don't cry." He brushes my tears away, catching them before they fall and ruin my satin dress.

"I'm so sorry," I say.

A few wedding guests exit through the front door and we shoot apart, sitting in silence until they disappear down the sidewalk.

"Can you at least tell me why, now?" Dawson asks.

"I told you that night," I say.

"There's no way that's all of it," he argues. "I want the *real* reason why."

"It's going to make you really mad." I bite my bottom lip. "And not just at me."

"I don't care. I need to know. Please."

Taking a deep breath, I tell him about my conversation with his dad at their house the night I went over for dinner. About Ed's threat, and his words, and how they snaked into my head and wrapped around all of the not-so-nice things I've always secretly thought about myself. Dawson listens with a clenched draw, his face growing redder and redder as his hand squeezes mine tighter and tighter.

"I fucking hate him," he spits when I finish. "How could I let him do this to us?"

"It's not your fault," I murmur.

"Why didn't you tell me sooner?" he asks.

I shrug. "I was scared. Of the influence he could have on Sunny Spirits. Of what he would do to keep us apart. Of losing you, and that ended up happening anyway."

Leaning my head on his shoulder, I let him come to terms with everything I've just said. Inside the B&B, the music changes from a group dance song to Phil Collins's "Can't Stop Loving You." I listen closely to the words, thinking about how insanely accurate they are to the situation.

I will never stop loving Dawson Aiken.

"I know we can fix this, Sage," he says. "I'll cut my dad off. I'll quit school. I won't let him do anything to you or your family. I will do whatever I need to do for *us*."

Lifting my head, I scoot away so I can fully look at him. Because there's something else I have no choice but to tell him.

"It's still not going to work," I say. "There are other things at play besides that now."

He frowns. "Like what?"

I spit it out, bluntly and honestly. "I just found out I'm pregnant."

His face stays expressionless and he shoots up from the swing, pacing up and down the porch. "Are you seeing someone else?"

"No!" I say, standing to join him.

"So how?" he asks, looking so broken I want to scream.

I tell him about Lucas, pacing next to him because there's no way I can sit still now either.

Eventually, he stops and turns to me. "I don't care, Sage. This doesn't change anything for me."

Sweet, sweet Dawson.

"I know you think that now," I say. "But it will eventually."

"It won't," he argues.

"You have to live your own life, Dawson." I lean against the railing of the porch. "You have so many good things coming to you. Better things than me. Better things than Larkspur, if you want them."

He stands in front of me, placing a hand on either side of my waist. His face is inches from mine and his eyes glisten in the dim light. "I don't want them."

His lips find their way to mine, and I don't have the willpower to push him away. So I let him kiss me, convincing myself that it's okay one last time.

CHAPTER 29

PRESENT DAY, DECEMBER 2022

" A toast!" Sawyer says, stepping onto a chair and holding his glass of champagne in the air.

The various conversations happening in Cole and Caroline's backyard cease, and everyone moves to grab their own flutes and form a circle. Dawson stands to my left and Dad to my right, followed by Ms. Knox, Eve, Cole, Caroline, and finally, Sawyer. Whitley, Maddie, and Cam stand in the center with plastic cups of sparkling cider. We all look up at Sawyer.

"First, a happy birthday to my sister," Sawyer says, and everyone whoops. "And of course, a huge congratulations to Dawson, the new owner of Larkspur's soon-to-be-ex old ice cream parlor. Not to mention, Sage and Dad who will soon have a brand-new space for Sunny Spirits. These are all things to be celebrated. Cheers!"

We go around the circle, clinking glasses and exchanging pleasantries, then I take a sip of cool, tingly champagne. I remove the glass from my lips and am swiftly met by a kiss from Dawson. The bubbles on his tongue intermingle with mine, and I smile against his mouth.

"Congratulations," I tell him.

"Congratulations to *you*," he says. "And happy birthday."

"Happy birthday, Mama!" Whitley throws her arms around my waist, spilling cider down my back.

"Thank you," I say, cringing and taking the cup away from her. "You've told me about fifteen times today and it sounds better every time."

"What's next?" Ms. Knox asks Dawson.

"Applying for permits. Finding someone to do the work. There's a long, long list, but it will get done." Grinning, he puts an arm around me.

Across the deck, I lock eyes with Sawyer. He smiles and nods. I finally told him about Dawson and me a few days ago. Being my younger brother, being there during the most vulnerable time of my life, I think he will worry for a while, while Dawson and I continue to reacquaint ourselves with the people we are now. But he'll also support me, and I can't ask for more than that.

"Sage, come help me!" Caroline calls. I leave Dawson to chat logistics and follow Caroline inside the house.

"What am I helping you with?" I ask. She leads me to the kitchen.

"Nothing really," she says. "While you're here you can help me carry the cake and plates out, but I mainly wanted to ask how things are going."

"Good." I look out the sliding glass door, at my friends and family and Dawson. "Amazing, honestly. I never thought I would say that again."

"I never thought I would hear you say that again." She opens the pantry and grabs a stack of paper plates.

"The only thing is I wish we could find more time alone," I say. "Between work and the parlor and Whitley, it's slim pickings."

Caroline shoves the plates at me. "Take these outside. And how about Cole and I keep Whitley for a while tonight?"

"You don't have to do that."

"Come on, Sage, you know we don't mind. Take Dawson home. Spend some time with him. *Boink*." She winks at me.

"What is with you and that word?" I laugh, opening the door for her so she can carry the cake out.

Caroline calls everyone over and makes them sing "Happy Birthday" to me, then forces me to make a wish and blow out the candles. I pretend I don't like it, but I can't deny that being surrounded by all of my favorite people as I turn 33 makes me completely ecstatic. I give Whitley a slice of cake, then carry a second over to Dawson.

"Remember that time you brought me birthday cupcakes?" I ask, sitting next to him.

"How could I forget?" He takes a bite of cake. "You didn't make a wish then. Did you make a wish today?"

I run a hand through his hair and let it rest on the back of his neck. "Once again, I'm not sure how much more I could wish for."

He feeds me a bite of cake.

"Also, I have a surprise for you," I say.

"For me? It's your birthday."

Leaning closer, I whisper into his ear, "Caroline is going to watch Whitley for a while...if you want to come over?"

The expression on his face changes from want to need. "Can we go now?"

I grab the collar of his jacket. "I don't see why not."

He shovels the rest of the cake into his mouth, and I make my rounds of saying goodbye and telling Whitley I'll be back to get her soon. Then Dawson and I rush out the front door and into my car.

"This makes me miss the moped," he jokes, placing a hand on my knee then sliding it up my thigh. "Do you still have it?"

"Unfortunately it's long gone." I squirm as his hand

climbs further. "Believe it or not, you couldn't fit a car seat on the back."

Laughing, he moves his hand over my hip and into the bottom of my shirt.

"Do you want me to get in another wreck?" I ask.

He kisses my neck. "If it somehow gets us home faster."

Home. The word sends serotonin flowing through my body. The cottage is my physical home. But Dawson is where my heart belongs. For the first time in a long time, the word means what it's really supposed to.

When I stop in the driveway, Dawson puts the car in park for me. We barrel out and rush up the steps. I somehow get the door unlocked on the first try, despite my shaking, anticipatory hands. Inside, Dawson takes the keys from me and drops them to the floor, then picks me up and presses my back to the wall, wrapping my legs around his waist.

His tongue tastes like champagne and cake. His hands feel like that same word—home. Pinning me to the wall with his hips, he pulls my shirt over my head and drops it to the floor with the keys. He carries me to the sunroom before sitting me down. We both pause to stare at the new Skeleton Beach window. The setting sun filters through it, painting the furniture in shades of blues and purples.

"It looks even better in the evening," he says.

"But it looks best with you in the room," I reply breathlessly, removing his shirt.

I run my hands over his stomach and up through the hair on his chest, re-memorizing every bit of skin, noting the new and improved differences. Walking a circle around him, I pause to kiss the faded ghost on his shoulder, then stop in front of him to plant another kiss in the center of his chest as he takes off my bra. He backs us closer to the couch.

Taking a seat on the edge, I pull his hips to me and unbuckle his belt. His jeans slide down easily, to a puddle around his feet, leaving him standing in a pair of black boxer briefs. He protrudes out of them and moves his hips closer to me, silently begging for more. I hook my thumbs in the sides, but before I can skim them off, he grabs my ponytail, pulling my head back and forcing me to look up at him.

The sudden movement makes me gasp. My hair falls around my shoulders as he slowly pulls the scrunchie out of my hair, his eyes dimming with every escaping strand. "Fuck, Sage," he says. "Time has only made you prettier." He runs his thumb across my bottom lip.

I return to the task of getting him out of his boxers, pausing to appreciate every square inch of the body painted colorfully by the light from the window. I kiss his lower stomach before taking him into my mouth. The sound that escapes him intensifies my need for him. His hands stay in my hair guiding me, assisting me until he can't take it anymore.

"Come here," he whispers, and I stand to meet him. He kisses me as he takes off my jeans and panties, leaving us both in our most vulnerable states.

Except with him, I don't feel vulnerable. With him there's only comfort. Reassurance and support, and relief.

He lowers his head and takes one of my nipples into his mouth, then releases it. "I have a condom in my pocket. I haven't been with anyone since Eliza, and I tested after that just to be safe."

I wrap my hand around him, stroking gently. "As you already know, it's been more than a decade for me." He smiles as I kiss him. "But I'm also on birth control."

"Are we on the same page if we skip the condom?"

"Yes," I say, impatient.

He moves around me and takes a seat on the couch, then pats his thigh. "Hop on, Ghost Girl."

"You're such a nerd." I laugh, placing one knee beside him on the couch.

He pulls my other one to the opposite side, then lowers my hips toward him. I hold my breath as he fills me inch by inch, releasing it only when every part of our bodies is connected. He kisses across my collarbone, then thrusts into me. I place my hands on his shoulders, giving myself leverage. He meets me move for move, his mouth never leaving my skin.

"You feel so good," he says against my cheek.

Suddenly, he rolls us to the side and flips me onto my back. A sound of surprise escapes me and he laughs, finding our rhythm again once we've rearranged. I look up at him, at the colors on the ceiling above his head. At the window over his shoulder.

"We've come full circle," I pant.

"Huh?" he breathes into my hair.

"Our first time was on Skeleton Beach. I remember the way the stars looked around your head," I say, taking his face between my hands. "Now I have the beach in my home, and here you are again."

His eyes glaze over. "That was the night I first told you I loved you."

"I know," I breathe, moving my hands down to draw him even deeper into me.

He pauses, his eyes on mine. "I loved you then. And I love you now, Sage. Even more."

I kiss him, hard and rough. "I love you too."

He begins to move again, this time with less urgency. I hold him close and kiss him, until I once again see stars.

CHAPTER 30
PRESENT DAY, JANUARY 2023

"Come on, girlie," I tell Whitley after grabbing two Spine Chillers from the counter at Beans. "Today is a big day!"

"Mama, what does 'renovation' mean?" she asks as we walk up the street to the old ice cream parlor, now better known as "our" building.

"It's when you make changes, usually to a house or a business," I tell her.

"Like to make it bigger?"

"Yep," I say. "Or different somehow."

"Oh, okay. So that's what's happening today?" She looks up at me, and it's one of the times when I see her dad in her. In the past, that often freaked me out. As I get older, I've learned to just silently tell him thank you. No one else has given me a better gift.

"It's starting today," I say. "Dawson is stressed so we're going to wish him luck."

"Cool," she says, then makes a gagging noise. "I still can't believe you have a boyfriend."

"Why? Is that gross?"

"Kind of. But at least he's cute. So good job with that."

I swear, this kid keeps me laughing.

Our building is teeming with people when Whitley and I arrive. Orange-vested men with jackhammers hang around outside and others walk around inside, following Dawson and Cole. The construction company Cole works for is doing the remodel, and he's the project manager. It's another one of those things that has worked out a little too perfectly.

Dawson's face lights up when Whitley and I come through the front door. "What a nice surprise!" he says, kissing me and lifting Whitley into a hug.

"We won't stay long," I say. "We just wanted to wish you luck, and give you this." I pass him the coffee.

"Beautiful." He takes a long sip. "Exactly like both of you."

"I know," Whitley says. We both laugh.

"Where's my coffee?" Cole asks, coming over to give Whitley a noogie. He plops his construction hat on top of her head and it falls down to cover her eyes.

"I wasn't thinking," I say. "I'll go get you one if you want?"

"Nah, I'm just giving you a hard time."

Whitley takes the hat off and gives it back to Cole. Something in the back of the room catches her eye, and she takes off running. "Grampa!" she yells. "What are you doing here?"

"Helping," Dad says, leaning to kiss her on the cheek before walking over to Dawson and me. "Also doing a bit of ghost recon. If there's something in here it's going to get pissed when we start knocking down walls."

I raise an eyebrow at Dawson. "Did you put him up to this?"

Dawson ignores me and looks around the room innocently.

"I also have something to show you," Dad tells me.

"What is it?"

He sticks a hand in his pocket and pulls out a piece of paper, unfolding it as he passes it to me. I take it from him and scan it. It's a printed email with the subject "Offer of Representation."

Happy tears spring into my eyes and I look at him. "Is this what I think it is?"

Grinning, he motions for me to finish reading. So I do.

Dear Gerald,

Congratulations! I have absolutely loved reading through your book, "Larkspur Island: A Haunted History." I would officially like to extend an offer of representation and help you find a publishing home for this work of nonfiction. Please let me know the best time for me to reach out for a call, and we'll discuss all of the details.

I'm so excited to work with you.

Best,
   Johnny Pulmer
   Literary Agent
   Pulmer Literary Agency

I throw my arms around Dad's neck, trying not to spill my coffee down his back. "Are you kidding me?" I say. "Oh my god, I don't even know what to say!"

"Say, 'finally,'" Dad jokes.

"What's going on?" Whitley asks. Dawson and Cole watch silently.

When I release him, a couple of my tears fall onto the email and I try to wipe them away before saying, "I'm so damn proud of you."

"I couldn't have done it without you, Wedgie," he says. "I know I suffer from a one-track mind, and I haven't given you the help you deserve over the years, but this accomplishment is just as much yours as it is mine."

Dawson takes the email from me and reads it, then claps a hand on Dad's back. "Congratulations, Gerald. This is huge."

"What is going on?!" Whitley yells this time.

I turn to her. "Grampa has someone who wants to help him sell his book."

"And that's really exciting?" she asks, not quite grasping the concept.

"It's *very* exciting," I confirm.

"I hate to break this up," Cole says, genuinely looking guilty. "But this wall is coming down soon and I can't have y'all in here when it happens."

"Oh, right right right," Dawson says, passing Cole his remaining coffee. "I'll walk them out so you can start and I'll be back soon."

"You got it, boss," Cole jokes, waving goodbye at Dad, Whitley, and me.

"Hey, Whit," Dawson says. "Should we go outside and watch them demolish the wall?"

"That sounds gnarly!" she agrees.

Smiling, Dawson takes Whitley's hand in one of his and mine in the other. He leads us outside with Dad, across the street and into the edge of the square. We stand huddled together in the January cold front, watching as Cole's crew starts their jackhammers. Whitley covers her ears to block out the noise, and dust begins to swirl spookily through the air.

I look up at Dawson. He's been back for months, but every time I see his face it still feels like I'm in shock. Feeling my eyes on him, he returns my stare and bends down to kiss me.

"Hopefully our ghost doesn't get too mad," he quips, turning back to observe the chaos. On his other side, Whitley and Dad look on, excited to be witnessing the start of new beginnings.

My eyes stay glued to my Ghost Boy.

EPILOGUE
JULY 2023

Dad and I hold the giant red ribbon taut while Dawson snips it in half with the biggest pair of scissors I've ever seen.

"Introducing," Caroline says, stepping to the side to display the front door, "the new home of Sunny Spirits Ghost Tours and Aiken Stained Glass Contractors!"

The small crowd gathered in front of our building claps, oohing and aahing over the real eyecatcher of the establishment: the large stained front windows. They sit on either side of the door: Dawson's a complicated, vibrant pattern of colorful diamonds and squares, and mine a gold background with three friendly ghosts in the center. Above the windows, our brand-new signs wave in the breeze.

"We did it," I say, jumping into Dawson's arms.

"Together," he murmurs into my hair.

"Hey, Dawson, Sage?" Dawson's new assistant Emily runs over. "Can I open the door and let people in now?"

"Absolutely," he tells her.

"Thanks." Grinning, she runs off in a flurry of red hair,

ever eager to do her job. Over Dawson's shoulder, I watch Sawyer's mouth fall open as Emily runs past him.

"Oh boy," I whisper to myself.

"What?" Dawson spins to see what I'm looking at. "I'll tell you later," I say, looping my arm through his.

We hang out on the sidewalk, waiting for all of our guests to go inside first. We're finally getting ready to walk through the door when I hear my name called from down the sidewalk. I look over my shoulder, my eyes widening when I see Mom and her husband Greg coming toward us. We run to each other, meeting halfway to hug. "You came!" I say.

"We wouldn't miss it." Mom squeezes me before moving to Dawson. "You look a bit different than the last time I saw you," she tells him jokingly.

"How ya doing, kiddo?" Gary asks, taking his turn with the hugs.

"Good, good," I say. "Let's go in! We have so many snacks and drinks and I know y'all had a long drive."

"I *am* famished..." He pats his round belly.

I open the door for them and Dawson grabs my wrist, keeping me from going in for a little longer. "What?" I ask as he folds me against his chest.

"I just want to take it all in for a second. In silence. With you."

We hold each other in the doorway that still smells like construction in the best possible way, wordlessly rocking back and forth.

"Your parents didn't come..." I say quietly.

"I didn't expect them to," he murmurs. "At least I can say I extended the invite."

"They'll come around one day," I tell him.

"Even if they don't, I'll be okay." He kisses my forehead. "I have you."

"I've been thinking," I say, looking up at him. "You should

move in with me and Whitley. You've already extended your lease once, and I don't see any point in you doing it again when you're with us all the time anyway."

He grins. "I've been waiting for you to ask that."

"No time like the present," I joke. "Buster will be so excited."

"When should I start packing?" he asks, letting me go and opening the door.

I peek back at him as I walk through it. "I was thinking...immediately?"

Laughing, he pats me on the butt and follows me inside.

ACKNOWLEDGMENTS

I can't begin to explain how much fun I had writing this book, and how excited I am to have it in the hands of readers. Like all of my projects, I couldn't have done it without the help of some amazing people.

Mama, Celia, and Stacy, thank you for reading my early drafts and providing the advice and encouragement I needed to bring this story to its final form. I'm so lucky to have people that I trust wholeheartedly with new ideas. The support the three of you continue to consistently provide is unmatched.

Kristen, thank you for helping me edit and format this baby! I can always count on you to check facts, share your knowledge, and help make my stories stronger. Forever thankful that we crossed paths!

Britt, thank you for the thoroughness and attention to detail you provided during proofreading. After finishing your final edits, I breathed a giant sigh of relief because I felt so confident about the final version of this book, and I think that's all any writer could ever ask for.

Kelsey, I still can't stop staring at this new cover. You absolutely nailed the vibes of Sage and Dawson and their story and I feel so lucky that I've gotten to work with you on this and the Sunny Spirits logo. Thank you!!

A huge thanks to my ARC team! Working with early readers and reviewers is one of my favorite parts of the process. Book people are the best people.

I'll finish things off with a general THANK YOU to my

readers, family, and friends. Y'all help this lifelong dream of mine come true every single day, and I get emotional when I think about the support I receive from people I've met during every previous part of my life— from my hometown, to college, to work, to the barre studio, and beyond. I love you all.

ABOUT THE AUTHOR

Miranda's earliest memory of writing goes back to a third-grade story competition, where she wrote about a cat and a horse who became best friends. Spoiler alert: it was bad and she didn't win. She's almost over it now.

These days, Miranda writes cozy contemporary romance novels. She lives in Florida, where she works in the travel industry and dreams about living somewhere with seasons. She hates raisins, and would put her life on the line for a good chocolate chip cookie.

instagram.com/authormirandav